TERROR TIMES TWELVE

Fire trucks and ambulances completely blocked Fifty-second Street. Well-dressed people stood behind the police lines holding each other and crying. The entire front of the *Globe* had been taken off by the explosion. A lone fireman stood in front of the building playing his hose into what was left of the lobby. Fifteen or so orange bags were scattered randomly around him covering the bodies.

We walked across the street in silence, the glass crunching underfoot. Kane bent down and pulled up a tarp.

The explosion hadn't killed the victim. It looked like he'd been shot about a hundred times with a twenty-two. Kane dropped the tarp and swept something up from off the sidewalk. He held out his hand. There were ten bent and blackened nails in it.

"Nasty," he said. "Very, very nasty."

UNBALANCED
Acts

JEFF RAINES

AVON BOOKS ◆ NEW YORK

For my mother and father

I'd like to thank Alice Turner, Bob Mecoy, Jim Landis, Bonnie Nadell, Marlene Wrankle, Zoltan Takach, Elizabeth Dudevoir, Terrance Kloeckle, Jim & Janice Gere, Ray Seed, Fred Hill, and Haresh Shah for making this novel possible.

UNBALANCED ACTS is an original publication of Avon Books. This work has never before appeared in book form. This work is a novel. Any similarity to actual persons or events is purely coincidental.

AVON BOOKS
A division of
The Hearst Corporation
105 Madison Avenue
New York, New York 10016

Copyright © 1990 by Jeff Raines
Published by arrangement with the author
Library of Congress Catalog Card Number: 89-91882
ISBN: 0-380-76008-8

First Avon Books Printing: May 1990

AVON TRADEMARK REG. U.S. PAT. OFF. AND IN OTHER COUNTRIES,
MARCA REGISTRADA, HECHO EN U.S.A.

Printed in the U.S.A.

RA   10   9   8   7   6   5   4   3   2   1

CHAPTER 1

Kane was stationed in front of the peephole and didn't show any inclination to move. He had been there, softly whistling "There Is a Rose in Spanish Harlem," for at least fifteen minutes. It was beginning to get on my nerves. We weren't anywhere near Spanish Harlem.

Josh sat patiently on a plastic milk crate holding his M16. He appeared to have blocked out everything: the truck, Kane's whistling, the automatic weapons the terrorists had been using. Fred spent his time taking inventory. His lips moved silently as he patted one pocket after another, making sure he hadn't forgotten anything. Wayne had an unconscious blank look on his face.

The beer distributor's truck we had borrowed for the raid was parked in front of a grocery store a half block down the street from the tenement where the CPF, the Caribe Peoples Front, was holed up. Kane had spotted one lookout sitting on the steps in front of the building and another at the end of the block. He was keeping an eye on them.

Wayne adjusted the groin flap on his Kevlar vest for about

the tenth time. It was an unconscious motion, not exactly a nervous twitch. Josh caught the motion out of the corner of his eye. "What you worried about, white boy?" he asked. "Take a pretty damn good shot to get yours."

Wayne jerked his hand away from the flap and turned red. Kane stopped whistling and looked back at Josh.

"You look pretty calm considering my granny could get yours with one eye closed in a strong crosswind."

Josh gave a low laugh. "Just because she hits it don't mean she gonna do any damage."

Kane grinned and turned back to the window. His blue baseball cap was turned backward on his head and I could see the gold initials embroidered on the front of it: "A.T.A.C."—Anti-Terrorist Action Command. He'd had six of them made after he'd seen *Nighthawks*, a Sylvester Stallone movie about the New York City Police Department's antiterrorism unit.

He would have had "E.A.T.U." (standing for Elite Anti-Terrorism Unit) printed on them, but it had a less fortunate pronunciation than ATAC. In the movie the ATAC leader is murdered by a beautiful terrorist and the Stallone character takes command and wipes the terrorists out single-handedly. Kane sees himself in the Stallone role.

The first thing he'd said to me at our headquarters that morning was, "Where's your 'attack' cap?"

I told him I must have left it in the "attack" helicopter, which shut him up for almost five whole minutes.

He had been remarkably cheerful all morning, considering that the CPF had begun blowing things up lately. In addition to robbing banks they had started delivering "midnight manifestos"—generally consisting of twenty to thirty pounds of TNT. It was an incredibly stupid thing for them to have gotten into. After one of their bombs went off in the Federal Building, it had suddenly, human nature being the way it is, become much easier to get the electronic surveillance authorizations we had been screaming for for weeks.

It had occurred to me some weeks previously that the CPF and the Corteze family might have come to some kind of understanding. No one on the street would talk about the CPF, and a large number of Colombians had started going back to Medellín in boxes—some in very small boxes. A sudden easing in probable cause standards had allowed me to put my theory to the test. It wasn't very long before we had a recording of Alfredo Corteze, the old man's grandson, offering to trade fifty pounds of dynamite and a few thousand dollars for the head of Carlos Hegerra.

It had then been simply a matter of trading Alfredo's head for the CPF. Which is how we came to be in Harlem, sitting in the back of a beer truck at six in the morning.

"Here's Lemkul," Kane announced.

I got up off the floor where I'd been busy doing TM relaxation exercises. I was much better at looking cool than Wayne was, but still had a long way to go to match Kane. I was mildly surprised that my legs worked as well as they did as I joined Kane at the peephole.

Bret Lemkul, my lieutenant, wearing an aloha shirt and chinos and looking very lost, was just getting out of his rental car. He appeared to be experiencing every white person's nightmare: car trouble in Harlem. He'd stopped the car, steam billowing out from under the hood, in the middle of the street and appeared to be looking for a pay phone.

Belinda Jonson was sitting in the passenger seat with a street map of Manhattan clutched in her hands. I could almost see the white knuckles. It had to be acting though, taking into account who she was. She'd arrested more rapists in the past year than most precincts managed in a decade. Most of the rapists were still walking funny when they got to their pretrial hearings.

"God," Kane whispered admiringly. "All they need is a couple of ears of corn sticking out of their pockets."

I looked back at Fred and hissed, "Driver."

Fred spoke softly into his radio. A few seconds later I heard the driver whistling as he left the market. He got into the cab and fired up the engine. He would be scribbling on his clipboard until Fred told him to get going.

Josh called out, "Lock and load." He slammed a magazine into his rifle and worked the action to insert the first round in the chamber. Kane and Fred followed suit while Wayne and I checked the safties on our pistols. Wayne had wanted to carry a rifle too, but he wasn't checked out and I didn't want him running loose with an automatic weapon.

Considering how early it was, it was amazing how fast the crowd gathered. And just like we'd figured, the two guards hadn't been able to resist the urge to go scare the pants off whitey. They were already halfway to the car.

"Roll," I said. Fred spoke into his radio and the gears clashed as the truck began moving. It didn't have very far to go.

The driver slammed on the brakes as we got to the tenement and we rolled up the doors and were out running. I looked over my shoulder to see how Bret and Belinda were doing. Bret had his man spread-eagled on the ground while Belinda had hers leaning into the car with his hands on the roof.

I took the steps three at a time and was gratified to find the front door unlocked. I heard Kane and Josh dropping the battering ram as I hit the inside stairs. According to Alfredo, who had been there, the CPF was holed up on the top floor. He had drawn us a floor plan and mentioned that the door was barricaded and a lot stronger than it looked. We were prepared.

Fred and I knelt down by their door and got to work. He dropped two quarter-pound blocks of TNT on the floor in front of the door and reached into a pocket on his Kevlar vest for a blast card. He peeled the back off the little card and stuck it to the bottom left-hand corner of the door. Then he attached one end of a spool of wire to the metal prong sticking out of the card and began unreeling it back to the third-floor landing.

In the meantime I was molding a rope of plastic explosive

around the door frame. Fred had braided three "demo" cords together and then cut a triangular groove along the length of the braid. It was about three quarters of an inch in diameter and looked like a lumpy garden hose. I worked it into the doorjamb—making sure the groove was up against the door. It took maybe thirty seconds. I poked the rope onto the metal prong in the blast card and wrapped the slack around one of the blocks of TNT. I jammed the other block into the cord on the other side of the door and then took the steps four at a time down to the next landing.

Fred had the other end of the wire in one hand and an electronic detonator in the other. He had told me the wire had a cordite core; if the detonator failed he would light the wire. I squatted down beside him and put my fingers in my ears. He inserted the wire in the detonator, released the safety and turned the handle. I had one last second to think about the Philadelphia policemen who had burned down an entire block of row houses doing something like this. I understand they've been permanently attached to the homeless decoy detail.

The flash from the explosion illuminated the landing for the first time in what was probably years. There was no appreciable delay between the flash and the concussive wave that followed it. But by the time the wave reached us my adrenaline was pumping out so fast that I didn't feel it as anything but a warm breeze. We pounded back up the stairs, and as Fred had promised, the door was missing. So was a good deal of the wall—giving us an excellent view of the two guys who had been sleeping in the room that opened up to the door. They were rolling around on the floor screaming in Spanish with their hands pressed against their ears.

The smoke from the explosion hung eerily around our waists as we entered the apartment. Fred told me later that the bottom of the door must have gone first, channeling the smoke along the floor. The acrid smell was everywhere though, along with the screams of the deafened men, which had become high-pitched wails. Everything seemed to be moving in slow motion, giving the scene an unreal aura. I was holding my right wrist with my left hand, steadying it, as I covered the men on the floor. My hand wasn't trembling, but I could feel a high-frequency vibration throughout my body. The bedroom door opened and a naked man appeared.

He seemed to be an island of sanity amid the unreality. He had dark skin and widely spaced, intelligent brown eyes under a high forehead. He seemed untroubled by his nakedness or the madhouse scene before him. He had a shotgun.

I had swiveled my gun around in his direction as soon as I'd seen the door opening. He turned to aim the shotgun at me.

"Drop it," I screamed. But he didn't seem to hear me.

Kane cut him in half. An M16 on full automatic fires faster than you can see. But I saw each bullet individually enter his body. The first hit him a few inches above his right hip and began to turn him. The second entered his belly, just to the right of his navel. The third entered at an angle just below his short ribs. The fourth entered his left side through his chest; the last through his shoulder. He was almost perpendicular to us by the time the last round hit him. His shotgun discharged into the wall and the recoil pushed his upper body backward. His shoulders hit the carpet and bounced while his legs spasmed, his body's reflexive attempt to restart his heart.

I went over his body low through the door he had come through with Kane just behind me. There was a girl in the bed. She was clutching the covers in both hands and her eyes were incredibly big. I swiveled to cover the bathroom door while Kane went for the girl. He grabbed her by the hair, pulling her out of the bed and throwing her up against the wall while I kicked in the door of the bathroom. It was empty.

Kane had turned to cover the outer room again, ignoring the girl, who was shivering against the wall. I dropped onto my belly to check under the bed and then turned to cover the closet Kane was standing next to. He reached out to pull the door open.

"Clear," I shouted.

"Right," he replied.

I couldn't detect any stress in his voice. There was no one in the closet. Kane ran to see how the others were doing before I could get off the floor. I turned to look at our prisoner.

She was naked and thin, too thin to be anything but a child. I doubted she was old enough to drive. She was shaking uncontrollably and she seemed to be trying to hold herself together with arms that weren't nearly big enough for the job. She wasn't crying. She was too scared to be crying.

My brain began to sort out the sounds that were filtering in through the walls. My own ragged breath was the first thing I noticed. It occurred to me that I must be hyperventilating, so I ordered myself to stop. The screams from the common room had receded to low moans and I began to hear the sounds of the distant sirens and the *whop whop whop* of the helicopters circling overhead. There was no sound of gunfire.

I put my gun away and pulled a sheet off the bed and wrapped it around the girl. I didn't want to leave her in the room. She might calm down long enough to drag a machine gun out of the closet and empty it in our direction. But I was reluctant to take her into the common area because her boyfriend was out there decomposing. Finally I decided I didn't have any choice and steered her out into the carnage.

Jonson was peering in through the hole where the door had been. She replaced her pistol in the holster she'd wrapped around her "I'm from Iowa" sundress and took charge of my prisoner. She put her arms around the girl and said, "There there, sugar, everything's going to be all right."

I pointed wordlessly at her weapon. She looked over at

me, real hurt in her eyes, and gave me an annoyed look. But she took her gun out and unloaded it.

I could hear Josh in the back bedrooms telling someone he really ought to be kissing the floorboards harder because that was the nearest thing to sex he was going to get for the next twenty years. They didn't need any help from me. I patted down the two guys on the floor. They were unarmed, but I found a pair of automatics concealed in their bedding that I unloaded and threw onto the couch.

Kane and Fred led the other prisoners into the common room. Fred was speaking into his radio, telling the SWAT teams that everything was cool. Wayne and Josh came in behind them with big grins on their faces.

Kane came up behind me at the window where I was watching the three-ring circus down in the street. The terrorists had boarded up the windows, but they had left spaces where they could keep an eye on things. There were around fifty cruisers parked out in the street. Add in a fire truck or two and some ambulances and it was beginning to look like the media event that it was. The uniforms had started pushing back the crowd and setting up barricades. Camera crews were just beginning to arrive.

"Thanks for saving my life," I told him.

"No problem, Chief," he replied. "Bastard would've gotten me too."

I let his answer hang there. The implication was that I had let him down. It had been my shoot and I hadn't taken it. The guy with the shotgun could very well have killed us both because I hadn't been able to make myself pull the trigger.

I looked over at the wall where the shotgun had discharged. There was an enormous hole in the plaster at about eye level. I just shook my head. He would have blown my head clean off my shoulders. The coroner's assistants would have had to scrape my face off the wall with putty knives. Kane probably would have lived through the first blast.

"Sorry," I told him. "I wanted him alive."

"Sorry don't buy you a new liver, Mike."

We watched the crowd for a few minutes. A limo pulled up to the barricades and was waved through. It stopped in front of the building and someone got out of the back followed by three or four other people in dark suits.

"Jesus," Kane said. "It's the mayor."

Hizzoner appeared in a few minutes. He must have run up the stairs but didn't look to be very winded. He walked into the room like he owned it, took one look around and seemed to get the whole picture in a glance. One of the men following him had a camera and started to bring it up to his eye to take some shots. Fred grabbed the lens and pointed it at the floor. "No pictures," he told him.

The mayor looked annoyed. As a good executive it's my job to look after my men, so I went over to smooth any ruffled feathers.

"Captain Kelly," I told the mayor. "Antiterrorism. I'm sorry, sir, but we can't allow pictures of me or any of my men to appear in the press. It would reduce our ability to prevent this sort of thing." I gestured around the room.

He nodded and gave me a once-over. I'd heard that he made spot character assessments and if yours didn't turn out so good you had better find a new city to work in. He turned to the photographer. "No pictures." Then he turned back to me.

"Well, Kelly, what happened here?"

I gave him the gist of it without mentioning Alfredo Corteze. I almost felt bad about letting Corteze off the hook. But I figure he would have beat the rap anyway because it really had been a weak warrant. Besides, it wouldn't take the Medellínes very long to figure out who had been doing what.

The mayor looked over at the hole where the door had once been but refrained from commenting. We aren't authorized to use explosive entry, but there had been a lot of esoteric weapons used in their bank robberies. I had thought it over and decided that I wasn't likely to be second-guessed one way or the other.

"Only one man killed?" he asked.

"Yes, sir," I replied. "Apparently their leader."

"Who did the shooting?"

"Sergeant Thomas Kane," I replied, indicating Kane over by the windows.

The mayor looked over at Kane, who was leaning against the wall. The light streaming through the boards across the window made it look like a scene from a men's cologne ad. Kane had his M16 slung over one shoulder and he'd loosened the straps on his bulletproof vest so that it hung loosely off the same shoulder. His .44 looked gigantic in its holster. I could tell the mayor wanted his picture taken with the macho police hero in the worst way.

"I'd like to go on record," I continued, "that without the strong support of officers from Manhattan North, especially Sergeant Jonson and Captain Jeffers, we could never have successfully accomplished our mission."

I had pointed at the couch where Belinda was sitting trying to comfort her young charge. The mayor looked over and his eyes lit up when they landed on Jonson. Macho cops may sell better than pretty women, but macho pretty women heros don't come along every day.

The mayor looked over his shoulder on his way over to pay a call on Belinda. "Manhattan North, you say?"

Kane and I watched with some amusement as the mayor and his flunkies wheedled Belinda into taking off her gun belt.

The mayor stayed for ten minutes or so. Had his picture taken a lot. Shook hands with everyone in the room who didn't have his hands cuffed behind him, and then made a dramatic exit.

It took another hour to get all of the prisoners carted off and the physical evidence tagged and bagged. We gave the arrest to Jeffers because he'd helped out without asking a lot of foolish questions. Apparently he hadn't thought it was all that unusual to get his SWAT teams ready for an early morning urban assault. He'd even thrown in some helicopters. Besides, he had a sergeant who was an ace at filling out paperwork. It probably wouldn't take him more than five or six hours to get the entire CPF processed.

"So how long do we have to stick around?" Kane asked me.

"Well," I said, "we have to wait for the FBI to snoop around for a while before we seal the place. And the postal inspectors will probably want to look around, but that's OK, they're pretty cool. And then there's Internal Affairs; they haven't been here yet."

"What do those assholes want?"

"Relax," I told him. "It's routine. They have to investigate shootings, and," I said, pointing at the sheet-covered lump on the floor, "you seem to have shot that one over there."

For the first time the enormity of the paperwork jungle he was faced with struck him. He gulped and his eyes got bigger.

"But," I said, "seeing as how you saved my life and everything, I'll fill out most of the paperwork for you." I paused and let him look relieved, and then went on. "Except, of course, the personal stress evaluation form, the request for psychiatric care form, the departmental history form, in triplicate, and the PBA report of departmental action form. You'll have to fill those out yourself. But I'll take care of the DA's office, the mayor's office, the community relations office, the coroner's office, the ballistics department and Manhattan North."

Fred came up and added, "Don't forget the chief of detectives; he's got an inquiring mind too." He threw his arm around Kane's shoulders. "Want my advice?" he asked. He held up about a yard of demo cord. "C4, my man, no paperwork at all."

"No worries," Josh reassured him. "They'll just put you on administrative duties for six months or so until they can get their heads out of their asses long enough to have a hearing."

"But don't worry," I told him, "we're behind you a thousand percent." I paused, peering into his face puzzledly. "Errr, what did you say your name was?"

Bret walked in with Jeffers. They stopped in the door to give the by now standard whistle at Fred's handiwork before coming in.

"You're an artist with that shit, aren't you?" Bret asked Fred.

Jeffers looked at me admiringly. "I have had my picture taken more in the past hour than I have in the preceding forty-one years of my existence," he told me. "I have had more microphones stuck in my face than I knew existed and I have been asked the same question by every reporter slime in this city." He paused. " 'Who is this Michael Kelly person who has saved our fair city, and why doesn't he want to have his picture taken?' "

"How 'bout the rest of us?" Josh asked, patting his hair into place.

"You'll be lucky if they get your name right," Jeffers told him. He looked around until he spotted Kane. "Except you," he said. "They want to know about you."

Kane looked like he'd just gotten the death sentence.

"Yeah," Jeffers said. "You're a hero. The mayor was down there telling them how you bravely risked your own life in defense of your leader or some such shit."

A reprieve. Kane looked up. "What?"

"Don't look at me," Jeffers continued. "I would have figured you did the guy for kicks, knowing you like I do. But the mayor's saying he's putting you in for the commissioner's medal, and that asswipe isn't likely to say no to the guy who appointed him. The rest of you are getting something too," he added. "Thanks of the city or something."

He turned to me. "Thanks for the collar. I gave it to Taylor. He's up for lieutenant and maybe it'll help."

The room fell silent as IAD arrived. IAD stands for Internal Affairs Division. Besides kicking twenty-five-year veterans out on the street without their pensions for accepting gratuities, IAD's other major preoccupation is second-guessing actual policemen. This guy was fat, poorly dressed and looked like a real asshole. And, proving that opposites don't necessarily attract, he was accompanied by Special Agent Mayes of the FBI.

The fat man paused in the doorway and touched the wall where the door frame had once been. He took the cigar out of his mouth and whistled. "You boys don't fool around, do you?"

He came in and showed me his ID; he was Captain William Sicular, IAD. "OK," he said, "where's the hero?"

Everyone looked at him like he was the boogeyman. Kane came over, looking a lot less casual than he usually does. He almost came to attention. "Me, sir?" he asked.

"No," Sicular replied. "I'm looking for your mother." He walked over to the body and lifted up the sheet and counted bullet holes. "Jesus," he said. "I've seen better-looking hamburger. So what happened?" He motioned his photographer over to take some pictures.

"Well, sir," Kane started, "I observed the perpetrator with—"

"Cut the crap." Sicular cut him off. "This shithead came at you with a shotgun and you blew him away." He pointed at the wall. "Take some shots of that."

"Yes, sir," Kane went on. "I truly believed that my and Captain Kelly's life were in imminent danger when I fired upon the suspect."

"Suspect?" Sicular looked incredulous. "What'd you suspect him of? Possession of an unlicensed weapon?" Now Sicular looked disgusted. I decided he wasn't your typical IAD asshole. He pointed at the shotgun and had his photographer take a couple of shots of it. Sicular looked over at me. "That the way it happened?" he asked.

"Yes," I replied.

"What the fuck were you doing? They didn't issue you a gun when you got out of the academy?" He didn't wait for me to say anything. "OK, it all looks pretty clear-cut to me." He picked up the plastic bag with the shotgun in it. "I'll just be taking this along. Get your reports in. When we have the coroner's report we'll wrap it up. We'll call you if we need anything." He pointed at Kane. "Try not to kill anybody till then; it always screws things up."

He turned to leave and nearly bumped into Wayne.

"I'm sorry, sir," Wayne told him. "You'll have to sign a receipt for the weapon."

Sicular didn't look particularly put out at having to follow regulations. He signed and left.

Mayes was over at the body. He'd taken the sheet from Sicular and was peering at the dead man thoughtfully.

"Know him?" I asked.

"By reputation," he replied. He looked over at Kane. "Well, you're a legend now. You've killed the poet laureate of the Caribbean." He dropped the sheet and dusted his hands off. "Ramone DeSilva Santiago, poet, dreamer, and fighter of lost causes. A personal friend of Fidel Castro up until he began to question Castro's devotion to the peasants." He shook his head. "A shame he had to go this way."

"You mean because he didn't get to take any of us with him?" I asked. Mayes and I are not friends.

"You were supposed to pool your information with the FBI, Kelly. I don't think a telephone call at five in the morning counts as cooperating."

"You want cooperation?" I asked. "How's this for cooperation? We got onto the CPF from the judge you went to for your wiretap authorizations. He seemed to think that maybe it would help if the local cops knew what was going on. He told me all about your hot tip on somebody named Luis Alviso and how you were following some Nicaraguan UN spy around all day.

"If you'd have come to me I could have told you who

Alviso is. He's an enforcement specialist for the Corteze organization, not a Sandinista desperate to make you look good. But it was too good an opportunity to pass up, wasn't it? They'd have loved you back at Headquarters if you could have pinned this one on Managua, and you weren't going to take a chance on having to share the glory with the local flatfoots, were you? You didn't care how many more banks they robbed or post offices they blew up or people they killed as long as you made the arrest and got to smother yourself in glory when it was all over."

He didn't say anything. He just turned and left. He gave the impression that we'd be meeting again, though. I wasn't looking forward to it.

I called the coroner's assistants in to haul the body— once poet, now fertilizer—down to the morgue. On the way out Fred told me how he'd managed the trick with the rental car.

"It was easy," he told me. "I just disabled the fan and told Bret to leave it in neutral and race the engine until the warning light went on. Then when he got to where he was going he just set off the M80 I had taped to the radiator: *voila*, instant steam."

I looked at him in awe.

"No worries," he told me. "We took the collision damage waver."

CHAPTER 2

I t was late by the time I got home. We'd gone out for Vietnamese food and stayed for beers. Josh and I packed it in around midnight when the bachelors had gone downtown looking for women. Josh dropped me off at my co-op on his way out of town.

The night doorman was nowhere to be seen. I waved at the video camera in the lobby and made a little bet with myself as to how long he had been asleep. The elevator was up at the penthouse, so I wandered over to the mailboxes to see who wanted me to buy what this week. As usual, the box was stuffed with catalogs and flyers, but at least all of the magazine subscriptions had run out.

There was a statement from the trust company that had been paying my bills for the past year. As I dumped the whole load down the incinerator shaft I wondered if I was living beyond my means. Somehow I didn't think so.

Our co-op, my co-op, is on the seventeenth floor, well above the worst of the traffic noise. It came complete with a gourmet kitchen, hardwood floors, one bedroom and a

terrace. It has more than enough closet space for a bachelor.
We had bought it, even though we really couldn't afford it,
because Jenny had convinced me that it was a great investment. The bank was happy because Jenny's parents had
been willing to co-sign for the loan. And since the bank
had prudently taken out mortgage life insurance on both of
us, we had all made out on the deal.

There were still two bottles left of the '83 Margaux we
had laid down for our retirement. I put one into the indus-
trial-strength corkscrew I'd fixed to the pantry wall back in
happier times and popped the cork. Just pull the lever and
presto: instant gratification.

I took a goblet out onto the terrace and sat in one of the
deck chairs. I propped my feet up on the railing and toasted
the lights on the other side of the park and brooded about
the morning's events. I played it back in my mind, trying
to figure out why I hadn't pulled the trigger. It wasn't
because I had a death wish, far from it; I had loads to live
for. Loads.

Eventually I got up to get the second bottle.

My pager went off before dawn. The only reason I heard
it was because it was in my jacket pocket and I was still
wearing my jacket.

It's the latest thing in twenty-first-century electronics. It'll
reach me anywhere in the United States or Canada, and has
a liquid crystal display for messages—in this case, Kane's
telephone number. It occurred to me that he had the watch
that night. Which basically meant the switchboard operator
would call him if they needed anything. I groaned. He
wouldn't be calling me if another junkie had overdosed
outside our headquarters. I stumbled into the kitchen and
called him. He sounded wide awake and alert, but then he
always sounds wide awake and alert.

"Somebody hit Toyon this morning," he told me.

Toyon, I thought. *Who the hell is Toyon?* He must have
been a UN person, but my brain was too foggy to remember

from where. At least it wasn't a Turkish name. A Turkish name would have meant the Armenians, and there was no way we wanted to mess with the Armenians.

"Who's Toyon?" I asked.

Kane didn't seem put out. "Not who," he said. "What."

And then it came to me. Toyon was an institution on Long Island: The New York State Prison for the Criminally Insane at Toyon.

"Oh," I said. The first thing that occurred to me was that some poor bastard had a real mess on his hands and that I sure felt sorry for him. Then I started wondering why Kane was calling me. "What the heck does that have to do with us?" I asked, even though I had already figured it out. I just wanted Kane to confirm my worst suspicions.

"They murdered three guards and snatched some loonies," he told me. "The politicians have this crazy idea that now they're going to want something in return for getting them back.

"The mayor," he continued, "has pledged full cooperation. And because he has, according to CBS, the best antiterrorism team in the country, he's lending it to the operation. There's going to be a chopper landing in the softball field across from your apartment in twenty minutes. See you there."

"Crap, crap, crap," I mumbled on the way to the bathroom. I felt old, old, old. Deck chairs, even Williams-Sonoma deck chairs, weren't meant to be slept in. I stripped and set the shower on "hurt me" and let the hot water beat some sensibility back into me.

There had been a can of Cherry Coke in the refrigerator for two years. I think Kane must have brought it over for a football game. I grabbed it on the way to the elevator and practiced reciting my mantra waiting for the elevator to creep up to our floor. I waved at the camera in the lobby again and hurried out into Central Park.

Kane was pretty easy to find. He was baiting muggers. He was leaning heavily against the backstop of the softball diamond, seemingly attempting to hold it up. Every few seconds his head would nod down to his chest and then bounce back up.

I snuck up behind him and asked, "Well, just suppose I was a mugger and I did mistake you for some lost yuppie on his way back from a club after a long night of alcohol and cocaine abuse? And I decided that maybe I'd have a little fun with you and make a tidy little profit on the side? What are you going to do about it? The helicopter's due in three minutes."

He turned around and gave me a dirty look. "You know," he told me, "you're the only guy I know who wouldn't have a good time at a sorority slumber party."

"You mean because I'm such a nice guy?" I asked. I popped the top of the soda and took a long pull. The gag reflex was barely controllable. I could feel my teeth rotting inside my head and I had to swallow three or four times to keep it down.

"Nice guys," he informed me, "never get laid." He took a close look at me. "You have a long night or something?"

"Or something," I agreed.

"They don't have windows that open on these choppers," he told me. "So if you're going to barf, you better do it here."

"Thanks," I told him. "I'll think about it."

He handed me the *Daily News*.

The banner headline on the front page said something about cops nabbing reggae terror group. The accompanying article compared me to Wyatt Earp and Kane to Doc Holiday.

It was a couple of minutes later that we heard the chopper. Kane heard it first. He's particularly sensitive to helicopter noises. I threw my half-empty can about twenty feet into a trash barrel and handed the paper back to him.

Kane wasn't particularly impressed with my shooting ability.

"You're going to wish you still had that in fifteen minutes or so when you start puking into your lap," he told me.

It was a ten-seat state police helicopter. Its searchlights blazed down on the pitcher's mound and it landed between the mound and second base. It was really loud. I wondered how many millionaire investment bankers it had just woken up. Not nearly enough, I finally decided.

The pilot was alone, and if he was put out at having to pick up city cops he didn't show it. He motioned to us to get in and took off with a stomach-churning jump. I surprised myself by keeping the soda down. I must have turned a little pale, though; Kane slid away from me on his seat on the way up.

Toyon is about halfway out on the island, built on the kind of real estate generally reserved for particularly successful doctors and lawyers. But it had all been potato fields when the state put up the mental hospital and prison. I'm sure they would love to unload the property to a developer and move the prison to the boonies. But, politically, it just wasn't going to happen. If they tried to move it every voter for fifty miles around the proposed site would be in a panic. It wouldn't matter where they wanted to put it. There's nothing quite like the threat of a prison to turn mass apathy into a feeding frenzy.

The pilot circled around the prison to give us a bird's-eye view. Even though it was five stories high, the building looked squat. It was surrounded on all sides by fifty feet of concrete slab and there were guard towers at the four corners of the fences. First light had just broken, but every light in the prison was turned up full. There were at least a hundred vehicles parked outside.

The chopper pilot put us down outside the main gate and then took off, leaving us there by ourselves. There was no welcoming committee.

The prison looked to be at least a hundred years old. It was built of red bricks with barred rectangular windows at regular intervals. The red bricks had darkened with age, giving it a sinister appearance that was heightened by the razor wire topping the chain link fences surrounding it.

The guard at the main gate checked our IDs and let us through. We passed an ambulance parked in the courtyard and were stopped by another guard at the door. He looked pale and just glanced at our IDs before waving us into the building. He didn't look like he wanted to chat.

We had to pass through two open gates and go up a flight of steps to find anyone. Kane pointed at the video camera focused on the first gate. "They must have known who they were letting in," he told me.

There was a large waiting room at the top of the stairs on the right. The room had the institutional feel that prisons acquire. The janitors would all be inmates and none of them had given a damn about anything for a long time. The room smelled of heavy applications of disinfectant, but dust balls were clearly visible under the pale green vinyl furniture. They were waiting for us there.

The various policemen stood around the bodies shuffling their feet and speaking quietly to each other. It didn't look much like they were searching for evidence. My eyes were drawn to the dead guards stretched out facedown on the floor at their feet. There were three of them and they had been cold-bloodedly executed, shot in the back of the head.

I pictured how it must have happened. The terrorists would have stood above them and then, on someone's signal, they had pulled their triggers. It had to have been planned in advance. They couldn't have stood around and debated it; one of the guards would have done something, turned to beg for his life, if nothing else.

They hadn't had to do it that way. There was no good reason for it. But they were sending us a message. Lives didn't mean anything to them.

"Uh oh," Kane said.

I turned and looked at what he was staring at. Someone had written "The lights go down on Broadway" across one of the walls. To show that he really meant it, he had apparently written it in blood. There was a beaker with a paintbrush stuck in it sitting on an end table. I turned back to the bodies. One of them had a slit throat. There were pools of blood scattered around him.

I felt something churn in my stomach. Only a raving maniac would have done something like that, but raving maniacs don't lead coordinated terrorist attacks involving complicated logistics and large numbers of men. They lurk in the bushes and wait for their victims to come to them.

So it had to be someone playing the part of a raving maniac. But anyone cold-blooded enough to play the part of a maniac was worse than a mere lunatic. I felt like a mouse who's just caught his first whiff of the cat. It wasn't a good feeling.

A state police captain spotted us from across the room and made his way over to talk. He stuck his hand out in my direction, which gave me a chance to read his name tag, "Dempsey." I remembered him from an FBI seminar on terrorist methods we'd attended in the Poconos the year before.

"Captain Kelly," I reminded him. "And this is Sergeant Kane."

"Yeah," he said. "I remember you." He pointed at the slogan. "Nice, huh? Think that's going to cause talk?"

"Well," I said, "I wouldn't want to be a drunk trying to find my way home tonight."

"Oh," he said. "It's a lot worse than that. There'll be a run on ammunition at the hardware stores this afternoon and we'll have at least three accidental shootings before dinner. I'll have to tell my men not to try to sneak up on anything and we'll have more panic calls than you can shake a stick at. If it's windy tonight it'll be twice as bad."

"How many are missing?" I asked.

"A dozen, we think," he said. "The staff's here now taking inventory. But whatever they lack in quantity they more than make up in quality. They got Wilbur, Roble, Stern, Twain and Whitman, to name just a few."

I recognized four of the names; they belonged to serial killers who had terrorized the entire state. Roble had wiped out three whole families upstate in the early seventies, butchered them and left them hanging on meat hooks. Stern had been a nurse. She had specialized in poisoning hypochondriacs. There had been several pages devoted to her in my deviant behavior text. Twain was the Nightclub Stalker. Even after he'd nearly put every club in the city out of business he was still picking up women and killing them. He had been the final nail in the disco coffin. Whitman had gunned down fifteen skateboarders one afternoon.

"Who's Wilbur?" I asked.

"Kindly Dr. Wilbur?" he said. "A little before your time maybe. He was a plastic surgeon in Scarsdale. He had an unusually high rate of complications. And he had it for a long time before he was caught. When they dug up his backyard it turned out he had been working at home too. Quite a scandal back in the sixties."

Imagining Dr. Wilbur lurking under my window brought the whole picture into clearer focus. I sleep seventeen stories up and have a number of guns around the apartment. But I knew I would still be thinking about kindly Dr. Wilbur lurking in the hall as I went to sleep that night.

If I was going to be worried, I could just imagine how the folks in suburbia were going to be taking it. That's why Dempsey was hoping it wouldn't be windy. If the wind blew branches up against their windows, people would be calling the police. Unless, of course, they had a gun. In which case they might shoot first and then call the police to tell them about it.

"Going to be a lot of overtime put in tonight," Kane said.

"How'd they get in?" I asked.

"You see that ambulance out in the courtyard?" Dempsey asked me.

I nodded.

"The ambulance company got a call from the institution

here at a quarter to twelve. A patient was having convulsions and they wanted to transport him to the hospital in Jericho."

"How often do they get calls like that in the middle of the night?" I asked.

"Don't know," he said.

"Is that the ambulance the company sent?"

"No," he told me. "And we haven't found it yet either. But that's how we found out something was going on. The ambulance didn't report back by two so the dispatcher called the hospital. The hospital said they hadn't seen it. So the dispatcher called the prison; no answer. So he called the police. A patrol car got here at two-fifteen. He saw the ambulance in the courtyard but couldn't get any answer from inside.

"He hooked a chain to the gate and busted it open. But the front door was locked. By this time he knew something was up and put out an alert. We had roadblocks set up by three-thirty but we were way too late."

"How'd you eventually get in?" I asked.

"The night manager at the mental hospital had a key.

"Anyway," he went on, "it was my unhappy duty to wake the governor up at quarter to four this morning and inform him that some of his wards were missing. I told him about that 'Lights go down on Broadway' business and he decided to call your mayor and inform him of the imminent threat to the peace of his city."

"Mighty white of the guy, seeing as how they hate each other's guts," Kane put in.

"Oh," he said. "You haven't heard anything yet. Seems your mayor called back fifteen minutes later."

I groaned.

"He told the governor that he figured you boys would be of invaluable assistance to the task force and volunteered your services." He paused. "And wouldn't you know it, the governor not only agreed, he decided the leader of this intrepid band of antiterrorists would be a crackerjack candidate to head up the combined task force that's going to catch these hoodlums and put them all behind bars."

"You mean put them all behind bars within the next twenty-four hours and keep the general panic down to an acceptable level and take all the heat if some voter somewhere gets hurt?" I asked.

"Kind of a hot potato, isn't it?" he said. "But I'd say you have more than twenty-four hours before you get fired and spend the rest of your life answering the telephone at some precinct house on Staten Island. More like seventy-two, I'd say."

"Unless somebody gets hurt," Kane put in.

"Of course," Dempsey said, "there's that."

It was going to be my job to go out in public and tell the world that there was no cause for alarm and that their police officials had things well in hand and that we were expecting arrests any minute now. There were a number of good reasons to say those things. If I didn't there would probably be widespread panic in which a whole bunch of people would get hurt. Plus it might cause the people holding the loonies to think twice about using them or it might even make them panic and do something stupid.

But sure as the sun was coming up the next day, people were going to get hurt and there wouldn't be any quick arrests. The public's fear would turn to outrage and I'd be sacked and replaced by someone who wouldn't make rash statements in public. And then in a month or so, the terrorists would slip up and we'd get them and everything would be hunky-dory. I'd be able to read about it in the local paper out on Staten Island.

Just when I thought things couldn't get any worse, Mayes strolled in accompanied by three other guys wearing blue suits.

He looked around and didn't seem to be particularly upset by the sight of the bodies or the writing on the wall. He saw me and came over. You'd have never known from his expression how he felt about me.

"I understand you're heading up the joint task force,"

he told me. ''You'll have the full cooperation of the federal government.''

''Good,'' I said. ''We'll need the FBI crime lab people up here immediately to go over the ambulance and prison. We'll need access to your files in Washington, although not until we get their demands and find out what we're up against. We'll need the cooperation of the customs and immigration people and possibly Interpol.'' I paused. ''Anything else you can think of?''

''No,'' he said. ''That seems to cover it. I'll have the crime lab people up here first thing in the morning.''

Assuming that Mayes had found out about the same time I had, he had had about an hour and a half to set things in motion. The important people at the FBI labs had pagers just the same as I did. They should have already been on the way to the airport.

I turned to Dempsey, Kane and the other blue suits. ''Would you gentlemen mind if I had a few words with Special Agent Mayes in private?''

They dutifully trooped over for a closer look at the bodies and I turned back to Mayes. ''Look,'' I told him. ''I cut you out of the CPF business because you aren't a team player. But you're going to be a team player on this operation or I'll see to it that you spend the rest of your career chasing moonshiners on Guam.''

''How,'' he asked sarcastically, ''are you going to arrange that?''

''Because I went to school with the attorney general's son,'' I told him. ''And I still play squash with the guy. That ought to get me your boss's telephone number. Then all I have to do is tell him I'm on my way down to the *New York Times* to tell them how you tried to pin the CPF bombings on the Sandinistas. Five minutes after the story hits the wires you'll be called in to explain how you came to discredit ten years of Central American foreign policy. And five minutes after that you'll be on your way to the Pacific.''

He turned pale, but he didn't say anything. He seemed

to be searching for something, but nothing came out. Finally he said he was going to call Washington and spun around on his heel and stomped out. Kane came back from the viewing and watched him depart.

"I thought I detected a little righteous anger over here," he said. "You didn't give him the works, did you?"

"Yeah," I admitted sheepishly. "I gave him the team effort speech."

I'd gotten blitzed once at a department function and done my imitation of the motivational speech the Columbia football coach had given us at the start of yet another losing season. I hadn't remembered doing it, but the next day when I crawled into the office an hour and a half late Kane had repeated it for me verbatim as I dribbled black coffee down my chin. I was lucky I hadn't given myself second-degree burns.

"You should be ashamed of yourself," he told me.

"Whatever," I said. "Can we move all these people out of here before they ruin some clue our friends the terrorists might have left behind?"

We trooped over to Dempsey and he suggested a conference room on the next floor. I sent one of the blue suits back for Mayes and stationed a pair of state troopers at the doors and told them not to let anyone touch anything. Then we eased everyone away from the gore.

The conference room was windowless and maybe thirty feet long. There was a single long wooden table in the middle of it with sixteen old-fashioned wooden armchairs around it. Evidently the state budget didn't have a line item for conference facilities at the state prison for the criminally insane.

There were plenty of seats. Since I had been elected I sat at the head of the table and had Dempsey sit next to me. I let everyone else find their own seats. The two FBI agents took up a block along the left side of the table with two chairs in between them for Mayes and the guy I'd sent after him. There were six other seats taken. Kane and a pair of uniformed state troopers leaned against the walls near the door.

"All right," I told them, "let's get started." I pointed at the nearest FBI agent, who had a pad out and was poised with pen in hand. "Can you take minutes and get copies out to the rest of us by this afternoon?"

"Yes, sir," he said.

I turned to face the rest of the table. "My name is Michael Kelly. I'm a captain with the New York City Police Department assigned to the antiterrorism unit. The governor has requested that I be placed in charge of this investigation due to the threat to New York City that we all saw painted across the wall downstairs."

I looked around to see if there were any unfriendly faces. There weren't. "This should not be taken as a slap in the face to anyone who might ordinarily be expected to take command of the investigation." I glanced apologetically at Dempsey, but he didn't appear to feel slighted.

Technically the FBI should have taken charge, but the governor had spoken and it's difficult for the Feds to tell a sitting governor what to do in his own state. Mayes hadn't decided to fight it anyway.

"As of the present this matter is strictly a local problem. However, the FBI has pledged full support for the investigation and we deeply appreciate any help the federal government may be able to provide. Special Agent Mayes is calling in technicians from the FBI crime laboratory now. I think we should wait for him before we begin the meeting. Are there any comments?"

"Just that you have the full cooperation of the state police," Dempsey began. "I'm sure all of us are more interested in capturing the bastards responsible for what happened downstairs than we are in who gets to appear on television tonight."

It was only a couple of minutes before Mayes and his subordinate appeared. He seemed to be surprised that we hadn't started without him. I made a mental note not to be late for any meeting he was chairing.

"OK," I said as Mayes was taking his seat. "Let's get started. I think we should begin by introducing ourselves. You all know who I am." I glanced at Dempsey.

"John Dempsey, captain, State Police Special Investigations Division."

"Buck Johansen, lieutenant, State Police Special Investigations Division."

"Roald Buchanen, governor's office."

I glanced at Buchanen speculatively. I was titular head of the investigation but was serving at the special request of the governor. Buchanen looked to be a career politician and was undoubtedly one of the governor's hatchetmen. Everyone in the state knew the governor wanted to be president someday. And it would be Buchanen's job to see to it that nothing got in the way of his boss's ambitions. There wasn't much doubt he would sacrifice me in a heartbeat.

I looked on to the next man but didn't really need an introduction.

"William Ostresky," he said. "I'm chief of police here in Toyon."

The next two guys were from Suffolk County and then it was over to the side of the table the FBI were monopolizing. While they were introducing themselves I sent Kane out to find the guy in charge of the prison. I wasn't quite sure what to call him; "warden" didn't seem right.

After the FBI had finished introducing themselves and pledging fealty to the investigation I turned to the local police chief. I figured it was his turf and we needed him a lot more than he needed us. I didn't see the terrorists returning to Toyon.

"Well, Chief," I said, "is there anything you want to bring up?"

"Just," he said, "that when we catch those bastards I want to be there and I surely hope they resist arrest. I knew the men they murdered and they didn't deserve to get shot down like that. Shot down like dogs."

I nodded. "I promise you'll be there, Chief. How many men did you have out on patrol last night?"

"Two," he replied. "Plus a dispatcher plus there's the county boys."

"They see anything suspicious?" I asked.

"Not until Bob got here at two," he replied.

"So," I said, "let me see if I've got the chronology down. The ambulance company got the call fifteen minutes before midnight. Somewhere between here and the ambulance station that ambulance got stopped. Figure the fake ambulance gets here at midnight. They'd want to be early in case the other ambulance got through somehow.

"Two fake ambulance attendants enter and overpower the guards. One of them waits here with the guards while the other goes back and opens the gate to let the truck in."

"What truck?" Ostresky asked me.

"They carted off twelve prisoners. They must have had a truck. They sure couldn't use a school bus. Anyway, they let the truck in and then at least two, probably three, of them come back here. That's when they would have murdered the guards."

"Why then?" Ostresky asked.

"They needed at least three men to pull the triggers," I answered.

"Why couldn't it have been one guy pulling the same trigger three times?"

"One of the guards would have done something." I looked around the table to see if anyone saw it the way I did. They didn't appear to. "I think it's important that everybody realize what we're up against here," I began. "They had to have planned killing the guards right from the beginning. They are cold-blooded, ruthless killers."

Nobody looked very impressed. I gathered that they had seen their share of cold-blooded, ruthless killers on television. "In case you missed it," I told them, "the guard

with the hole in his throat was already dead when they
chopped him open. He wouldn't have bled very much so
two of them would have had to lift him up by his ankles to
drain him. That's how all the blood got in his hair.'' That
got their attention. One of the Suffolk County sheriffs looked
like he was going to be sick. I continued.

"On an extremely tight schedule they broke into this
prison, executed three men who didn't have to be executed,
and kidnapped what will probably turn out to be the dozen
most psychotic killers in the state. They were in and out in
probably half an hour and have now vanished into thin air.''
I paused. "When they reappear you can be sure it won't
be in a letter to *Newsday*.''

There was an uncomfortable silence around the table.
Finally Chief Ostresky spoke up. "What about the ambulance attendants?''

"They're dead," I replied. I wasn't certain, but it seemed
like a real good bet. "The dead guards are a message," I
told him. "They're telling us that they're serious and we
better believe them when they make their demands. They're
also telling us that they're careful. The possibility that any
of the guards might have noticed something meant more to
them than the guards' lives. And finally, they're letting us
know that they don't care. They've already maxed out as
far as the courts are concerned. Nothing they do from now
on is going to make their sentences any longer.''

"Where do we start?'' Dempsey asked.

I looked down at the county people. "The first thing
that'll have to be done is to look for witnesses. Anyone who
might have seen anything between midnight and . . . say,
one-thirty. Gas station attendants, convenience store clerks,
that sort of thing. You men know the area. My guess is that
they headed straight for the expressway, but don't limit
yourselves to that.''

"You got it," the senior of the two replied.

I turned to the chief. "These creeps are professionals.
They wouldn't have come in here without intelligence. Ask

around at the library and the local newspaper about strangers who might have been asking questions about the prison. They must have had a good idea how the ambulance company operated as well. Check their records for job applicants over the last year. Check any apartment that has a view of the ambulance station. They probably had someone watching the prison. Look for indications of that.''

He nodded. He was taking this personally and was glad I was giving him something to do.

Dempsey pointed out that they must have had a tap on a phone, either at the ambulance company or the prison. Mayes said he'd have a specialist look for it.

I turned to Mayes. "This stinks of paramilitary. We'll need file information on paramilitary extremist groups. It could be survivalists, Palestinians, white supremacists, black radicals, Colombian cocaine dealers or anybody else who wants something real bad but doesn't stand a chance of getting it.'' I looked around the table without much hope. "I guess I don't have to say that we shouldn't be mentioning any of this to the press."

They all nodded.

I turned to Buchanen. "We'll need administrative help from the state to tie the task force together.'' "Administrative help" was a code for money. He knew there wouldn't be a nickel forthcoming from the city until someone was butchered outside Gracie Mansion.

"No problem,'' he said. "There are contingency funds available for emergencies." He looked around the table. "I don't think there'll be much debate in the legislature that this constitutes an emergency. Just let us know what you need.''

Kane reappeared with a nervous man, who had to be the prison director, in tow. The director was slightly overweight and had a head full of thick black hair. He was wearing a conservative brown suit with a purple shirt and a wild paisley tie. He was pretty clearly from the Indian subcontinent.

"This is Dr. Gopinath," Kane introduced him. "He's in charge of the facility."

"Well, Doctor," I said. "Who and what is missing?"

He sat down and took out a handkerchief to wipe his forehead. His English was faultless although it had a British slant to it. "There are twelve inmates unaccounted for," he began. He shook his head. "It is quite serious. Quite quite serious. They have taken everyone on the Q wing."

"And whom do you keep in the Q wing?" I asked.

"Q stands for quiet," he replied. "Patients whom we feel, for one reason or another, to be untreatable are kept in the quiet wing. By untreatable I mean patients who are unresponsive to therapy and must be kept isolated from the rest of our patients."

"Are your patients allowed to congregate?" I asked.

"Some are," he replied.

"What's so special, then, about the Q wing prisoners?"

He didn't reply for a moment. Looking for a delicate way of putting it. Finally he shrugged his shoulders. "The staff here is quite limited. Some of these prisoners are quite dangerous. We keep them on the Q wing because we are afraid of them."

His admission of fear had a chilling effect around the table. I saw the county people look at each other nervously. The FBI men looked straight ahead but I detected a tightening about their shoulders. Kane was admiring his manicure. He seemed to be thinking about his plans for the weekend.

"Who exactly is missing?" I finally asked him.

He didn't have to consult a list. He knew who was missing. "Branner, Crothers, Durand, Kairos, Lasuen, Moore, Roble, Roth, Stern, Twain, Whitman and Wilbur. All of them are extremely dangerous. I can only compare them to bombs waiting to go off."

"Did they take anything else?" I asked.

"The pharmacy has been rifled," he replied. "We are not certain what is missing, although they seem to have taken a great deal. The safe has been destroyed and the contents are missing.''

"Can you put together a list of what's missing?''

"In time,'' he replied. "I'll have the pharmacist do an inventory.''

"We think they were well organized,'' I told him. "It seems likely that they knew exactly what they were doing every step of the way. That leads us to believe that they had inside information. We need to know about recent employees and any visitors the prison may have had in the past year.''

"There have been no new employees,'' he said. "We have a very stable work force. The pay is rather high because of the nature of the facility and the work is not overly taxing. We have had a number of interns from various medical schools come through. I can give you their names and adresses.''

I nodded to him.

"We do not encourage the press,'' he continued. "It is the policy of the state corrections department that the less publicity about institutions such as ours the better.'' He paused and a sick look came over his face. He reached into the inside pocket of his suit coat and pulled out his pocket schedule. He leafed through it for a moment until he found the page he'd been looking for. "On February third a Columbia student by the name of Eric Degangi called and asked for a tour of the facility. He claimed to be doing his senior thesis on the psychiatric treatment of the criminally insane.'' He flipped forward a couple of pages. "He visited us on the tenth. He was very interested in the Q wing.''

"Can you describe him?'' I asked.

"I can do better than that,'' he replied. "We have his picture on file.''

"Do you photograph all your visitors?'' I asked.

"No, but we cull pictures of all our visitors from the video monitors and keep them on file.''

"Why?'' I asked.

He seemed embarrassed. "Because it was one of the selling points when we bought the video system," he replied. "We do it because we can. I have a whole file folder full of pictures."

"That may be their first mistake then," I told him. "Can you get us the folder?"

He picked up the phone and called upstairs. "It's on the way," he told me.

"Any chance that the tape from last night is available?" Mayes asked.

"No," the doctor replied. "The tape was missing this morning. It was the first thing I checked."

I looked over at Mayes. "Can you get duplicates made of the doctor's photo file for distribution? We'll need to see if any of them ring any bells with anyone." He nodded. "We'll also need the FBI to run down the interns. It's pretty unlikely, but maybe one of them will remember someone who was unusually curious about this place." He nodded again.

"OK," I said. "We all know what we're supposed to be doing. I suggest we break here and meet again this afternoon at two at FBI headquarters in Manhattan. By that time the press should be worked up to a fine lather and we'll have to make some sort of statement to reassure the public." I looked over at Buchanen but he was busy examining the ceiling. "I hope we'll be able to tell them more than to keep their doors and windows locked."

"I think it would be better if I stayed with my patients this afternoon," Gopinath began. "They are extremely upset over what has occurred."

Dempsey looked over at him. "And just when was the last time one of your patients got well enough to leave?" he asked sarcastically.

The doctor looked at him. He was both embarrassed and angry. "Of course, it is unlikely that any of them will ever be allowed to leave this place," he replied. "But that does not mean they do not get better here."

"Dr. Gopinath," I said gently, "there may be many lives at stake. Thugs who can kill as casually as these people do won't hesitate to release your patients where they could harm innocent people. We have to catch them, and we have to do it soon."

He seemed to deflate in his chair. They were his patients, and to his mind, his responsibility. The thought of what they might do seemed to weigh heavily on him. "The wives of two of the guards called this morning. They wanted to know why their husbands were late returning home. I will do anything I can to help."

"We'll need the complete medical histories of the missing patients," I told him. "I want you and a friend of mine who teaches at City College to get together and try to guess how each of the patients will react if he or she is released. Do you think you can get to the city by noon?"

"I am not sure," he replied.

"I can get you to the city in half an hour," Dempsey assured him.

"Then I will be ready."

A secretary came in and handed Gopinath a manila folder. It really did bulge it was so full. We all dutifully trekked up to the next floor and waited for the machine to warm up so the good doctor could photocopy the somewhat blurry picture of one Eric Degangi. None of us recognized him. He distributed a copy—even more blurry and in black and white—to each of us, and gave the original, along with the rest of the folder, to Mayes. Mayes assured us that with a little help from a computer he could give us copies that a professional photographer would be proud to call his own.

We had to pass by the waiting room on the way out of the building. I noticed that most of the men in front of me didn't look in on the way by. I did; nothing had changed.

We found an angry medical examiner out in the courtyard. I had to assure him that he would eventually get to see the bodies, but not before the FBI crime lab. Chief Ostresky took him aside to calm him down.

A uniformed state trooper came running up to Dempsey while Ostresky was trying to calm down the ME. "We've found the ambulance, sir," he reported. "One of the choppers spotted it parked behind a grocery store. The attendants are dead, sir."

"Same MO?"

"Yes, sir. They were shot in the back of the head."

"Well, seal the site up and wait for the crime lab people. You didn't drive around back there and mess up any tire prints, did you?"

"No, sir," the trooper said with some emphasis. "We're detouring traffic around the store now and knocking on doors in the neighborhood to see if anyone saw anything."

Dempsey nodded and said, "Good work." The trooper saluted again and hurried away to help knock on doors. "Good trooper," Dempsey told me. "We'll need men like that if we're going to break this case."

"Nah," Kane said. "These guys are jerks." Kane had his hands in his pockets and his aviator sunglasses on and was doing his "too cool to qualify" routine.

"Whadda you mean?" Dempsey asked.

"Shit," Kane told him. "You take all the people that these loonies have killed between them and what does it amount to? Fifty, sixty people? Me or any one of a hundred thousand other guys could walk into a hardware store with forty dollars and make a bomb that would ruin the whole day for an entire floor full of people at a department store. This business with the loonies is just a stupid gimmick."

"No, you're wrong," I told him. "It's not how many people you kill that counts. It's how many people you can scare. People aren't rational about what they're afraid of. They may have six sets of locks on their apartment doors but won't think anything of speeding down the freeway not wearing their seat belts with a cigarette in one hand, a beer in the other.

"You may run into a maniac outside Saks tomorrow, but that won't affect how you sleep tonight. But the thought that there might be a maniac with a straight razor lurking outside your window, waiting in the shadows for the last light to disappear . . . waiting and waiting until there's no sound from the house, and then stealthily trying the doors and maybe forcing in that basement window you've been meaning to fix for the past year, and then creeping into your young daughter's bedroom with the razor raised above his head . . ." Dempsey's hand came crashing down on Kane's shoulder and Kane jumped about a foot and a half and gave off a strangled "Yipe."

"Of course," I concluded, "some people may be more affected than others."

Kane straightened out his sunglasses and gave me a dirty look. "If it wasn't for all those *Friday the 13th* movies it would be even more of a stupid gimmick," he told us. "But we'll still get them. They're jerks."

CHAPTER 3

Dempsey provided a chopper to take us back to the city. Kane and I got into the rear seats and fastened our seat belts and I had a chance to relax for the first time all morning. Relaxing was a mistake. I'd been so preoccupied I'd forgotten how hung over I was. Lift-off brought it all back in a rush.

I was so busy concentrating on keeping my stomach in its usual position vis-à-vis my teeth that I didn't have time to take in the scenery. Unfortunately, Kane wasn't as preoccupied.

"Hey," he shouted. "Take a look at that." He was pointing out his window. He motioned for the helicopter pilot to circle around for a better view. The pilot threw the chopper into a tight circle while we were still climbing like an express elevator at the World Trade Center.

"Urghh," I managed to choke out.

The pilot had the chopper tilted at a forty-five-degree angle so Kane could get a better look at the mass of media vehicles being held back at the gate to the institution. Kane turned to me. "You ought to see this."

I desperately shook my head. But he ignored me. He motioned to the pilot to bring it around so I could take a look. Obligingly, the pilot threw it into a tight figure eight.

"Arggh," followed by a moan, echoed in the cabin. The chopper rocked violently as the pilot straightened it out and pitched it down at forty-five degrees in my direction. I leaned forward and stared at him desperately. He turned to look at me and then very gently straightened the chopper out. He pointed at the airsickness bag in the pouch on the back of the seat in front of me and kept the chopper on the straight and level all the way back to the city.

We landed at the East Sixtieth Street heliport thirty minutes later and he ordered us out. We hit the concrete crouched over and ran for the terminal door. The pilot waited for us to clear the main rotor before he took off but the wash from the blades still came close to knocking me over. There was a Pepsi machine inside the terminal. I had left all my change on the bureau at home. Kane, in his role as Mr. Helpful, lent me seventy-five cents. I used the quarters to buy a soda and sipped at it, trying to settle my stomach.

"Someone seems to have forgotten who fills out his annual evaluation forms," I said to no one in particular.

"Ah," he said. "You don't think anyone would think I could buy you off for a lousy seventy-five cents, do you? Jeesh, everybody knows the going rate for captains is at least twice that."

"That isn't what I was referring to," I told him. "And if you think you're getting your money back, forget it."

I headed for the door with Kane following me at a safe distance.

"Hey," he said. "It's not like it's my fault. I mean, I did warn you about the windows in those things. But hey, does anyone ever listen to me?"

I ignored him so he answered his own question. "No,

no one ever listens to the sergeant. Not until it's way too late.''

A shuttle had just gotten in from one of the airports and a long line of millionaires had formed at the cab station. I walked to the head of the line and showed the attendant my badge and got into the next cab. While I was telling the driver where we wanted to go Kane paused in the door and looked back and addressed the jet set slugs.

He pointed at them and said: "Police emergency, citizens, just doing our jobs." He got into the cab and slammed the door.

"You enjoyed that," I accused.

"Bet your ass," he answered. "But if you think that was fun, you should go downtown some night and try busting stockbrokers." He made an odd "hee-heeing" noise. "You don't even need a warrant. All you have to do is have a couple of beers in one of the bars and wait for a likely-looking lad to take a long time in the men's room."

His voice took on the tone he used in answering defense attorneys. "Having had two beers over the course of approximately two hours and fifteen minutes I felt the need to visit the men's facilities, where I observed the defendant engaged in snorting a white substance which I believed to be cocaine."

"So what do you have against stockbrokers?" I asked.

"Gee," he responded. "Didn't they teach you anything at Columbia? Don't you know that the history of mankind is the history of class conflict in which the poor oppressed members of the working class—represented by my humble self—struggle for justice against the cruel masters of capital—represented by dorky stockbrokers?"

I wouldn't admit to having learned any such thing. "Well anyway," he said, "that's known as the Marxian interpretation of history."

"Groucho or Harpo?" I asked.

"What is that," he responded, "a trick question? Everybody knows Harpo never talked."

I groaned and then hammered on the bulletproof glass and shouted at the driver that if he hit one more pothole he was going to jail for the rest of his natural life. He shouted back something about no speaking no English and sped up.

Seeing as how there were eight or nine reporters gathered around outside our headquarters, I paid the driver off—rather than stiffing him—and got a receipt for my expense record.

The NYPD's "elite" antiterrorism unit has its headquarters, such as it is, in what had once been a junior high school on East Fourth Street, in what the natives cheerfully refer to as Alphabet City. When we first moved in we had shared the building with a VD clinic. But at least now we had the place to ourselves—a recent development attributable to the sudden influx of dollars into the city's venereal disease control program.

The city had shut the school down in the early seventies to rip out the asbestos ceiling tiles, and then hadn't replaced them due to the fiscal crisis. All of the windows were broken and had been replaced with sheets of plywood and we were lucky if the toilets worked on alternate Tuesdays.

The department had set up our group in 1986 after a local got himself killed in the Rome airport. I was the third lieutenant on the promotion list to captain, but the two guys on the list ahead of me had declined the honor. They were holding out for a precinct command. I had needed the money.

I was allowed to select my own team from among "volunteers not serving in vital positions." Which basically meant that I could ask for volunteers, and if they were useless or had pissed off their supervisors, I could have them. I opted for people who had pissed off their supervisors.

I rescued Kane from the Times Square "Pussy Posse." He'd been exiled to Times Square when his boss had begun to doubt that there were really that many muggers who resisted arrest.

Kane put me on to Josh Leonard. Josh had taken it into his head that he was going to clean up the Bronx all by himself. His boss decided to save his life and let me have him.

I got Fred from the bomb squad. He hadn't exactly pissed off his boss. More like scared the pants off him.

I took Wayne on as a charity case. He had testified against a group of detectives who were using electric cattle prods to coerce confessions. Nobody in a uniform had talked to him since. He seemed endlessly grateful that we would. He idolized Kane.

The department assigned me Bret. A typical PD bureaucrat, he wants to put in his twenty years and retire so he can start working on a second pension.

The neighborhood we work in isn't great, but then we all have guns. Standard operating procedure requires that at least one person keep an eye on the projects across the street while the gate is being opened or closed. We'd turned the basketball court into a parking lot and it hadn't won us any friends in the neighborhood. They all had guns too.

Looking over our shoulders wouldn't be required today, I realized as we got out of the taxi and were immediately surrounded by reporters. It made me yearn for the street gangs that usually hung out in the neighborhood. I gathered that the general consensus of inquiry was "What the fuck is going on out on the Island?"

I held up my hands and told them that at this point I couldn't make a statement without approval from the governor but that if they came down to FBI headquarters we would probably have a statement ready after our two o'clock meeting. It didn't seem to satisfy them, but Kane was offering to break arms so they didn't press me too closely.

We left the reporters outside the gate. I think that pissed them off more than the lack of a statement. As we walked across the parking lot I could see Bret and Fred watching the crowd through the peephole they'd cut in the plywood covering our windows.

"Jesus Christ" was the unanimous response when I told them what had happened.

"It's a lot worse than people think it is," I told them. "We're going to have widespread panic in a couple of days. The only thing people will be thinking is that they personally are going to get to star in their very own slasher movie. They're going to be shooting at shadows, their kids are going to have nightmares and every police department on the East Coast is going to be swamped with crank calls. And the buck is going to stop right here with us."

I let that sink in for a few seconds. Then I told them what we could expect in the way of help.

"Thanks to his excellency the governor, it's going to be us on the hot seat. It we don't produce results fast, we can be certain our friends in the FBI will be more than willing to take over. And considering what a jerk Mayes is, we can just about forget about any help from that quarter."

"Do we need their help?" Josh asked.

"We need all the help we can get," I told him. "Think about it; they're holding everyone in the Northeast Corridor hostage. Everybody's favorite phobia is out there tonight: psychotic killers, baby rapers, sadists, perverts. But what's really going to send the public off the deep end is the idea that the psychos are going to be getting help. It's one thing to keep an eye out for some sick weirdo following the kids home from school, but how are they going to stop terrorists from hijacking a school bus and feeding their kids one at a time to Dr. Wilbur?

"And you can be sure our pals in the media are going to be stirring the pot as fast as they can," I added. "There's nothing quite like mayhem on a wide scale to sell newspapers."

Wayne spoke up. "What do you think the terrorists are going to do with the loonies?"

"It looks to me like they're setting us up to look like real chumps with that crap about the lights going down on Broadway," I told him. "If we put three hundred cops at the

corner of Broadway and Forty-second and they unleash
Branner in the express train to Times Square the press will
wonder how we could have been so stupid. But if we don't
put three hundred cops in the theater district and they give
Whitman a machine gun and let him loose outside Sardi's
we can all expect to be handing out parking tickets in Queens
next week.''

Branner had gone berserk with a saber on the observation
deck of the Empire State Building—he had said that the
mayor of New York had ordered him to kill all the tourists.
It had been real bad for the trade. Whitman had been a gun
nut who lived in Brooklyn. He had finally decided that he'd
had enough of the skateboarders in his neighborhood and
had let loose with an AK–47 in an effort to keep the sidewalks passable.

"So what are we going to do?" Wayne asked.

"I'm not sure," I told him. "It would help if we knew
who we were up against, but we don't. They seem to have
a penchant for publicity so I expect them to do something
splashy. We don't have nearly enough manpower to cover
everything. But we can be pretty sure that they'll strike
here. Because," I added, "as everyone knows, this is the
media capital of the Western world."

"So what do we do now?" Fred asked.

"Josh, see if there's any word on the street. These people
are bad; see what your contacts have to say about the worst
dudes they ever knew. Fred, go see Roark at Interpol. He'll
be glad to help, although this stinks of being homegrown.
Wayne''—I handed him the picture of Eric Degangi—"this
guy paid a visit to Toyon last February, claiming to be a
Columbia student named Eric Degangi. Go down to Columbia and find out if he really does attend and where he
lives. Watch his apartment and see who comes and goes."

"Columbia's out for the summer," he pointed out.

"There'll still be plenty of students. Don't flash the picture around and don't make any moves without us. Bret,

stay here and man the phones. Everybody else report in on the hour. Any questions?''

"Yeah," Kane said. "Why do you think they're home-grown?''

I shrugged. "Whoever thought this up must have a great notion for how Americans think. If they were foreigners they'd have just set off a bomb at Children's Hospital and left it at that." There weren't any more questions. "Let's roll," I told them.

I went to my desk to call Dempsey and saw the message from Chief of Detectives Goldman. I gave Bret a nasty look for not telling me right away and dialed the number. Goldman is reputed to be the smartest man ever to put on a blue uniform and he isn't famous for his patience.

"About time you called, Kelly," he told me. "I didn't get you this assignment so you could keep me in the dark. Now what's going on?"

That at least solved the mystery of how I'd come to get my plum position. Of course, Goldman probably really did look on it as a plum: my chance to shine. I brought him up to date on the situation at Toyon and what I surmised about the people we were looking for.

"Shit," he told me. "That stinks. Well, you better haul your ass over to City Hall and tell the mayor. He's kind of anxious to hear about it himself."

"Yes, sir," I told him. I didn't bother to ask what time. He meant haul my ass now.

I wasn't surprised to find Goldman, along with his boss the police commissioner, cooling their heels in the mayor's office. They were sitting on opposite sides of the waiting room studiously ignoring each other. It was an open secret in the department that they despised each other. I sat down by the chief while Kane went to investigate the mayor's secretaries.

"It's bad, Kelly," he told me. "I think you're right about them setting us up to look like chumps. And what's worse," he added, glancing over at the commissioner, "I got this feeling somebody else is already setting us up to take the fall for it."

"How's the mayor taking it?" I asked him.

"Not real well. He suspects that there's going to be a lot of people who decide to spend their Labor Day weekend somewhere else this year. There's a big ABA convention due in town Tuesday, and as you know, the United Nations is back in session. I think he's taking a lot of heat."

"Nobody's supposed to know anything yet," I pointed out "So how is he getting any heat?"

He gave me a withering look. "If nobody knows anything," he asked, "how come the *Post* is reporting that the hero cop who so lately saved the city from the Caribbean menace is now running the state task force in charge of the 'Deranged Dozen' investigation?"

"They're just doing what they do best," I told him, "guessing. They'll probably have Son of Sam on the loose by the time the afternoon editions come out."

"How's the investigation shaping up?" he growled.

"Mayes, the FBI guy, is going to be a jerk. But the state police captain is a stand-up guy and Suffolk County is co-operating, for all that's worth. How much help are we going to get from the city?"

"You," he told me, "probably not much. But every man on the force is going on OT this weekend. We're sending them out in force to reassure the public."

One of the mayor's secretaries came out of his office and beckoned us toward the inner sanctum. I had to pry Kane away from his target-of-opportunity. I figured the mayor would remember him.

The mayor's office was decorated in the fashion of a Victorian-era lawyer's office. It suited his personality; he'd always reminded me of a Dickens character. The walls were light blue down to the white wainscoting and built-in cabinets. The walls were barely visible they were so cluttered with the memorabilia of his thirty years in politics.

He had been talking with one of his political assistants, whose name escaped me. I'd seen the guy on television a lot, but always in the background. He was staying for our meeting. I allowed the various big shots to grab seats and then took one off to the mayor's left behind Goldman. Kane sat behind me and the secretary behind the mayor. She took out a pad and prepared to take notes.

The mayor looked up from his report over at Goldman. "Well, Sy," he began, "what's happening?"

Goldman shook his head. "It's not good. It's already turning into a media circus. We can expect about the same story we had during the last of the Son of Sam business, only multiplied by twelve. Tourism will be way down, absenteeism way up. We're going to get killed with police overtime. The hotels will suffer and nobody's going to be singing 'I Love New York.' "

The mayor turned to the commissioner, who looked down at a page of notes he had in his lap and started reading them.

"The switchboards are already jammed by cranks with hot tips. I've canceled all vacations and we're gearing up to put more manpower on the streets. Sy's set up a command post at One Police Plaza and we're drawing men from all precincts to staff it. We're going to concentrate heavily in lower Manhattan since that seems to be the most likely target. But we're also assigning men to other high-visibility areas like the Statue of Liberty and the bridges. We're withdrawing all uniformed patrols from the theater district and we're going to saturate it with plainclothesmen starting tonight."

Goldman nodded. "We'll have the city sealed tight as a drum by this evening. We already have extra men out on the streets and we're going to use the rookies in the academy to handle routine duties. We're prepared to help the state task force in any way possible. We'll be interfacing with them through Captain Kelly." He looked over at me and I took that to be my cue.

"The terrorists appear to be highly efficient and ruthless. The FBI crime lab people are going over the prison now, but frankly we don't have much hope of finding any useful physical evidence. The state police and Suffolk County are cooperating fully and we expect to have integrated all local and county police departments into the task force by Sunday.

"We're investigating what leads we do have and are in contact with Interpol for any help they can give us. Captain Dempsey of the state police is setting up his command post in Mount Vernon to handle the organizational details of the multistate task force. By this evening it will be the largest combined police action in the history of the United States."

I didn't tell him that it was mainly going to sit around and wait for people to die and hope that the terrorists screwed up somehow.

The mayor leaned forward in his chair. "Is there anything I can do personally to help?" he asked.

"Yes, sir," I told him. "A statement by you asking the public to remain calm would be most helpful. We're expecting a busy night ahead all over the state."

"I'll call a press conference for this afternoon," he told us. He ignored his political flack, who seemed to have something he wanted to tell him. "Let me make one thing clear to everyone in this room. I want these bastards caught. And I want them caught soon and I don't care what you have to do to do it. This is my city and I won't have my people being held hostage."

He glared around the room waiting for one of us to threaten to take his people hostage. When none of us offered, he went on "All right, get going."

We dutifully trooped out, leaving the mayor and his assistant to work up a reassuring, but noncommittal, speech for the mayor to read at six o'clock, just in time to be the lead story on the six o'clock news.

"By the way," Goldman told me on the way to the elevators, "that was good work you boys did up in Harlem yesterday."

"That's right," the commissioner added. "We have a lot of faith in you."

That was rich; he probably hadn't known he had an anti-terrorism unit until the press started asking him questions about it. "Thank you, sir," I told him.

"You really going to be able to get those Connecticut assholes to cooperate?" Goldman asked me.

"Well," I told him, "Dempsey said he would take care of it, and he's the kind of guy you have to believe when he says he's going to do something. The task force is having a meeting at two at the Federal Building. Would you like to come along, sir?"

"No," he replied. "I'm so busy now I probably won't get home for a couple of days. How about you, Jamie?" he asked the commissioner.

The commissioner shook his head and looked blank and then regretfully declined.

Kane and I didn't have much time before our two o'clock meeting so we grabbed hot dogs from a pushcart and headed over to Federal Plaza. We had to show our badges to get past the metal detectors in the lobby at FBI headquarters. And even then they made us stand in front of a video camera until somebody upstairs could identify us. I gave the man on duty the name of one of Mayes's flunkies. I didn't give them Mayes's name because we didn't want to cool our heels in the lobby for twenty minutes.

The agent I'd asked for came down to the lobby to escort us. He gave us visitor badges and was agonizingly polite.

"I'm sorry, sir," he told us. "Special Agent Mayes is on the phone with Washington. Your friend Dr. Pearlroth is upstairs with Dr. Gopinath, though."

"That's fine," I told him. "Can you take us there?"

He agreed that that was within his abilities and inserted a cylinder key in a lock where a button should have been and opened the elevator doors.

Sheldon and Gopinath were cloistered away in a conference room three floors up. They weren't speaking to each other and you could sense the tension between them. I should have figured that Sheldon and Gopinath wouldn't get along. Sheldon has an unsurpassed ability to piss people off within five minutes of meeting them. He has a frenetic personality and is one of the most self-centered human beings I've ever met. On the other hand, I understand he's great with spastic kids. Maybe they can identify with him.

Sheldon looked up as we entered. "Mike," he said. "I owe you, buddy. This is going to make the best case study of mass hysteria in the literature. And I'm going to be right there to get the scoop." He looked like a kid anticipating Halloween.

"Yeah," I told him. "It's really going to be great when a couple of kids get butchered. I expect that'll bring out all kinds of hidden psychoses in the public."

His face fell. "Jeez," he said. "That's the trouble with you laymen, you can't get the proper perspective on these things. It's not like I'm responsible for what's going on. But since it's there, we might as well reap what benefits we can."

"Thank you, Dr. Schweitzer. What's going on in here?"

"Well, for one thing," he replied, "real bad medicine." Dr. Gopinath's eyes were boring holes in him and I could see that the prison director was barely holding back his rage. Sheldon was oblivious. "You don't have to worry much about the missing inmates doing anything soon. They probably won't even be walking for a few weeks."

I raised an eyebrow.

"You wouldn't believe the drugs they've pumped these people full of. This is polypharmacy at its worst," he said, holding up a file folder.

I looked over to Dr. Gopinath.

"If Dr. Pearlroth," he said acidly, "had ever stepped for even a moment out of his ivory tower, he would not be so quick to make these accusations."

Sheldon turned around to face him. "Are you trying to tell me that any of these people," he said, pointing to the stack of folders, "can do anything but feed themselves . . . slowly?"

"If we did not heavily sedate some of these people," Gopinath defended himself, "they would harm either themselves, their fellow inmates or members of my staff. Possibly all three."

"In the past each of these people, and I mean people, not stacks of manila folders, would have been placed in restraints twenty-four hours a day. Have you any idea what becomes of someone strapped into a bed twenty-four hours a day? Bed sores, atrophied limbs and disease. Staff members would have had to scrape the feces off their bodies on a daily basis and their life expectancies would have been less than five years.

"Drug therapy has allowed us to improve their lives immeasurably and I will not stand to have some know-nothing professor accuse me of abusing my patients."

"How can you call a permanent state of drug-induced stupor an improvement?" Sheldon asked him. "It's inhuman."

"If you had any love for humanity," Gopinath replied, "you would work with real human beings on occasion rather than staying in your antiseptic laboratory trying to pretend that college students make up a representative cross section of the human race."

"That's enough, you two," I told them. "Sheldon, get off his case. He's doing the best he can with the crap the state gives him. And you shouldn't act so high and mighty anyway. I doubt you'd want the AMA to know about your early drug experiments." Sheldon had been a chemistry major as an undergraduate and before the FDA had started controlling raw ingredients he had synthesized all sorts of interesting compounds for us.

"We have a job to do," I went on. "We have to get Dr. Gopinath's patients back where they belong. And in case you've forgotten—the slimes who took them killed five innocent people in the bargain. The one thing this task force can't stand is dissension. We're a team and I expect each of you to . . ." I nearly lost it there. Kane was mouthing the words as I said them. "Give one hundred percent for the team and help each other out regardless of your personal feelings."

I considered making them shake hands. But since it was only Sheldon who was acting like a two-year-old I decided not to subject Gopinath to the ordeal. They made noises about how of course capturing the terrorists came first and they would do everything in their power to accomplish it. Kane raised his fist in the air and mouthed, "Now get out there and knock their fucking jocks off."

CHAPTER 4

The FBI had plenty of money to spend on conference facilities and it showed. Everything from the carpets to the ceiling fixtures had that expensive boardroom feel to it. All that was missing were windows.

The *Post* was still reporting that I was running the investigation, so I took the chair at the head of the table. Mayes didn't seem to be particularly annoyed. I got the impression he was waiting, though. Waiting for the scent of blood and then it would be over faster than a shark attack in a kiddie pool.

Besides all of the attendees from the morning, there were Dempsey's opposite numbers from Connecticut and New Jersey, as well as a couple of faces I didn't recognize. A secretary of some sort sat down behind me and prepared to take notes. He crossed his legs and opened a steno pad and leaned forward and asked me to be sure to have everyone identify themselves at the start of the meeting.

Reading the minutes from the morning's meeting gave me something to do while we waited for everyone who was

attending to sit down. What each of us was supposed to
have been doing was spelled out on the first page. It made
chairing the meeting that much easier.

"Ahhemmm," I began. "I'm Captain Michael Kelly of
the New York City Police Department antiterrorism unit.
Please identify yourselves for the record so we can get
started."

They went around the table identifying themselves. The
only one missing from the morning's meeting, as far as I
could tell, was one of the Suffolk County guys. As far as
I could tell, because they could have switched the Feds
around all day and I'd have never noticed.

The new faces belonged, respectively, to an assistant
attorney general who had Ivy League shark written all over
her, and a special assistant to the secretary of state who said
she was there in case the terrorists turned out to be of foreign
origin.

"Special Agent Mayes," I began, "could you bring us
up to speed on what the crime lab's found and any progress
with Dr. Gopinath's photo file?"

Mayes looked down at some notes he'd spread across the
table in front of him. He didn't bother with addressing the
chair or any of that business. "All five of the victims were
killed by forty-five-caliber rounds fired from a distance of
between six and eighteen inches. Each of them was shot
twice in the back of the head. The damage is consistent
with the muzzle velocity of a MAC 10. Ballistic reports are
incomplete, but it appears that five separate weapons were
used in the killings.

"We've managed to match tire tracks found at the garage
where the ambulance attendants were murdered with tracks
at the prison. They belong to fifteen-inch Goodyear radial
truck tires consistent with light trucks or parcel vans.

"Footprints found at the garage site leading away from
the real ambulance are consistent with size-eleven military
jump boots. They apparently tracked grease from the lot
into the Q wing, where we've found trace amounts that

match the gas chromatograph response of the grease found on the pavement behind the grocery store.

"The second ambulance was purchased last March at a used-car lot in New Rochelle for cash and was registered to the Jasmine Delivery Service. Jasmine Delivery listed a post office box in White Plains as its mailing address. We obtained a search warrant for the box this morning but it appears to have been some months since the box has been opened. No one at the post office can recall anything about the people who opened the post office box. The salesman at the used-car lot vaguely remembered the man who bought the ambulance. We have him looking at file photos now, but we aren't optimistic.

"The Motor Vehicles registry lists no other vehicles in the name of Jasmine Delivery. A computer search indicates that no other commercial enterprise uses the post office box as its mailing address. There was nothing in the box not addressed to either Jasmine Delivery or 'Box Holder.'

"The writing on the wall at the institution is consistent with a left-handed individual between five feet eleven and six feet three inches in height. We're having a handwriting expert examine it at this moment and will have a report available by this evening. The blood apparently belonged to one of the guards. His carotid artery had been cut, also apparently by a left-handed individual. The medical examiner reports that he was already dead when his throat was slit—confirming Captain Kelly's analysis." He looked up. "He also reports that there were abrasions on the dead man's forehead. Apparently they just dropped him when they had sufficient blood." He looked back down at his notes. "There were no latent prints on the dead man's ankles.

"A courier flew to Washington with the Toyon photograph file this morning. As of quarter to two this afternoon, no match had been made with any known criminal or terrorist. We're flying the head of security at the prison to Washington to identify the individuals in the photographs.

We'll run a background check on each of them and let you know if anything unusual turns up.

"Eric Degangi is a student at Columbia. He lives in an apartment at Four-one-nine West Hundred-and-fifth Street in Manhattan and is originally from Kansas City, Missouri. He works part-time as a waiter and pays taxes consistent with his vocation. He is not known to belong to any extremist organizations and, in fact, is not even registered to vote. A passport was issued in his name in 1987. The picture from the State Department files doesn't match the one taken at Toyon."

Dempsey spoke up. "We pulled his license at Motor Vehicles; same name and address, different face."

"We have his apartment under surveillance," I told them. "When he gets in we'll talk to him. Anything else you can add?" I asked Mayes.

"No, other than that we're going to establish a base here for the crime lab people. They'll be ready when the terrorists strike." He looked around at all of us. "So please don't screw around at the scene." Dempsey and Kane winced; I didn't say anything. There wasn't much any of us could do until the terrorists killed someone. It was just unpleasant having Mayes put into words what all of us were thinking.

"Chief," I said, looking in Ostresky's direction.

"You were right about them staking out the ambulance company. Someone calling himself Richard Harris rented out old man Jensen's five-and-dime six months ago. It's right across the street from the ambulance company and it had been vacant for a couple of years. The owner never actually met Harris. He paid six months rent in advance with a money order drawn on Citibank. The only thing we found in the building was a stool in an upstairs office that had a view of the ambulance company. The stool was parked in front of a window.

"Nobody recalls ever seeing anyone entering or leaving the store. We figure they must have dropped off somebody at night and then relieved him the next night."

"They didn't leave any garbage behind?" I asked. "No coffee cups, no cigarette butts?"

"Nothing."

"Have you found where they were keeping the fake ambulance?"

"Not yet."

"Any word on witnesses then?"

"We've found a baker who thinks he remembers seeing a panel truck heading for the expressway. He was due at work at two A.M., which would put the sighting at approximately one-forty. We had him look through the book and it could've been a Ford delivery van."

Dempsey spoke up. "We're running a computer search now for light trucks registered as commercial vehicles with addresses given as post office boxes," he told us. "We're going to feed that through a relational data base at NYNEX to compare it to Yellow Page listings and another data base in Albany of companies registered in New York that have filed sales tax records. We'll run down the names that don't appear on all three lists. The postal inspectors are cooperating and they'll tell us which boxes haven't been opened for a long time."

"How many trucks is that going to be?" I asked.

"Probably hundreds." He grinned. "Most of them will probably turn out to belong to people running businesses off the books. When we're through we'll turn the list over to the tax boys." Every one around the table nodded their heads approvingly. Tax cheats are a sore subject for public servants.

Buchanen harrumphed and drew everyone's attention to a copy of the *Post*. It looked like they'd had to get out the wooden type again. The headline was "*NIGHTCLUB STALKER ESCAPED*." The headline covered three-quarters of the front page, leaving enough room at the bottom for his picture and a few lines of the story. The Loverboy Killer was Marcus Twain and he had really boosted circulation a few years back. It looked like he was about to do the same this year.

"The governor," Buchanen told us, "is not very happy about what's going on and expects a quick resolution. He wishes it to be known that every resource of the state is at your disposal." No one had much to say to that. The FBI evidently had pressure coming from other directions.

The assistant AG spoke up. "And, of course, every resource of the federal government is also at your disposal."

"Well, I guess you all know we're going to need all the help we can get," I told them. "It appears they've been planning this thing for at least six months. There's no way they could have done that without a lot of money. And even worse, six months of planning requires six months of discipline. I'm afraid we can't count on them making many mistakes."

"It's even worse than that," Dempsey pointed out. "Their six-month lease runs out at the end of the month. They must have established their time table six months ago. It's a sure bet they've got the rest of the operation planned out as well. They're acting and we're reacting and they're way ahead of us."

I let Dempsey's dark warning hang there for a moment. "All right," I said. "Doctors Gopinath and Pearlroth have a presentation to give."

Sheldon got to his feet and without a glance in Gopinath's direction launched into lecture mode. "We've prepared a brief summary on each of the missing patients and how he or she is likely to react under different circumstances. We'll give you the list in order of potential dangerousness, starting with the least dangerous and working forward."

He asked for the lights to be dimmed and fired up a slide projector. I guessed he was probably practicing for the next meeting of the American Psychiatric Association. Sheldon had never been too happy about teaching at City College and he probably figured this might be his opportunity to make it to the big time.

"The least dangerous of the inmates are the true psychotics," he began. "The hebephrenic schizophrenics: Lasuen, Branner and Whitman." As he spoke their names he flipped forward through their pictures, stopping with Whitman. The pictures all appeared to be old, probably taken when they were first admitted. "I know calling someone who murdered fifteen teenagers with an assault rifle the least dangerous sounds peculiar, but in these circumstances it's appropriate. Each of these men is clearly insane and easily recognizable as so by the public. They may be extremely violent, but it will be difficult, if not impossible, for the terrorists to control them. To get them to do the things they'll want done."

Dempsey had a question. "My understanding is Whitman lived in the same neighborhood for more than twenty years and was never thought to be anything but slightly odd. That doesn't exactly square with what you've just told us."

"Unfortunately, dementia is degenerative," Sheldon began. "It's possible he was nearly normal for fifteen years and slowly over time became unstable without anyone noticing. His present condition, according to his charts, is one of very significant psychosis. Unless heavily sedated he becomes impossible to control and extremely violent. He hears voices that order him to do terrible things and he's constantly in fear of the spirits of the boys he killed.

"Branner and Lasuen are the same way. As you recall, Branner felt the mayor had ordered him to kill all the tourists and Lasuen had gotten similar orders relating to the Jews— and from an even higher authority. Neither of these gentlemen has gotten any better at Toyon. In fact, their conditions have worsened to the point where everyone is now either a tourist or a Jew."

"And you don't think these guys are dangerous?" I asked.

"Oh no," he answered. "They may be extremely dangerous. On the other hand, they may not. You see, they aren't capable of rational thought and they don't take orders from anyone, especially from someone who has kidnapped them and is probably treating them badly. They obey an inner voice and it's doubtful the terrorists will be able to influence them. It they let Whitman loose with an M16 he might use it to shoot Martians he thinks are hiding inside streetlights. On the other hand, he may think they've disguised themselves as babies.''

"And what would happen if they gave Lasuen a MAC 10 and dropped him off in front of Temple Beth Israel on Saturday?'' I asked.

"Lasuen believes his testicles are large diamonds and the Jews in the diamond district are out to get them. If you dropped him off in front of a synagogue he might hide, or beg to be taken back to Toyon, where he would think himself safe. On the other hand, he might kill as many people as he has bullets. The point is, no one knows how he would act. And even if it was to kill people, he'd only be able to act once and then not in any predictable fashion. The true psychotics are incapable of rational planning. The other ones are quite capable of it and are, hence, that much more dangerous.

"Kairos, for instance.'' He used the remote control to advance the projector to a picture of a brooding, melancholy monster. "Seven feet one inches tall and suffering from paranoid schizophrenia. He felt short people were out to get him. He had barricaded himself in his house and was apparently the butt of a lot of neighborhood jokes. One day he came out with a sledgehammer and killed seven people, including one man who was six foot two.

"I feel he is more dangerous than the first three in that he is perfectly capable of planning an assault. Although, if the terrorists were to release him, he would probably try to go to ground. Which, considering his height, would be extremely difficult for him.

"They have four masked schizophrenics: Stern, Durand, Crothers, and Roth,'' he lectured as he advanced the slide projector. "These people are extremely dangerous in that it's very difficult to differentiate them from the general public. If you get to know them you'll probably be able to feel a strange sense of otherness about them. Generally, they're social outcasts, loners with a long history of personal problems. Nobody's ever very surprised when the police start digging up their backyards.''

He reversed the projector and backed to a picture of a harried-looking little man in a white lab coat.

"Durand, for instance, was an extremely well-paid computer scientist. He was well respected by his colleagues and had an important position and an admirable work record. And then one day he went berserk and killed three technicians and destroyed millions of dollars worth of computer equipment. They found his young son, who he was reportedly very close to, murdered in his bed. Apparently he had concluded that automatons had been substituted for the entire human race and that it was his duty to kill them all. In retrospect some of his colleagues said he had seemed somewhat odd. But no odder than most computer scientists.

"Stern," he said, forwarding to the next slide, "as you probably recall, was somewhat of a social outcast who nonetheless was able to kill at least forty people over a period of more than a decade without bringing suspicion down upon herself.''

Stern looked a little dumpy and pale. As if she'd grown up in the fifties and never quite realized that Ike wasn't president anymore.

"She developed a fixation about patients she didn't think were, in her words, 'good sports,' '' Sheldon continued. "Patients who complained or were unable to control their bowel movements or who needed medication at odd hours. Finally she moved on to patients in general, inducing cardiac arrest in random individuals. When she was caught her colleagues were shocked, although they had no trouble believing the evidence.

"Crothers was an obsessive loner," he began as the projector flashed to the picture of a skinny teenager wearing a plain white T-shirt. "No one was very surprised when he was arrested for child murder. He may have abused and killed as many as five children. Note that it was only through sheer luck he was captured. A retired police officer in his neighborhood decided he fit the bill for the killer and started following him.

"It's important for you to see the difference here between this group and the psychotics. Crothers lived more than thirty miles from the nearest of the killings. Raping and murdering children was something he was driven to do. But that didn't stop him from planning each of the killings in detail. That's a far cry from a psychotic opening up with a machine gun on his front doorstep.

"Roth," he said as another picture flashed on the screen. "Murder, rape, kidnapping, assault, sodomy; he did it all. And he'll do it all again if he's let loose; he enjoys it.

"All of these people, if released, would present a nightmare problem. They enjoy what they do or are driven to it and will attempt to continue doing it until killed or recaptured. Tracking them down could be difficult if the terrorists provide them with cover. Within the week there could be panic on a national scale.

He pushed forward once more to a picture of a kindly middle-aged man with salt-and-pepper hair. He was deeply tanned and his face was creased with smile lines. His blue eyes positively twinkled.

"Looks like Marcus Welby, doesn't he?" Sheldon began. "This is Dr. William Wilbur, possibly the most sadistic killer in the medical annals. They found parts of seventeen bodies buried in his backyard, and additional parts scattered around his house. He had installed a complete operating theater in his basement and was probably performing transplant operations years before anyone else. His success rate was low, however, and it wasn't just because he refused to use anesthetics.

"He was out playing golf with some colleagues when a short circuit in a homemade surgical light started a fire in his basement. Guess what the firemen found when they got there?

"Or how about this guy?" he asked as the picture of a clean-cut young blond with a toothy grin flashed on the screen. "This is Marcus Twain, better known as the Nightclub Stalker or the Loverboy Killer. He was from a very wealthy Boston family and had loads of hilarious stories about all the prep schools he'd been thrown out of for childish pranks. Every single woman in the city was staying at home nights and he still didn't have any trouble picking up victims. He was captured after a transvestite nearly killed him first.

"Florence Moore," he said, pressing the Forward button. "Here's a case. Too bad she didn't get picked up by young Marcus. She apparently enjoyed having men fight over her. She graduated from that to collecting penises. And as beautiful as she is, she accumulated quite a collection. Talk about unlucky. The last hotel she checked into with one of her victims made X-rated videos for the export business. They filmed her in action.

"And last, but certainly not least. Jonathan Roble, insurance salesman. He had a way of making people regret not going for the whole life after all." Roble looked like a young William Wilbur. He had that sincere "you'll be glad you did someday" look. I bet he sold a lot of insurance. Especially after people started hearing about all the families he had butchered.

"It wasn't sheer luck he was captured," Sheldon continued. "But the investigation lasted more than a year and required the full resources of the FBI and several mandecades of labor.

"You'll note," Sheldon continued, "that these last four have an awful lot in common. There is no way for anyone, including trained analysts with years of experience, to differentiate any of these people from a normal human being. As Cleckly put it so succinctly, they wear the mask of sanity.

But, ladies and gentlemen, believe me, there is nothing human behind the mask.

"They are, for the lack of a better term, psychopaths: subtly constructed reflex machines who can mimic the human personality exactly. You could talk with a psychopath all day, and you probably have, and you would never for a moment dream he or she had a serious mental illness. It is only by observing a psychopath in action that you can detect one."

Buchanen spoke up. "You talk as if they were quite common. That doesn't sound right."

"But they are quite common," Sheldon told him. "It's just for the most part they have a limited effect on society. Your typical psychopath will ruin the lives of her immediate family, borrow money from friends with no intention of ever repaying it, perpetrate small frauds on society, skip from job to job and generally lead the life of a ne'er-do-well. But in general, a true psychopath will avoid committing crimes serious enough to have herself sent to prison for long periods of time.

"A typical psychopath can mimic love and whisper all the sweet nothings expected of a lover and convince some poor, unsuspecting soul he is deeply in love with her. Only to leave her the next day for the lowest prostitute. And sadly," he added, "there is no defense mechanism that prevents us from falling in love with a psychopath.

"The annals are filled with case histories of men and women who have been arrested a hundred times. They've spent their lives in a never ending cycle of prison to asylum to freedom to prison again. It isn't that they are incapable of telling right from wrong. Many of them are extremely intelligent. It's just that they are totally incapable of experiencing any complex human emotion or feeling any empathy whatsoever for other human beings. However intelligent, they can only assume other people feel the same facsimiles of emotion or pseudoemotion known to them.

They can't distinguish adequately between their own pseudolove and the genuine responses of a normal person.''

"Well, if psychopaths are so much like my brother-in-law," Dempsey began, "incompetent, lazy, harmless sons of bitches, how do you explain a sadistic monster like Wilbur?''

Sheldon thought that over for a second and sighed. "Did you know sadists aren't as uncommon as you might think? They're actually not uncommon at all. But in these enlightened ages we're trained to suppress our enjoyment of the sight of suffering. It was different in the Middle Ages. Public torture was a form of light public entertainment. Large crowds would gather to watch traitors being broken on the wheel and then dismembered while still conscious.

"Those urges are still inside us. Totally repressed in most cases, but still there. Some of them are expressed in socially acceptable forms." He paused. "It's one of the dirty little secrets of the medical profession that some surgeons enjoy their work more than others." My appendectomy scar began to itch like mad.

"One of my patients"—he stopped and gave a significant look at Gopinath—"is a well-respected member of the community who has urges to torture dogs. These urges cause him great pain. He believes himself to be sick and contemplates suicide to save the world from himself. He's worried that someday he may try to fulfill his fantasies.

"These urges, dark and ugly to us, would not stop a psychopath for two seconds. He would simply go out and fulfill them. Incapable of feeling any sympathy for his victims, he could torture and maim children all day. Or until he grew bored with their screams and killed them. That explains Dr. Wilbur. Not one, but two demons haunt the good doctor. He's a psychopathic sadist, a combination both deadly and rare.

"When a psychopathic killer is captured no one can believe it. John Wayne Gacy molested and killed more than twenty young boys in Chicago. He used to dress up like a clown and entertain neighborhood children. Juan Corona killed twenty-eight farm workers in California. There are still people who know him who insist, despite incontestable evidence, that he couldn't have done it. Theodore Bundy may have killed more than a hundred women across the country. The Green River Killer in Washington has murdered more than forty women. He'll probably turn out to be your average joe next door.''

He flipped the projector back to Twain. ''We think he did it for the excitement. He did it for kicks. He murdered fifteen women for the hell of it. He had sex with a few of them, just to pass the time waiting for the main event. He ended fifteen lives, mainly painlessly, for the thrill of it. He couldn't have thought of them as human beings. Not being a human being himself it was probably easy for him.''

He flipped to Moore. ''As for Moore, apparently she is capable of one emotion. She hates men. We'll probably never know why with any certainty, but it's almost certain she was abused as a child.''

He flipped to smiling Jonathan Roble. ''Believe it or not, Roble's motive was greed. He committed some of the most heinous crimes in history hoping to boost his commissions. I wish we had a few pictures of some of the bodies.'' He paused for a moment. ''He hoped to create widespread panic in which he figured it would be easier to sell life insurance. A few dollars meant more to him than the lives of the people he killed.'' He paused for a few moments. ''Recently a stock speculator was arrested for tampering with cold pills in a supermarket. He figured he could make a quick killing in the market by driving the price of the cold pill company's stock down.'' He shuddered slightly.

''But anyway, Roble should give you a clearer idea of how the psychopath thinks. He apparently got no enjoyment out of the killings and dismemberments. He murdered eleven people in order to qualify for a free trip to Florida, where he was presented with a plaque honoring him as New York life insurance salesman of the year.''

"Do you have anything to add, Dr. Gopinath?" I asked.

He got to his feet and looked at each of our faces intently.

"I would just like to say that, despite the nature of these people's acts and how you personally may feel about them, they are still very sick people. I realize that in today's climate mental illness is not widely regarded as a sufficient excuse for mercy, but I would beg that you attempt to take my patients alive. They are truly not responsible for their actions."

"There are not now," I assured him, "nor will there ever be, 'shoot to kill' orders on the missing patients. Cops are people too, Dr. Gopinath. They don't kill unless they have to."

I turned back to Sheldon. "Do you have any guesses as to how the terrorists are planning to use the missing inmates?"

"Do you have any idea what they plan to accomplish?" Sheldon shot back.

"No specifics on demands," I answered. "But a good guess is they'll want publicity. They seem to have a talent for getting people's attention."

"In terms of public response," he began, "they'll probably want to do something as soon as possible." He paused and thought it over for a few moments. "I doubt they'll use one of their real stars, like Wilbur or Moore. They wouldn't want to risk having one of them captured. They'll want to keep them in the bank, so to speak. Terror is that much greater when it's unknown. My guess is they'll turn one of the psychotics loose. They'll probably shoot one of them full of amphetamines and let him loose here in the city."

"The police department is at full alert," I told them. "All leaves and vacations have been canceled. Starting this evening we're going to be patrolling the theater district with plainclothesmen. The transit police will be concentrating on Grand Central and Penn Station. We'll have patrolmen at all the bridges and tunnels. Saturday we'll cover the synagogues and diamond district. Sunday we'll switch them over to the cathedrals and bigger churches. Security at the UN is at full alert and all missions, especially the Israeli, Turkish, British, Soviet and American missions, have been warned to be on the lookout. The Port Authority police are patrolling the rivers constantly. The park rangers on Ellis Island have been reinforced with federal marshals.

"The city is pretty well buttoned up, gentlemen. The question is, what do we tell the public? Or," I added dryly, "is there anything left to tell the public that they don't already know?"

"I think it is important that some measure be taken to calm the populace," Buchanen told us.

"I think it is even more important to let the public know what's out there," I told him. "It won't do any good to hold back information. The press will just make it up if we don't tell them and that'll make things worse. I'm surprised they haven't told people Son of Sam is loose."

"They already have," Dempsey told us. "I heard it on the radio on the way over."

"That cuts it. I'm going to call a press conference for three o'clock and then we'll have Sheldon give them his presentation. That's just the way it's got to be." Buchanen refrained from saying "On your head be it." But I knew that was what he was thinking.

The meeting broke up. Ostresky and the county boys headed back for the Island. Probably they were beginning to get the idea that it wasn't their problem anymore and were heading for cover. I didn't blame them. The Connecticut and New Jersey state police captains headed back to their respective states. I was surprised they hadn't suggested quarantining New York. They had promised to cooperate prior to leaving.

We had a few minutes before I had to go face the press. Dempsey and Sheldon gathered around me outside the conference room to see what I was planning.

"What are you going to tell the press?" Dempsey asked.

"That we're actively pursuing leads and expect to have the crips back in their cages by Monday," I told him. Sheldon winced.

"Don't call them that," he urged.

"Sorry," I told him. "We'll have the unfortunate mental patients back under medical supervision by Monday."

"Much better."

"What makes someone become psychopathic?" I asked.

"We don't think you become a psychopath. We think you're born that way." He shrugged. "It usually becomes apparent during adolescence, but probably only because psychopathic children are harder to distinguish from normal children than psychopathic adults are from normal adults. It could be a defect in the brain, although no one's been able to show it. It apparently isn't congenital and it isn't learned behavior either. I can't think of any cases of psychopathic siblings.

"There is no cure and I can't think of anyone who's ever even claimed to have made much progress. A few optimists claim to have made changes, but I think all they really managed to accomplish was to make their psychopaths better facsimiles of human beings. They didn't actually change them."

He shook his head. "The only good argument I've ever heard for the existence of God is based on psychopaths." He grinned at our puzzled looks. "The psychopath cannot be told in any physical sense from a human being. However, there is little doubt that indeed he is not a human being. If there is a difference, it must be something internal that we can't measure. For lack of a better term, let's call what's missing a soul. If human beings, alone in the animal kingdom, have souls, we must have got them from God because how else do you explain it? It certainly isn't something you can point an evolutionary finger at. Therefore, God exists."

"You believe that, Sheldon?" I asked.

"I said it was a good argument," he replied. "I didn't say it was convincing."

"So how did the psychopath lose his soul?" I asked.

He looked at me impatiently. "I just told you, no one knows. Although it's really a horrible thing. Psychiatrists hate to see psychopaths. They make us feel useless. There's nothing worse than having to explain to some parent that their daughter is not just going through a rebellious phase, she is completely insane. And not only is she insane, she's never going to get better and there's not a damn thing any of us can do about it.

"They never believe you." He shook his head. "The patient always seems sane, just troubled. He always seems to be reasoning correctly and isn't hearing voices or acting psychotic. I tell people it isn't their fault and that the patient does not, regardless of what he may tell them, feel the same way about them that they feel about him. But it's really hard to disown your kids."

I wanted to press him further, but Kane appeared and told me the press was assembling downstairs. Sheldon grabbed the slide projector and hurried off to set up. He wanted to look good on TV.

CHAPTER 5

The press had gathered in full force in the Federal Building's auditorium. The photographers were sitting on the floor in front of the rostrum, flanked on either side by television news cameras. A dozen extra microphones had been attached to the podium with what appeared to be electrical tape.

"I guess it's too late for me to fall back on the camera-shy routine, isn't it?" I hazarded.

Kane slapped me on the back. "Hey," he said pointing into the glare of the TV lights, "isn't that Mike Wallace back there?"

"Anybody else care to get their picture on the front page of the *Times*?" I said.

Dempsey proved to be a stand-up guy and followed me up to the podium. There was a momentary deafening clash of shutters closing and film winding as fifty cameras went off at once. I could see, but not hear, the broadcast people speaking into their microphones. It occurred to me that we were undoubtedly going out live to every station in the tri-state area. I had a momentary urge to drop my pants.

I didn't start talking until after the camera noises had died off to an isolated whir. I looked down at the minutes from the morning's meeting and began to extemporize. "Ladies and gentlemen," I began, "I am Captain Michael Kelly of the NYPD antiterrorism unit." There was another spasm of camera noises as the photographers reflexively snapped off a few more pictures of yesterday's man of the hour. "I regret to inform you," I continued, "that at approximately one o'clock this morning, eastern daylight time, a group of armed individuals broke into the New York State Institution for the Criminally Insane at Toyon and kidnapped twelve of the patients. In the process they brutally murdered the three orderlies on duty as well as two ambulance attendants who were on their way to the facility to remove an injured patient.

"As of yet, we have no information as to who these armed individuals may be or what their demands for the return of the patients are. Police authorities from New York, New Jersey and Connecticut are cooperating fully in the investigation. By this evening the combined task force will involve more than one thousand officers from every federal, state and local police organization in the tri-state area and it will be the largest such task force in U.S. history."

I paused to catch my breath and think of what I was going to say next. Which gave an enterprising news hound a chance to ask whether Son of Sam was one of the missing inmates. Which at least gave me a chance to quash that rumor before I forgot about it.

"For everyone's information, David Berkowitz is not, was not and has never been a patient at Toyon. The irresponsible rumor mongering that has gone on in the media today must be ended immediately. Calming the public and following up false leads requires taking valuable manpower away from our investigation and it is extremely detrimental to our effort. There is nothing you can do that would be of greater service to the kidnappers than to continue spreading wild stories."

Naturally they all shouted out at once asking about any true leads we might have. I'd been careful not to use any loaded words like *terrorist* or *lunatic* and I'd called the prison an institution and the guards orderlies. But it quickly became apparent that I was just whistling in the dark.

"We are currently following up a number of promising leads," I told them. "But I hardly think it would be appropriate to mention them here. I would like to make one additional statement before I turn the microphone over to Dr. Sheldon Pearlroth of City College. I would ask that the public remain calm and that the media not overreact to what has occurred. The men who have perpetrated this action would like nothing better than widespread panic and banner headlines. We will arrest those responsible for these heinous crimes and return the kidnapped patients to Toyon."

"What worries the public the most," one of the reporters called out, "is that the terrorists will start releasing the maniacs. What are you doing to prevent that and where do you think the terrorists will strike first?"

I thought about telling him the terrorists were certain to start releasing the loonies right here in New York City. I figured if I were to tell them something along those lines the terrorists would be tempted to make me look bad by starting in White Plains—or even better, in Connecticut. But I couldn't do it to Dempsey.

"It is by no means certain," I told her, "that the criminals responsible for this are planning to release their prisoners or that they have some political end in mind. It is nothing but dangerous idle speculation on your part to assume any such thing. But," I continued, "we are acting on the presumption that the public is at risk, and for that reason we are on alert for any possible action the kidnappers may take. It would be foolish for me to speculate as to where they might act, if they were to act. But," I added, "it would be dangerous for anyone to assume that his or her city is not in danger.

"The most important thing the press and public can do to help us is to remain calm and watchful and report any unusual occurrences. A special hot line is being manned around the clock." I turned to Dempsey, who leaned forward and gave the number. "Local police agencies can also be contacted. We would especially ask that anyone who might have been in the Toyon vicinity last night and seen anything, no matter how unimportant, give us a call."

I turned to Sheldon. "This is Dr. Sheldon Pearlroth. He received his Ph. D. from Yale in 1979 and at present teaches psychology at City College. He is an expert in deviant behavior and is going to brief you on the missing inmates."

Sheldon called for the lights to be lowered, infuriating the TV people, and launched into lecture mode. He seemed to be doing a better job of it the second time around, but we didn't stick around to hear him. As soon as the lights were lowered we snuck out.

"What'd you think?" I asked Kane.

"You sounded too much like William Buckley and not enough like Melvin Purvis," he told me. "I think it would have been more reassuring to know there was a cop heading up the task force rather than some effete eastern Ivy League snob."

"Glad you liked it," I told him.

I found a phone and called the office and was pleasantly surprised when someone answered. Bret reported that Fred was back and that Wayne hadn't seen anyone matching the Degangi photograph entering the apartment building. I told Bret about what Dempsey had found by pulling Degangi's license at Motor Vehicles.

"Have Wayne go up and see Degangi," I told him. "Maybe he'll recognize the guy in the picture. Tell him to stick tight and we'll be along shortly. Have Fred meet us there."

"Sho'nuff," he told me. I wondered if he was beginning to get the idea that I didn't trust him to do anything important.

We headed uptown into the usual traffic nightmare, which, logically enough, thinned out appreciably once we got into the Columbia area. Wayne and Fred were leaning on Fred's car watching a wiffle ball game in progress. Gentrification in the Columbia area had proceeded rapidly enough that they didn't look too far out of place. But there wasn't much doubt everyone on the block knew they were cops. No one was dealing crack anyway.

"Well?" I asked.

"He knew the guy in the picture," Wayne told us. "He was in one of his classes and remembers the guy borrowing his ID card to sneak a friend into a basketball game as a student. He's kind of pissed off."

"Name?"

"Bryce Worthington, and he's apparently doing pretty good. The student directory has his address listed as 926 Park Avenue."

"You never can tell," I told him. "If he really does live there it could be rent-controlled. Let's go check it out."

We got into our respective cars and headed back downtown into the traffic. It only took us twenty minutes to traverse the forty blocks. But that was mainly due to Kane's driving. The apartment building we pulled up in front of was definitely not rent-controlled. The doorman eyed us suspiciously.

I showed him my ID and I might well have been the head of his union for the sudden change in attitude he showed. His backbone stiffened and his head went back and he gave off a "Yes, sir" that would have done a marine proud. It looked like the word had hit the streets about that new police hero, Mike Kelly, and his band of courageous lawmen.

"Is there a Bryce Worthington living in the building?" I asked him.

"Yes, sir," he shouted again. "Two of them. Young Bryce is in residence. His father, Bryce senior, is, I believe, in South America. They live in number fourteen, sir."

"Is the young one upstairs right now?"

"I do na know, sir. He hasn't come in this way but he would most likely have come up through the garage."

"What kind of car does he drive?"

"A BMW, sir. A black M6 it is, sir. The license plate reads 'BEAMER,' sir. And he would be parking in either stall thirty-one or stall thirty-two."

"Check out the garage," I told Fred. "Wayne, stay here. When we're in position buzz his apartment and see if he's at home." Kane and I headed for the elevators.

"Is young Bryce in trouble?" I heard the old man asking Wayne. I didn't hear his reply.

The elevator was fast and quiet. The doors opened and we found ourselves in a large vestibule with a number of expensive-looking chairs that didn't look particularly comfortable. There were fresh flowers on an antique table and a number of carefully placed mirrors so one could check one's coiffure prior to entering into the august presence of the Worthingtons.

"We're here," I spoke softly into the walkie-talkie.

"Damn right," Kane added. "Deep in the heart of the capitalist oppressor's lair. Built, no doubt, with filthy lucre stolen from the sweat of the brows of the working class."

I looked at Kane puzzledly. "I can understand why it would be filthy," I told him. "But why on earth would the working class keep their lucre on their brows? Don't they have mattresses for that sort of thing?"

"Ho ho ho," he responded. "See if you're still laughing when it's the bourgeois, running dog lacky's turn to go up against the wall."

"He's in there," Wayne informed me via walkie-talkie. "But he says go away and come back with a warrant."

"You want to try pounding on the gates of the capitalist establishment?" I inquired, looking at Kane. We'd had a dozen bench warrants issued in the name of John Doe that morning.

Kane pounded on the door, more for sizing up its sturdiness than for attracting the attention of the inhabitants. "Open up," he called. "In the name of the law." He turned back to me. "I've always wanted to say that."

It was one of those things you couldn't say when you expected the person on the other side of the door to open up with a machine gun. If Worthington had been an old movie buff he would have known his line was, "You'll never take me alive, you dirty coppers." Evidently he hadn't. He just told us to go fuck ourselves.

Kane had evidently decided the door wasn't all that sturdy. He took two steps back and one step forward and planted a size eleven next to the doorknob. The door shattered at the lock and sprung open.

"Viva the revolution," I called out. And followed him into millionaire land.

Apparently the Worthingtons kept the good stuff inside and left the old ratty stuff out in the vestibule for the trade. We found ourselves in an elegant hallway and the mystery of the missing fifteenth-floor button in the elevator was solved by the grand staircase heading upward. The walls were covered with original art and I felt a momentary twinge of regret at having taken Art Appreciation pass/fail.

Young Bryce was halfway down the stairs and looking peeved at having his front door kicked in. I could understand that. What I didn't get was why he would be wearing a Che Guevara T-shirt.

"You fucking pigs," he screamed at us. "You are going to fucking regret this for the rest of your fucking lives you—"

Kane cut him off with a light punch in the stomach that left him curled up in a fetal position gasping for air at Kane's feet. I knew it had been a light punch because he wasn't throwing up all over the Orientals.

"Bryce Worthington," Kane intoned. "You are under

arrest. You have the right to remain silent. You have the right to an attorney. Should you not be able to afford an attorney, and I fucking doubt that, the court will appoint one for you. Anything you say can and will be used against you in a court of law.''

Worthington was still grasping his stomach and no doubt thinking that this wasn't how they used to do it on "Adam 12.'' There were tears in his eyes and his breath was coming out in ragged gasps. "On what charge,'' he choked out.

"Well,'' I told him, "besides resisting arrest, there's five counts of first-degree murder and twelve counts of kidnapping. Which ought to get you seventeen life sentences without possibility of parole.''

"But,'' Kane told him, "since it's probably your first offense and you can undoubtedly afford a good lawyer, the judge will probably let you serve them all concurrently. Hell, you may even like Attica.''

Kane grabbed him under one arm and threw him up against a wall and cuffed his hands behind his back. "Have you seen *Deliverance*?'' he asked. "Can you squeal like a pig?''

"I haven't done anything,'' he informed us. "And I want a lawyer and you're the one going to Attica.'' He glared at Kane. "You assaulted me.''

"Oh?'' Kane asked him. "You got witnesses that're going to corroborate your version of you resisting arrest?''

He turned to me and I pointed a finger at myself and looked innocent. "Me?'' I said. "Well, I don't know. What's it worth to you?'' He couldn't think of a sufficiently high bribe so I sent them on their way.

I picked up the telephone in the hallway and called the Columbia University information number and had them connect me with the provost's office. After only a little persuasion I had them put me through to Dr. Pendar, whom I knew slightly.

"Captain Kelly,'' he boomed. "So good to talk with

you. It's always nice to see an alum doing great things in the world."

I made appropriate modesty noises and then described our recent arrest. "Seems like I remember a Worthington serving on the Trustees," I told him.

"Yes," he told me. "This could be quite embarrassing for the university. Bryce Worthington, class of forty-something. Wealthy industrialist. He's been very active in the university for more than twenty years and has been a trustee for more than ten. Very bad that his son should be in this much trouble. Thank you so much for informing us in advance." He sighed. "It's always worse when you get a phone call from some journalist asking for your reaction."

"Well," I told him, "it may not be all that bad. We need his cooperation in the worst way and maybe we can make some kind of deal. Though I get the impression he isn't going to be very cooperative. He's wearing a Che Guevara T-shirt and was calling us pigs. I thought that sort of thing had gone out of fashion."

There was a pause from Pendar's end. "It did," he told me defensively, "until about eighty-three or four. Since then there've been protests against apartheid, aid to the Contras, abuse of laboratory animals and the university's gobbling up local housing. Nothing particularly disruptive or violent. They're just out to draw attention to things they feel should be changed. And frankly, I think it's a lot more healthy than a campus full of junior achievers hell-bent on their MBAs."

"Any ideas what young Bryce was particularly upset about?" I asked, mentally crossing my fingers and hoping it was lab rats.

"No, I'm afraid not," he told me. "I was only vaguely aware he was here. I would have guessed he was mostly concerned about getting into the right business school. But I guess you never know. I can check around and call you back. Would that be acceptable?"

"That would be fine," I told him. "And if the family

lawyer's a sensible chap interested in keeping young Bryce out of Attica, you should give him a call as well.''

"Will do," he told me. "How can I reach you?"

I gave him the number and told him to try back in an hour.

I figured it was time to call in and tell Goldman what was happening. I had only a modest amount of difficulty tracking him down.

"Well, Kelly?" he asked. "Case cracked yet?"

"Not quite, Chief," I told him before filling him in on what I'd been doing.

"Think this Worthington character knows anything important?" he asked.

"Maybe," I told him. "Probably not. But maybe we can use him. Do you have enough pull with the mayor to have him announce we've made a major arrest?"

"Maybe. What'll that do?"

"They might get antsy and decide to check and see who's missing. Maybe we'll be able to trace the call."

"That's pretty weak."

"Yeah," I told him, "but the only other thing we have going is that the FBI crime lab technicians are standing by to analyze dead bodies."

"I'll do what I can," he told me.

"Anything else happening?" I asked.

"*Newsday* is reporting the 'Lights go down on Broadway' business."

"Hmmm," I said, speculating on who might have leaked that bit of inflammatory information. "Well, Chief," I told him, "this might be the night to get out and see *The Jetsons*. I bet there'll be plenty of seats available." *The Jetsons*— based on the Saturday morning cartoon—was the hit Broadway musical of the season. Tickets were impossible to find, but somehow I didn't think it would be so tough tonight.

"Thanks," he said dryly. "But I'm going to be busy tonight."

I heard the elevator doors opening and turned to see Fred

sneering at the low-tech job Kane had done on the door. I said good-bye to the chief.

"Wayne's on the way to see the judge about a search warrant," he told me. "Kane's downstairs trying to get the kid to tell him where all the money for this place came from. He's raving about the wonders of capitalism."

"Whatever happened to the idealistic young Marxist we've come to know and love over the past couple of days?" I asked him. "Stick around here and wait for Wayne. When you go over the place, dust for fingerprints. Maybe something interesting will turn up. And if you find a video camera pointed at the front door, erase the tape of the past half hour."

He took a two-foot length of demo cord out of his pocket and twirled it around his index finger. "No sweat," he told me.

"You think you can trace any phone calls young Worthington might be getting in the next few hours?" I asked him.

"Sure," he said. "I just have to call a buddy down at the phone company."

"Will he still be there?" I asked.

"Doesn't matter," Fred told me. "He's got a pager and he owes me a big one. I let him fire off a LAW once."

LAWs are shoulder-launched antitank rockets. They aren't the kind of thing you can mail-order from Georgia. I was almost tempted to ask where he had got them (there had to be more than one, because Fred wouldn't have given away his only antitank rocket). But I decided I really didn't want to know. I'm convinced that the brotherhood of gun nuts is going to take over the Masons, and hence the world, someday. They're everywhere and pervade all levels of society. They owe each other favors. It's a scary thought. I made a mental note to start subscribing to *Guns and Ammo*.

The doorman was nowhere to be seen when I got down to the lobby. He was probably too embarrassed to be around to watch young Bryce getting carted off to jail. There was also the small problem of having betrayed him to the flatfoots. He was probably making up for it by making a call to the president of the building's owners' association.

Kane was in the backseat of our police special with the prisoner. Worthington was leaning forward in the seat, seemingly intent on what Kane was telling him, but actually trying to get his weight off his hands. I slid into the driver's seat and cranked the engine. I had to pump the accelerator pedal a dozen or so times before it started.

"Look," Worthington was telling him. "My father got rich by working Central American laborers twelve hours a day for about fifteen cents an hour. It's not like he thought up some product that the consumers hadn't realized they couldn't live without.

"He exploited poor people in Guatemala so he wouldn't have to pay minimum wages in this country and meet the minuscule worker-protection regulations the federal government enacted after manufacturing labor became too scarce to just throw away after industrial accidents."

"Hey," Kane told him. "All I know is that this is the greatest country that ever was and that it's a land of opportunity where one man acting alone, without interference from the government, can control his own destiny and share in the profits of industry."

I started humming "God Bless America."

"A nation where any young person, no matter how humble his origins, can rise to the highest political office. A nation united in shared beliefs in dignity, freedom and equality. A nation striving ever forward in the belief that the future will be better for our children."

Worthington leaned in my direction. "What planet?" he asked me, "has this guy been living on for the past twenty years?"

"Hey," I told him, "quit complaining. The rubber hoses won't seem so bad after this."

* * *

It took the better part of an hour and a half to get back to the school through the evening commute. We were all annoyed by the time we arrived. Worthington because he was under arrest, Kane because Worthington refused to see the beauty of the American way of life, and me because I'd been driving. There was a note on my desk telling me that Pendar had called. I called him right back. I was only slightly surprised that he was still in the office. He was apparently the only one still there, because he answered the phone himself.

"Well," he started, "young Worthington seems to have developed quite a social conscience. Which just goes to prove that they aren't congenital." He paused and seemed to be shuffling papers.

"He was arrested earlier this year outside the South African consulate and also in the offices of ITT. He's active in the Democratic Socialists of America as well as the Sanctuary movement. He's a volunteer at a shelter for the homeless and is a founding member of a group that tutors underprivileged youths in the Columbia area. And as you know, there's no shortage of underprivileged youths in the Columbia area.

"Earlier this year he went to Nicaragua for spring break, where he helped rebuild the National University. He's written a number of passionate, albeit well-reasoned, articles pushing divestment for the *Spectator*. He's well liked by his professors and even people who have no use for his politics all agree that he's a likable sort not given to being holier-than-thou."

"How's he doing scholastically?" I asked.

"That's confidential, of course," he told me and paused long enough for me to make discretion noises. "He gets As from a certain subgroup of history and political science professors. But has managed to accumulate an impressive record of no-credits in a great many other required courses. He was on academic probation all of last year and has asked for, and been granted, a leave of absence for all of next year.''

He paused. ''For what it's worth, I think he's a good kid who's just overanxious to change the world for the better. I don't think he meant to do any harm.''

''Five people are dead,'' I told him. ''He helped.''

''Yes.'' He sighed. ''I suppose he did. If there's anything else I can help you with, please call.'' He gave me his home phone number and his private extension at school and hung up.

Bret threw me a package of slides. ''State trooper dropped these off earlier. Said a guy named Dempsey thought you might like to have them.''

I pulled a slide out of the packet and held it up to the light and found myself looking at a close-up of the back of someone's head. I squinted and saw the hole and realized it was from Toyon.

''No need to ruin your eyes,'' Bret told me. ''There's a brand-new deluxe Bell and Howell slide projector in that Executone cabinet over there.'' He pointed out a beige cabinet against the wall next to the door that hadn't been there this morning. ''Present from the chief of detectives,'' he added. ''They carted it all in here this afternoon.''

We set up the projector and fiddled around with it a few minutes trying to figure out how it worked. We had just got it all figured out when we heard honking. Bret walked over to our newly glazed windows and glanced out in the street.

''Know anyone who has a chauffeur-driven Mercedes limousine?'' he asked me.

''No,'' I told him. ''But I'm always willing to expand my circle of friends. You better go let him in before someone in the neighborhood claims him first.''

While Bret was out opening the gate I pointed the projector at a wall and flipped through the slides. They were disgusting. For some reason police photographers don't think they've done their job unless they get at least a couple of shots that are too gross even for medical textbooks.

Bret came back in with a distinguished old gentleman wearing a banker's blue suit. He had given in to fashion and dispensed with the vest and his tailor had done an admirable job of taking in the jacket so that you couldn't tell that there'd ever been one. Apparently Dr. Pendar had decided that Worthington's family lawyer was a sensible fellow.

"John Haergreve," he informed me, presenting his card. "Of Haergreve, Tressider and Jordan."

"Pleased to meet you," I told him.

"What is this nonsense I've heard about young Bryce?" he asked. "Some foolish, trumped-up charge without a trace of evidence, no doubt."

"Not quite," I told him. "He's charged with five counts of accessory to murder and twelve counts of accessory to kidnapping. If this were Florida he'd be sitting in a gas chamber next year—Haergreve, Tressider and Jordan or no."

"First of all," he told me, "the good citizens of Florida have chosen to use the electric chair to dispose of those of their fellow citizens who happen to be too poor to afford adequate counsel. And second of all, if you have any interest at all in advancing in the New York City Police Department, you will be more careful about slinging reckless charges about with such wild abandon."

I took out the picture of young Bryce culled from the prison photo file and handed it to him. "Last February Worthington junior visited the State Institution at Toyon under the name of Eric Degangi. He wasn't aware that they collected pictures from their video monitors. The head of the institution says he was quite interested in the wing where they held the inmates who were kidnapped this morning."

I had to hand it to the old guy, he didn't miss a beat. "That's Worthington the fourth," he told me. "And I am sure there is some perfectly logical, innocent explanation behind all this, which you did not bother to obtain from Bryce."

"There may be a perfectly logical reason," I snapped back, "but young Bryce was too smart to try and think it up for himself on the spur of the moment. He wanted to call in the family lawyer to think it up for him. But remember," I added, "no matter how logical it is, we only have to get one of the terrorists alive to blow it all to pieces."

"May I see my client then?" he harrumphed.

I motioned for Bret to take him back to the janitor's closet we had converted into a holding cell and they trooped out together.

The phone rang just as I began to start twiddling my thumbs. It was Fred. "He just got a call," Fred told me. "The caller was male, no distinguishing accent. When I told him Bryce was in the can he hung up."

"Did you trace it?"

"Of course we traced it. It came from a Ho Jo's on Ninety-five just west of Darien. I already called the Connecticut state troopers. Maybe they left fingerprints."

"Which side of the highway?" I burst out.

"What's the diff?" he asked.

"Were they going east or west, you idiot?" I screamed.

"Oh," he said. "Hold on, ahhhh . . . they must've been going west, 'cause there isn't a Ho Jo's on—"

I had already hung up so I didn't hear the rest of his sentence.

I dialed the emergency hot line number Dempsey had given me and cursed myself for not having gotten his number; and I must have three hundred business cards in my Rolodex. The friendly state police operator came on the line and asked if I would hold. I identified myself and explained in the calmest voice I could muster that no, I couldn't hold, and that I absolutely had to speak with Captain Dempsey immediately. And then in a moment of inspiration added that if Captain Dempsey wasn't available I would talk to Buck Johansen.

There was a slight hesitation on the other end. I held my breath and then expelled it as he told me to hold on and he would put me through. Dempsey came on the line a second later.

"Dempsey," he said curtly.

"It's me," I told him lamely.

"Well why the hell didn't you call my office?"

"Because I didn't have the number," I told him. "Look, we just got a call from what we think may have been the terrorists. They were at a rest stop on the Connecticut Turnpike just west of Darien. They're on the westbound side of the highway, so they've got to be headed here."

"You want that maybe I should throw up a roadblock and arrest them along with the other hundred thousand or so people who're headed this way?"

"No," I told him calmly. "I want you to set up a video camera on a highway overpass and record all the license plates as they whiz by underneath. And then I want you to compare those numbers to a list of—" I heard the phone dropping on the other end.

He came back on in a few minutes. "Sorry about the sarcasm," he told me.

"No problem," I answered. "They'll be here in thirty minutes. Is that enough time?"

"The commute's going to take a little extra time tonight," he told me. "It seems there's been a work action by the toll takers at the Larchmont toll plaza and kind of a bad accident in New Rochelle. What did the terrorists have to say?"

I explained about Worthington and the mayor's press conference. "It sounded like a suspicious call, anyway."

"Worth a shot. I hope it's not just some cheapskate who wanted his nickel back."

"Well," I told him, "we'll find out."

"I'll call the boys in Connecticut and get them working on a list of vehicles registered to post office boxes. Something they should be doing anyway."

"If it really is them," I pointed out, "they're coming for a reason."

"I'll let your people know," he told me. "Maybe we should all get together in the city."

"Can you set it up?" I asked.

"Ten o'clock OK?" he asked.

"That's fine," I told him. "And, ah, Dempsey?"

"Yeah."

"The operator who put me through to you. Promote him."

"Yeah," he said. "Not a bad idea."

Before he hung up he made sure I had his private number. He made me repeat it back to him.

I called Fred back and apologized for calling him an idiot. He seemed a little put out. You have to watch yourself with Sicilians. I explained what Dempsey was doing.

"I can't believe you traced a five-second phone call," I told him. "How'd you manage it?"

"In case you ain't heard," he told me smugly, "the future is here. You been watching too many old cop shows on channel nine."

"Good work," I told him. "If anyone else calls, or if they call back, let me know."

"Will do," he said.

Haergreve had been watching me in action for some time.

"Investigation proceeding smoothly?" he asked.

I couldn't tell whether he was getting ready to beg for clemency or sue the city for its last subway token.

"I can't comment on that," I told him. "How's your client holding up in durance vile?"

"Very well, thank you. It is possible that Bryce may have information that could be of assistance to your investigation. However, as his legal counsel I will have to insist that he not reveal any information that could be misconstrued as incriminating unless some form of an arrangement could be worked out in advance."

"Cut the crap, Counselor. I was married to a lawyer and

I can smell it a mile away. Your client's guilty or you wouldn't be in here offering deals and you know as well as I do that I can put him away forever."

"Perhaps," he said. "But perhaps not and in the meantime innocent lives are in danger." He leaned forward. "What are you offering?"

"If he cooperates I'll drop all charges."

His eyes narrowed to slits and he seemed to lean even farther toward me for a better view. "You don't have the authority to do that."

"So," I said, "maybe not. But I've been around long enough to know how life works. You probably sleep at the DA's house three nights a week and the kid's father probably spends the rest of the week there. You can work something out and make it stick as long as the arresting officer doesn't squawk."

"And you're the arresting officer, I presume."

"Sure," I said. Actually Kane was. But the arresting officer is the guy who signs his name on the paperwork and I'd have been pretty surprised if Kane had gotten around to it. At least he didn't say anything while I was telling Haergreve my little story.

"Very well," he said.

I motioned for Wayne, who was looking pretty disappointed in me, to take Haergreve back to see his client. We waited around for almost twenty minutes in dead silence till they got back. Kane wasn't asleep, he was just watching the ceiling intently.

Worthington didn't look particularly cowed at having spent time in the holding cell. But then this was his third arrest. He sat down defiantly and looked over at Haergreve.

"I have advised my client," Haergreve told us, "to cooperate fully with the authorities."

"Hit the lights, Wayne," I told him.

I ran through the slides again. I paused at the gorier ones. The almost artistic shots of exposed brain material and the close-up of the slit throat with the carotid artery exposed.

The shots from different angles of the slogan they'd painted with the dead guard's blood. I heard Wayne swallow and finally leave. Haergreve didn't say a word. He'd probably seen worse in court. The last picture was of a large, ugly black man with a sneer on his face.

"Who, might I ask, is that?" Haergreve asked.

"That's Joshua X," I told him. Kane got the lights. "He used to stick up convenience stores and then beat the clerks half to death for kicks."

"That is if the clerks were men," Kane added. "He did other things to the women."

"He's doing life in Attica right now," I told them.

"And he's likely to stay there, because he's killed a couple of guys since he arrived," Kane added.

"And what does that have to do with anything?" Haergreve asked.

"Well," I said, flipping back to a picture that had the three dead guards in it, "these guys and the guards at Attica all belong to the same union."

Kane leaned down and stared at Worthington, who to his credit had turned pale during the slide show. "Guess who your new roommate's gonna be?" he asked.

"There is no need for theatrics," Haergreve assured us. "My client," he looked over at Worthington, "will be cooperating."

I took out my Walkman and set it on Record. I noticed Bret shaking his head. He walked over to the magic Executone cabinet and brought out a big Sony reel-to-reel and plugged it in.

Bret turned the machine on and told it the date and time and explained who was here and what we were going to be talking about. Then he rewound it and played it back to make sure it was recording properly. Just for kicks I left my Walkman on.

"OK," I said. "Start from the beginning, unless you know something really important, and tell us everything you know about Toyon and the people who sent you there."

I'd have been amazed if he knew anything important. So it wasn't a surprise when he started at the beginning.

"I do volunteer work at a shelter for the homeless in Harlem," he began. "The shelter's run by David Abrahms. He was one of the leaders of the student protest movement at Columbia during the Vietnam war. After the war ended he decided to dedicate his life to public service. He's totally apolitical and a really cool dude.

"One night I saw this guy talking to him. I recognized him from an anti-Contra rally I'd been to. He was trying to convince Dave about something but Dave just put him off. Finally Dave walked away. It's like I say, Dave's totally apolitical. The guy looked really mad and started to storm out."

"Describe him."

"He was about forty, in pretty good shape. About six feet tall. He had short, brownish blond hair. No mustache or beard."

"Any accent?" I asked. "Any distinguishing marks?"

"No and no," he answered. "Anyway, I went up to the dude to see what the problem was. He was like really steamed. He told me that Dave was turning his back on the movement.

"That just blew my mind, 'cause Dave always harps on how political movements never solve anything and if we really want to change the world we have to do it ourselves, by ourselves. So I tried to explain all that to the dude, but he wouldn't listen.

"So I got to talking with the dude and mentioned that I'd seen him at the rally. He found out I was a student at Columbia and we talked about that for a while. He denied it, but I think he must have attended at one point, 'cause he sure knew his way 'round campus.

"We went out to get coffee."

"Think back about that," I told him. "Did he pick up his cup with his left or right hand?"

He squinted and tried to recall. "I can't remember, and what difference does it make anyway?"

"The slogan writer was left-handed," I told him.

"Anyway, he told me that the CIA was using Toyon to hold political prisoners." We all started. Even Haergreve looked up at the ceiling. Worthington turned red and looked embarrassed. "Everybody knows about the CIA's drug experiments in the fifties," he said defensively. "The guy told me they had perfected the drugs and were using them at Toyon to reprogram captured Sandinistas. They were going to send them back to Nicaragua to assassinate Ortega.

"He told me all that propaganda the government puts out about Soviet mental institutions is just cover in case they find out what we're doing over here."

Haergreve was rubbing his forehead.

"So I went to Toyon and cased the place. They told me they were going to try and sneak a guy with a camera in and they needed me to do reconnaissance. I went in and there weren't any problems. They wouldn't let me onto the Q wing.

"I met the guy at the same coffeehouse the next week and reported what I'd seen. He took notes. About a week later he called me and told me they were planning on infiltrating a team into the prison to rescue some of the prisoners and alert the *New York Times* about what was going on inside."

"And you believed that crap?" I asked him.

He looked even more embarrassed. "Everyone knows it's the kind of thing the CIA does. I should have known they wouldn't have done it so close to New York, though."

Haergreve started rubbing his eyes. "Just go on with the story, Bryce. We can tell each other fairy tales at bedtime."

"Anyway," Worthington continued, "they wanted me to brief the strike team. They picked me up in a white van and brought me to a farmhouse out in the country somewhere. I was blindfolded and hooded and they kept me in the back of the van so I don't have any idea where we went."

"Did they have a radio on in the van?" I asked.

"No. They didn't even talk to each other."

"Did they stop at tollbooths?"

"I think so, at least one anyway. It was hard to be sure. We drove for a couple of hours but I have a feeling some of it was just driving around aimlessly to throw me off."

"Did you pass through any tunnels?" Kane asked him.

"I don't think so."

"Did you see the house?" I asked.

"They took my blindfold off on the front porch and my eyes weren't adjusted to the light yet, but I think I could identify it if I saw it again."

"What happened inside the farmhouse?" I asked.

"It was really spooky," he told us. "They were all gathered in an upstairs bedroom. There were blankets across the windows and they had a bright light shining in my face. They told me it was best that I not be able to identify them if I were captured. It seemed cool at the time.

"I told them what I'd seen and then they showed me plans of the prison and asked what modifications had been made. They were real interested in the video system. They asked questions about lines of fire and things like that. I asked them why they needed to know about lines of fire and they said it was just in case something went wrong. They pointed out that they were going up against special agents of the CIA and that they couldn't be too careful."

"Did you get any impression about their leader?" I asked.

"He seemed professional. But he was really sincere. He talked to me for a while about the suffering of the people of Nicaragua and how it was up to brave men like the ones who would be risking their lives at Toyon to see that they got justice. He was really inspiring."

"Have they tried to contact you since?" I asked him.

He looked embarrassed. "I was just getting to that. About a week ago the original dude—the one I met at the shelter—

he called and asked me to meet him at Grant's Tomb the next morning. He told me to wear jogging clothes.''

"Why didn't you go?" I asked.

"I overslept and then I was in London for a week." He shook his head. "How'd you know I didn't make it?"

"Because, you simpleton," Haergreve snarled at him, "you're still breathing."

I sighed and signaled for Bret to turn off the recorder. Wayne took Worthington by the arm and started to escort him back to his lonely cell. Just as they got to the door, Josh, sometimes known as Joshua X when he's undercover, came through it. Worthington jumped about two feet backward and made gibbering noises. I didn't blame him; he was having a rough day.

Josh leaned forward and yelled at him. "What's your problem, boy?" Then he recognized Worthington from the picture and sniffed. "'Scuse me if I don't offer to shake hands." He walked past him and sat down next to Haergreve in the chair Worthington had just vacated.

"You been show'n that picture again?" he asked Kane suspiciously.

"Ah come on, Josh," Kane wheedled. "You got to admit it's a great picture."

"My ass." Josh looked over at me. "Well, I heard some great stories, but nothing particularly relevant."

"We're making progress, though," I told him. "What do you know about a guy named David Abrahms?"

"The Saint of One Hundred and Forty-ninth Street?"

I nodded.

"Not very much. He runs a shelter and soup kitchen. He leaves it about once a year to go pick up some humanitarian award or appear at a fund-raiser. The best thing this side of Mother Teresa, I hear."

"Bret," I said, "have a couple of guys go sit with Father Dave. Tell them to stick to him like glue and if he doesn't like it then arrest him for something and put him in a cell and watch him there. Make sure they understand his life's in danger.''

Bret got busy on the phone.

I turned to Haergreve. "Would it be all right if we held young Bryce in protective custody and saved the noble Worthington clan the embarrassment of having to come up with ten million dollars bail?''

"That would be acceptable,'' he told me. He got up to leave. "I know this isn't going to go over very big with you. But young Bryce is worth five of his father. We all have high hopes for him.''

I told Wayne to escort the lawyer to his car.

"Now what?'' Josh asked. "We all go home?''

I looked at my watch and then told him about the phone call to the Worthingtons' residence. "If it was really them, they should be here by now—accident in New Rochelle or no accident in New Rochelle. It's going to be a long night.''

They took me at my word. Kane and Bret started up their permanent Rummy game—Bret up by a couple thousand points but Kane still has high hopes. Wayne called out for pizza and Josh called home to tell his wife he would be late. The phone started ringing long before the pizza arrived. Bret picked it up and then had to push a couple of buttons before it stopped ringing. His shoulders tightened and he gripped the phone harder. "Yeah,'' he said. "Thanks for calling. We're on our way.''

He looked over at me. "There's been an explosion outside the Empire Globe Theater. Every ambulance in the city's been called.''

My knees suddenly felt weak and I was glad I was sitting down.

"What's playing there?'' Josh asked.

"*The Jetsons*,'' I whispered.

CHAPTER 6

We were almost out of the building when I had a sudden vision of a *Daily News* headline, "PRISONER EATEN BY RATS WHILE COPS AWAY." I had Wayne get Worthington out of his cell.

Traffic Division was diverting cars east on the island, giving the ambulances a clearer path to the hospitals. They saw our lights flashing in the distance, though, and had the barriers removed before we got to them. Our lights couldn't help us at the theater: fire trucks and ambulances completely blocked 52nd Street. We parked and walked the longest three blocks of my life to the Empire Globe.

The blast had blacked out the buildings along the north side of the street. It was eerie walking toward the burned-out ruin. The marquees and storefronts all along the south side of the street, except for the ones directly across from the Globe, were all still brightly lit in stark contrast to the dark hulks facing them.

Well-dressed people stood behind the police lines holding each other and crying. The fire trucks still had their lights flashing and firemen were playing searchlights along the upper floors of the theater looking for signs of fire. The trucks cast long shadows that disappeared into the gloom.

The entire front of the Globe had been taken off in the explosion. A lone fireman stood in front of the building playing his hose into what was left of the lobby. Fifteen or so orange bags were scattered randomly around him covering the bodies.

We walked up to the battalion chief, who was on his radio telling the outer boroughs not to send any more ambulances or apparatus. His lieutenant nudged him and he turned around to face us. He seemed to recognize me.

"Careful where you step," he told us, turning back to his assistant. "We only had enough bags for the big pieces."

Worthington looked down and then jumped quickly off to the side. He put his hands across his stomach and began to look sick—I didn't think we'd have any more problems with him cooperating.

"How many dead?" I asked.

The chief turned back to face me. "Who knows?" he replied. "Maybe twenty, maybe more. If it'd gone off a half hour earlier it would have been hundreds. But, as it was, everyone was inside in their seats." He shook his head. "It's an old building. If it was new it probably would have come down on their heads."

I looked around helplessly. I couldn't believe how easily we'd been suckered. We'd been so sure of what they were planning that it hadn't occurred to anyone that they might not limit themselves to the obvious. I had a feeling we were going to look pretty stupid in retrospect. God knows, we had been.

The chief turned back to me. "Go look at those bodies over there," he said, pointing across the street.

We walked across the street in silence, the glass crunching underfoot with every step, reminding me of the roar of a distant and angry crowd. Kane bent down and pulled up the tarp. The explosion hadn't killed the man under it. It looked like he'd been shot about a hundred times with a .22.

Kane dropped the tarp and went over to the building, where he bent down and swept something up off the sidewalk. He came back to us and held out his hand. There were ten bent and blackened nails in it.

"Very nasty," he told us. "This is what I meant by forty dollars at a hardware store."

And then it hit me. We were being set up.

"Kane," I said, "why didn't the bomb go off at quarter to eight, when there would've been hundreds of people milling around out here?"

"Maybe they screwed up."

"No," I told him. "Remember this morning you were saying what jerks they were for kidnapping loonies instead of setting off bombs. These people don't make that kind of mistake. It wasn't a time bomb. It must've been radio controlled. They set it off late because Dempsey screwed up traffic on the turnpike."

"But why would they have to come all the way in here to set off a bomb?" Wayne asked.

I ignored him for a second and walked up to the nearest plainclothesman. He had his hands in his pockets and was chewing a toothpick watching the show.

I identified myself and asked him where he was supposed to be.

"Ahhh, well," he said. "I'm patrolling."

"And where are you supposed to be patrolling?"

"The theater district," he told me. He was probably thinking I was a bastard for taking my frustrations out on him. I looked around and counted fifteen other guys who almost had to be ours.

I turned to Kane. "How many guys do you think actually stayed at their posts and how many of them are standing around here gawking like tourists?"

"You can't really blame them," he pointed out. "A couple of our guys must've been here when the bomb went off."

I started running for the car.

We jumped in and I reached for the ignition. Kane handed me the keys.

"Where we going?" he asked.

"It's been almost thirty minutes," I pointed out. "That ought to be enough time to get every reporter in the city here. And it's only nine blocks to Times Square."

We were halfway there when the call came through on the radio.

We were the first units to arrive. A cruiser was parked in the north end of the square with its lights flashing. We pulled up alongside it and piled out of the car with our guns drawn.

A crowd had gathered on the other side of the cruiser and I spotted a lone patrolman trying to push it back. He wasn't having much success. A look of vast relief crossed his face when he saw us coming to his rescue. He recognized me at first sight and identified himself as Cadet Williams, on loan from the academy to Traffic Division.

"I think it must be Branner, sir," Williams told me. "He came screaming out of nowhere with a fucking sword."

The body was stretched out facedown in the street alongside Williams's car. Branner was still gripping the saber tightly and I suspected the morgue attendants were going to have to break his fingers to get it loose. Someone had used duct tape to fix headphones to his ears. At least ten turns of the stuff were wrapped around his head like an obscene parody of the bandages a cartoon character with a toothache would wear.

The tape player they'd attached to his belt was still running. As I bent down to put my ear next to his head to hear what their choice of music had been, I got a closer look at the body. The exit wound gaped in the back of his head and there was foam leaking out of the corners of his mouth bordering a thin trickle of blood.

"Kill the tourists," I heard. "Kill the tourists." It was

repeated over and over and it was the mayor's voice.

"Good work, Williams," I told him as I got back to my feet. "I'll see you get a commendation for this. Did you see where he came from?"

He looked suddenly embarrassed. "It wasn't my shoot, Captain."

I looked around for his partner and didn't see anyone. He pointed into the back of the cruiser and I turned to find myself staring into the defiant eyes of a small black kid. I turned and looked questioningly at Williams.

"Well, sir," he began, "I was directing traffic in front of the Port Authority Terminal when I heard about the bomb. So I drove down here to try and clear traffic for the ambulances. I was out of the car trying to turn people east when I heard screams from over here and then a shot. I drove over and found the kid there with a smoking pistol in his hand and a dead body stretched out in front of him. When he saw me coming he tried to run but I caught him.

"He won't talk to me," he finished lamely.

"You'll still get a commendation," I told him.

I opened the car door and the kid came along with it. Williams had cuffed him to the armrest so he couldn't get away. I motioned for Williams to cut the kid loose but had him put the cuffs back on him. I didn't want to find myself chasing a skinny black kid through one of the welfare hotels that line the Times Square district.

Williams handed me the gun. It looked very familiar. It was a Belgian-made nine-millimeter automatic. The kid must have had to use both hands to fire it. I took my own out and compared the two. His looked slightly newer. Probably because he wasn't required to take his down to the police firing range once a month and prove he knew where the trigger was.

"So," I said, "I paid four and a quarter for mine."

He didn't say anything but from the smug look he gave me I got the impression that he had gotten a considerably better deal. But then he probably hadn't been able to deduct the cost of his as a reasonable and necessary business expense.

"Nice shot," I told him. "But in official competition you don't get any points for head shots."

He still didn't say anything.

"You don't have much to say for yourself, do you?" I asked.

He didn't even demand a lawyer. He was probably thinking about all those statistics about the likelihood of a black man being executed for killing a white person. Black kids in New York grow up knowing those things. If they didn't they might wander into Howard Beach by accident.

I scanned the crowd looking for a reporter. It only took a second to find one. I turned to Williams and pointed the reporter out to him and told him to go get him. By this time at least sixty uniforms had shown up and were doing an admirable job of crowd control.

I turned back to the kid. I pictured him standing there, all eighty pounds of him with his pistol gripped tightly in both hands, with a slavering white maniac bearing down on him. I had to admire his guts. He'd done better than I had. "If you don't at least tell me your name," I told him gently, "I'm going to have to identify you to the press as a small black child. That ought to give your friends a good hoot."

"Kinta," he told me. I raised one eyebrow. "Kinta Jones."

Williams came back with the reporter, whose name completely escaped me. It didn't matter; they were all interchangeable.

I pointed to Kinta and introduced him to the press. "This is Kinta Jones," I told the reporter. "He heroically saved the lives of dozens of innocent bystanders. With no thought at all for his own safety he took on a slavering maniac three times his own size and won. No pictures," I added, putting my hand over his camera lens.

"What's it worth to the *Post*," I asked, "for the exclusive rights to interview Mr. Jones and relate his story to the public?''

"*Newsday,*" he said. "I'm with *Newsday*." He licked his lips and agonized. "I can't go higher than twenty grand on my own," he told me.

I'd been watching Kinta out of the corner of my eye. I would have sworn his ears stood up straight at the mention of the twenty thousand dollars.

"Unfortunately," I told him, "that's not enough. You'll have to go at least fifty."

"I can't," he said.

I started scanning the crowd again. "There must be a guy from the *Post* out there somewhere," I said to no one in particular.

"Look," he told me, "five minutes, give me five minutes." He ran for a pay phone.

New York has three tabloids: the *Daily News*, the *Post* and *Newsday*. All three of them have massive circulations, and they are all involved in a fierce battle to steal each other's readers. I didn't think there was much doubt that *Newsday* would swing for the fifty K. They'd have had to pay a lot more in an auction. But I didn't have time for an auction.

I turned back to the kid. "You look like you've been arrested before. So I guess I don't have to explain the routine to you, do I?" He shook his head. I could tell he wasn't listening to me. He was wondering who he was going to get to chauffeur him around in his new BMW. "Better start thinking now, Kinta," I told him. "When was the last time they let you make a phone call down at Juvenile Hall?"

Suddenly, I had his full attention.

I held the automatic up in front of his face. "Last time I checked they weren't giving permits for these to ten-year-olds," I told him. "You won't go to jail for it, but I can make you disappear off the face of the planet for a week. And guess what the Kinta Jones story is going to be worth in a week?"

He guessed, correctly, that it wouldn't be worth anything. "What you want?" he asked.

"What happened?"

"Dis crazy white dude come out'a nowhere wit dat pig stickah an I blow'd his head off. What you think happen?"

"Did he have anyone with him when you first saw him?"

"Jes the dudes in the phone truck."

"A NYNEX truck?"

"New York Bell," he told me. "You happy now?"

I was overjoyed. Williams handed me the microphone from his car's radio and I called it in. "They've only had ten minutes," I said. "They can't have gotten very far."

"Not with traffic at a dead standstill all across Manhattan they won't," Kane told me.

"How's that?" I asked.

"When the call came in about the nut with the sword, Terry closed all the bridges and tunnels outbound," he replied. "But he left the inbound lanes alone. There's not a car moving anywhere."

"God," I said. "That took guts." Fifteen minutes with the outbound arteries closed and traffic would be screwed up till way past midnight. But Terry had always had guts. That's how the best young police captain in New York had ended up in the Traffic Division. He'd told the commissioner where to stick it one night and ended up in Traffic the next day. An object lesson in boat rocking for all the other hotshots on the force.

For a second I thought about going out and looking for the telephone truck. But they could have gone in any direction and I wanted to be in the center when it was found. Not that they were likely to get anything but an empty truck.

I turned back to Kinta. "How many telephone guys did you see?"

"Two."

"And what did they look like?"

"They looked white."

"Did they have telephone company uniforms?"

"Yeah."

"How tall were they?"

"They wuz big."

"Did they have any facial hair?"

"No."

I gave up. It occurred to me that to a ten-year-old black kid living in the Times Square area all white adults looked exactly the same. Probably why he'd taken to carrying a nine-millimeter pistol. He'd probably been the least surprised person in the city to find himself being attacked by a slavering white maniac.

Just because I'd given up didn't mean Worthington had to.

"So where are your parents?" he asked.

The kid just shrugged.

"Where are you staying?"

"Around."

"When was the last time you saw your mother?"

The kid looked over at me. "I haf to take dis shit?"

I shook my head. The kid looked at Worthington triumphantly.

Worthington turned to me. "You can't just give him the fifty grand," he pointed out. "He'd be dead ten minutes after he got back to this shit."

Kinta looked at me suspiciously, expecting I was going to cheat him out of the money. I rubbed my chin reflectively. Of course Worthington was right. Kinta's life really wouldn't be worth a nickel if the word hit the street that he had fifty thousand dollars. It wouldn't matter whether it was in a bank or under his mattress.

"You gotta lawyer?" I asked him.

"Maybe," he replied.

"You gotta lawyer who won't try to cheat you out of as much of the money as he possibly can?"

He didn't say anything.

Kane leaned against the cruiser and looked down at him. "Let me tell you what's going to happen," he began.

"You're going to go up in front of a judge who's going to stick you in a home for boys. Probably the same one you ran away from last time. Only this time, because you have money, they're going to charge you for staying there, whether you run away or not."

It was such an outrageously unfair thing to do that Kinta knew it had to be true. Some of the money would probably still be left when he turned eighteen. But not a whole heck of a lot and I knew it would be tough to convince him that there'd be any.

"But since you're a sharp operator and have money now," Kane continued, "you'll probably be able to find some junkie whore who'll swear she's your mother and have the judge release you to her. But since you're only ten, guess who's going to get control of the money?"

"I'm thirteen," he lied, making himself three years closer to being eligible for the dough.

"Doesn't matter," Kane told him. "Five years is plenty of time to spend whatever the IRS leaves you with."

"What you need," I told him, "is a lawyer you can trust." I turned to Worthington. "Haergreve do much pro bono work?"

He snorted.

Kane looked up. "Chopper."

I told Willliams to look after Kinta and Worthington and headed down the square to the open area where Seventh and Broadway intersect. I looked back and saw Worthington telling Kinta something. I hoped it was good advice.

Kane started dropping flares—which he must have gotten out of Williams's cruiser—in the roadway. He didn't bother telling people that they ought to move; they got the idea. The helicopter turned on its spotlights and began to descend. It looked like all the rules about helicopters in the city were getting thrown out the window.

I was almost happy to see Mayes getting out of the chopper because he was followed by three guys carrying medical bags. I was mildly surprised to see Dempsey following them.

We all gathered around Branner.

Mayes looked at me suspiciously. "You haven't touched anything, have you?" he asked. I told him no.

The lab guys began opening their bags and putting on rubber gloves. One of them had a small vacuum cleaner that he played over Branner's clothes. He stopped when he got to the shoes and changed the bag in the vacuum before he continued. Another began to take pictures while the third held a ruler next to the body to give the pictures a scale.

"Twenty-three dead at the theater," Dempsey told me. "Another six dead at the hospitals and four more not expected to make it till morning."

It didn't cheer him up any when I told him he'd probably saved two hundred lives by tying up traffic.

"How could we have been so stupid?" he asked me.

"They made it easy for us," I told him. "We're just lucky that it's only thirty-three. If it wasn't for you and a pint-sized Matt Dillon it could have been much worse. And then we'd really have a mess on our hands."

"It's only going to get worse though, isn't it?" he asked. "They told us where they were going to act this time. Next time we won't be so lucky."

"You check out his pig stickah?" Kane asked me.

"No," I told him. "Anything special about it?"

"It's not one of those tourist-special samurai swords," he told me. "It looks like an antique cavalry saber. It's razor sharp and it looks like somebody rubbed shit all over the blade. A nasty thing to get cut by."

"Great," I said. "They don't miss a beat, do they?"

The lab guys began to turn the body. I was vaguely surprised that they didn't dust him for prints but I guessed they would want to do that in the privacy of the morgue.

There was a note pinned to his shirt. They'd put it inside a plastic letter protector. They'd probably figured it would get bloody and they were doing us a favor. The note read,

"The Front for the Total Independence of Nicaragua greets the bloody hegemonistic oppressors of North America. The revolution has been brought to you and now you know the tears that have been shed for centuries in Nicaragua. The United States has twenty-four hours to denounce its imperialistic war of terror in Nicaragua or your tears will know no limit. Long live Sandino."

I turned to Kane. "Sounds mighty familiar, Kane."

"Don't look at me," he replied. "That's not my handwriting."

"It's typed," I pointed out.

"So, I don't know how to type. You know how long it takes me to fill out paperwork."

I could sense Mayes beginning to lick his chops. This was really too juicy. First the terrorists make the local cops look like complete idiots and then they turn out to be working for the FBI's number-one villain. The only problem was that I didn't buy it for a second.

The five of us—Kane, Fred, Wayne, Josh and I—turned as one. The police radio had been on in the background the entire time but we had tuned it out. But no cop misses a 10–13, the code for "Assist Patrolman, a report of an officer shot." The dispatcher gave the address as East 36th and Madison and we all started running.

I could hear Dempsey pounding away behind me. I didn't turn around, but figured Mayes wouldn't be too far behind. Kane cruised up beside me.

"So?" he asked. "Does squash really keep you in good shape?"

I was already beginning to breathe heavily so I didn't answer. He smirked at my predicament and spent the ten minutes it took us to get to 36th and Madison explaining what a real physical fitness program entailed.

The action was over when we got there. Two of Williams's classmates from the academy were dead and the telephone company truck was riddled with bullet holes. Five or six guys in uniform were trying to push the crowd back while a couple of others tried to resuscitate the fallen officers. A priest knelt down next to one of them giving him the last rites.

We knelt down next to the third body. A blond man, dressed in a telephone company uniform, he was well over six foot and appeared to have lifted weights for a hobby. He was only shot about two dozen times. I was transfixed by the number of bullet holes. Kane took out a pencil and used it to push back the sleeve of the dead man's T-shirt, exposing a tattoo. A screaming eagle diving out of the sky clutching a swastika in its talons.

"Shit," I said. It was the only thing that came to mind.

CHAPTER 7

I t was ten-thirty by the time we all gathered at the Federal
Building. The crew from the morning, with the exception
of Gopinath, were all present along with a few additional
faces. The commissioner had sent along one of his yes-men,
Ron Gagliardi. We had pushed pencils together in the commissioner's office in years past and had developed a fine
loathing for one another over the years. He was sitting next
to Mayes.

The State Department had sent along an official assistant
secretary of state for Latin America. And in a move guar-
anteed to piss off Mayes, the FBI had sent in their antiterrorism specialists.

I knew Hank Wallace and his band of gangbusters from
the various FBI training programs we'd attended. My father
refers to guys like Hank as ''stand-up.'' It's the nicest thing
he ever says about anyone. Hank almost makes up for
Mayes. While Mayes looks like a corporate lawyer, Hank
looks like an up-and-coming corporate vice president.

Which is ironic because Hank really is a lawyer and Mayes's degree is in accounting.

Dempsey had managed to talk the Connecticut and New Jersey state police captains into returning. They were sitting near the end of the table and seemed to be having trouble combating fatigue. They didn't appear to think of our current problems as affecting them any.

"The number of dead at the theater stands at thirty with at least three additional deaths expected before morning," I began. "Some of the bodies may never be identified, but at least four of them were officers of the New York City Police Department in plainclothes.

"William Branner was killed in Times Square thirty minutes later by an armed ten-year-old child who lives in the area. Two police officers were killed approximately fifteen minutes after that by an individual who was placed in Times Square just prior to Branner's attack. He was subsequently gunned down by other officers. There were no identity documents found on his body.

"Captain Dempsey of the state police has some videotape to show us," I concluded.

Dempsey's assistant punched a button and then froze the action at the beginning of the tape. The screen filled with the familiar-looking face of a television reporter I recognized from the six o'clock news. He was standing in front of the Empire Globe.

"They were taping in front of the theater at ten past eight," Dempsey began. "Keep your eyes on the white van parked next to the theater."

His assistant pushed the Pause button again.

"Ordinarily," the reporter told us, "the street would be bustling outside the Empire Globe theater, where the hit musical, *The Jetsons*, is playing to sold-out audiences. But this morning's tragic events in the sleepy hamlet of Toyon and the chilling threat leveled at Broadway have left these usually crowded streets as empty as Albany's on a Friday night."

The camera panned back and forth at the relatively empty sidewalks. I recognized a couple of unmarked cars and at least one familiar face was leaning against a lamppost. He waved at the camera.

"The theater manager reports that although there are no tickets available for this evening's performance"—he paused and grinned—"many of the ticket purchasers are spending their evening elsewhere and their sixty-dollar seats are vacant." He grinned into the camera. "And a few brave New Yorkers have ventured out to see if they couldn't pick up a bargain."

The camera pulled back, revealing a young couple. They were both wearing tight jeans and Members Only jackets. His was black with red trim and hers was gray. I guessed that they'd both have been wearing boots. He had probably been a lineman on the high school football team. She had probably been a cheerleader. The unspoken assumption was that they would be sneaking in at intermission.

The reporter stuck the microphone in their faces and I had a momentary feeling of almost uncontrollable sadness. They were less than fifty feet from the van.

"Frank Tadeutcher and Mye Sinatra from Queens," he introduced them. "You apparently aren't worried about the Deranged Dozen."

Frank laughed and put his arm around his girl's shoulders. He leaned forward over the microphone with a huge grin pasted across his face. "Hey," he said, "what's twelve more in a city—"

Dempsey's assistant had hit the Slow Advance button. But the wall of flame coming out of the van was too fast for the videotape to pick up. In much less than a second the flames had washed over them and the screen went black. They had both been smiling. The assistant hit the Pause button.

"We're checking all the other stations to see if anyone has a shot where the van's license plate was visible," Dempsey said.

"Don't bother," I told him. "There were two parking tickets on it."

"Oh," he said.

Gagliardi said he'd have the license number by morning or someone's head would roll. I wondered who else's head was scheduled for rolling.

Dempsey signaled for more tape and we all turned back to the screen.

"This is the telephone van that Captain Kelly put the alert out for after the Times Square killing," Dempsey went on. I made a mental note to thank him for the plug. The camera moved to the back of the van and showed the license number. "It's registered to the Easy Payment Company of North Tarrytown. The address is Post Office Box 1287 in North Tarrytown. This is the only vehicle registered to that name." He paused. "It was on our list of candidates, by the way."

The camera panned over the body of the truck. There really were a lot of bullet holes in it. Most of the bullets had probably already passed through the guy with the tattoo. The scene changed momentarily to a view of a superhighway. The perspective was evidently from a highway overpass. Traffic was lighter than you would normally expect, given that you knew it was I–95 on a Thursday evening. I didn't have any problem spotting the van as it whizzed by underneath.

"This is Interstate Ninety-five in Pelham," Dempsey continued. "At seven-thirty-four this evening." The assistant reversed the tape and then froze it on the telephone van. "The same van. We're running checks on all the license plates that passed this point between seven-twenty-five and seven-fifty and hope that maybe they were in a convoy."

"How in God's name did you get that tape?" Wallace asked him.

Dempsey looked over at me.

"We arrested a Bryce Worthington the fourth this afternoon,'' I told him. ''He's a rich kid with a social conscience. He was the one who infiltrated Toyon under the name Eric Degangi. He believed he was doing reconnaissance for a group involved in pro-Sandinista activities. He's downstairs right now going through the FBI files trying to identify the people he worked with.

''Anyway, we asked the mayor to announce his arrest this evening, hoping that the terrorists would call around attempting to see what damage had been done to their network. The mayor's announcement came at six o'clock and someone called the Worthington residence at seven-oh-five asking for Bryce and immediately hung up when he wasn't available.

''We traced the call to a westbound rest stop on the Connecticut Turnpike just west of Darien and immediately called Captain Dempsey, who set up the surveillance camera in record time.''

At the mention of Darien, the Connecticut state police captain sat bolt upright and began to suddenly look a lot more interested in the proceedings.

''And couldn't you have thrown up a roadblock as well?'' Buchanen asked.

''You have even the vaguest notion what traffic is like on that particular stretch of highway?'' Dempsey asked him.

''If we had thrown up a roadblock on the highway,'' I interrupted, ''besides being ineffective we would have been telling the terrorists that we knew where they were hiding. This is the best break we've had so far and I mean to exploit it.'' I looked around the room. ''I don't suppose I have to tell anyone that if this information is leaked to the press it could lead directly to the loss of innocent lives.''

''And even if I can't make it stick,'' Dempsey added, ''I'll arrest the cocksucker who leaks it for accessory to murder and do my damnedest to ruin his fucking life.''

''I don't think that's an appropriate remark,'' Buchanen told him.

"Maybe not," Dempsey replied. "But I made it." He waved at the guy operating the VCR.

The action began with a close-up of the note they'd pinned to Branner's shirt. The camera zoomed out to a full body shot so we could see that the note was still fixed to his body. His mouth was frozen in a grimace and the foam on his lips had dried but you could see the residue if you looked. The action froze just as the bullet hole in his forehead came into the frame.

"If anyone's curious," I told them, "I'm informed that he had probably been shot full of PCP before being released. There were marks on his body from the restraints. Apparently they had to cut them off him." I turned to Wallace. "Any thoughts about the note?"

He shook his head. "We're all very puzzled. It would be unbelievably stupid of the Sandinistas to get themselves involved in something like this. I for one," he told us, totally ignoring the dirty looks from the State Department people, "don't believe for a second that they were. Or even that they knew anything about it.

"It's considerably more credible," he continued, "that some of their friends in this country think that they're doing them a favor. And I'm tempted to say something like they need more friends like those.

"If the note's genuinely from friends of the Sandinistas," he continued, "and more about that later—they're probably from the loony Left in this country. Although it's not out of the question that they could be from some foreign organization."

"How likely are they to be foreign?" I asked.

"Well," he said. "I don't think they are. My guess is that they're homegrown. I'd be certain they were homegrown except that they're so damn good at it that it makes me think they must have been trained abroad."

"Why couldn't they be homegrown and trained abroad?" I asked.

He looked uncomfortable and glanced over at the State

Department contingent. The assistant secretary gave an almost imperceptible head shake.

"It's very unlikely," he told me. From the look that accompanied the words I got the impression that it was more than unlikely but that I didn't need to know why.

"In any case," he continued, "if they aren't homegrown there are a number of unpleasant possibilities. The Palestinians are known to have worked with the Sandinistas. And the Red Brigades are in debt to the Palestinians. And, as everyone knows, Qaddafi is rather unhappy with us."

"What about the IRA and those German thugs?" Buchanen asked. I could see why he wouldn't want us to dwell too long on the Italians.

"The IRA's main source of revenue is donations from Irish-Americans," Wallace told him. "Any IRA man foolish enough to get mixed up in terrorism aimed at this country would be executed by the IRA directorate—there would be no appeal. As for the Baader Meinhof Gang"—he looked over at the State Department people again—"well, let's just say that it's very unlikely.

"One interesting possibility," he told us, brightening at the thought of interesting possibilities, "would be the ERP, the Ejercito Revolucionario del Pueblo, from Argentina. They've been with the Sandinistas right from the very beginning. But I don't think they're any more likely than the rest. They're too close to the Sandinistas. They wouldn't get involved without letting the Sandinistas know about it. And as I mentioned earlier, I don't think the Sandinistas have anything to do with it."

"Why not?" one of the State Department officials asked.

"Because the Sandinistas are rational," he answered. "And if this were from the Sandinistas it wouldn't be rational. If the note claimed to be from the Iranians I'd believe it. But not from the Sandinistas. I mean really, we've invaded their country twice already this century. They're not going to give us an excuse to do it again.

"Besides," he added, "there's the one that got killed."

We all turned back to the television as the scene changed to the dead blond man. The camera panned from his bloody crew cut to his bloody work boots. I didn't try to count the bullet holes. The camera turned back to the tattoo on his upper arm and zoomed in. Kane's hand was visible holding back the T-shirt sleeve. The assistant froze the frame on the tattoo.

"I think we all agree," Wallace continued, "that it's unlikely we'd find this sort of tattoo on a dedicated Marxist."

Buchanen spoke up again. "Then the note's obviously from some other group out to make the Sandinistas look bad."

"Well," Wallace hedged, "that's a distinct possibility, but not a hundred percent sure thing.

"First of all, there are a great many people around the world who're still fervent admirers of Adolf Hitler and all that he stood for. The Palestinians, for instance, probably wish that he'd been more thorough and they'd be happy to give him another shot at it if they could." He paused. "But then this fellow doesn't look much like a Palestinian, does he?"

No one thought that he did.

"If we assume," Wallace continued, "that he indeed is—err, was, a white supremacist, that still doesn't get the Sandinistas off the hook. Terrorists belong to a rather exclusive club, and they all have a lot more in common with each other than they do with any legitimate government. They've also developed a degree of sophistication over the past decade. And I'm afraid that many of them have adopted the philosophy that the enemy of my enemy is my friend."

"But what on earth," I asked, "would some loony Left organization seeking justice in Central America have in common with an even loonier organization trying to bring back Hitler?"

"Humm," he said. "Well, I told you we were all puzzled. But, as you'll recall, three Japanese terrorists from the Red Army Brigade shot up Lod Airport outside of Tel Aviv back in seventy-two as a favor for the Palestinians. Qaddafi is known to have supplied arms to the IRA, and the Baader Meinhof Gang helped organize and train the Red Brigades, in Italy. The South African secret service is supporting at least five black guerrilla armies, three of which are hard-line Marxist in orientation. Both the United States and Iran supplied the guerrillas in Afghanistan with arms. And both the Israelis and the Syrians supplied arms to the Iranians during their war with Iraq.

"And if you think any of that's odd, consider that the Ku Klux Klan donated money to the Nation of Islam last year." He paused and looked around to see if we all knew what the Nation of Islam was. We didn't. "The Nation of Islam, for those of you who don't know," he informed us, "is a black Muslim group dedicated to racial segregation and the destruction of Israel.

" 'Strange bedfellows' doesn't even begin to describe some of these relationships. So the idea of a white supremacist slash pro-Sandinista organization isn't as weird as you might think.

"Jake Kinsella's our expert on white supremacists," he concluded. He looked over at a thin, balding man with a giant nose. "Jake," he said, pointing to the television, "any idea who this fellow is?"

Jake got to his feet and looked at the television for what looked like the first time. He was amazingly tall but sort of stooped over. He jammed his hands into his pockets and we all had to lean forward to hear him.

"It's not certain," he told us. "But I checked with the guys in Washington and he pretty nearly fits the description of Gary Lee Hopkins, who was last known to be living in northern Idaho. If it is him, he's affiliated with the Righteous Arm of Jesus Chapter of the Knights of Aryan Chivalry." He reeled off the organization's name with relish, as if it were the punchline to a particularly rich inside joke. "Which is a radical offshoot of the Christian Identity Movement."

He looked over at his boss. "You want me to give 'em a rundown on the CIM?"

Wallace nodded.

Jake stretched without taking his hands out of his pockets and addressed his remarks to the ceiling. "The Christian Identity Movement is a relatively recent phenomenon in the ever popular lunatic fringe. Its roots extend back to the forties, when it was founded by Wesley Swift. Old Wes was the foremost proponent of the British-Israelite theory, which holds that the British are the true descendants of the ancient Israelites. That's a convenient notion that allows them to get around this Jesus-was-a-Jew business.

"Their main goal is a racially separate nation free from federal controls and uninfluenced by what they refer to as Zionist ideology. They wish to protect"—he paused and sucked air in and seemed to be desperately trying to stifle a laugh—"their seed line.

"Although they draw many of their members from the Ku Klux Klan and similar racist hate organizations, there's some important differences between the two.

"The KKK, for instance, purports to being a patriotic institution. They see themselves improving the United States through policies of racial segregation—which is what they have in common with the Nation of Islam, by the way.

"But the Christian Identity Movement is the exact opposite of patriotic. They want to overthrow the government—which they refer to as ZOG, the Zionist Occupation Government—and replace it with something else. And they're prepared to use violence to do it.

"The first of these groups that came to our attention was the Posse Comitatus, founded by Gordon Kahl. The Posse didn't recognize any government on a larger scale than counties. Seeing as how they felt the entire federal government was a tool of Satan they refused to pay any income tax. Not just," he added dryly, "that portion being spent by the Defense Department.

"Naturally this brought them to the attention of our colleagues in Internal Revenue and Mr. Kahl was singled out for prosecution. Not recognizing the right of the federal courts to try him, he ignored all the subpoenas and whatnot the IRS sent his way. Then he murdered two federal marshals and a deputy sheriff who'd been sent to arrest him. In the ensuing standoff a tear gas grenade ignited Mr. Kahl's house. He chose to remain in the house, rather than surrender, and was incinerated.

"He wasn't the last martyr, if you can call him that, of the CIM. After the Posse Comitatus debacle we began to subject white supremacist organizations to a higher level of scrutiny. In 1984, in Ukiah, California, ten men in military uniforms took three-point-six million dollars out of an armored car. Naturally we became interested immediately.

"To make a long story short, the robbers turned out to be members of the Order, a radical offshoot of the Church of Jesus Christ Christian–Aryan Nations, which could hardly itself be described as moderate.

"They started out with counterfeiting and moved from there into bank and armored car robberies. Their operations were generally well planned and executed. But they weren't real strong in the security area—they liked to brag about their heroic deeds, for instance—and we tracked 'em down pretty easily. We killed their leader in a firefight on Whidbey Island in Puget Sound in late 1984.

"White supremacists ain't too bright but they more than make up for it in fanaticism. Robert Mathews, their leader, also chose certain death rather than surrender.

"Over the course of the next eighteen months we penetrated the rest of the organization and arrested all of its members and prosecuted them under the RICO act. Of the original twenty-four members, all of them are either in prison or dead."

"Well at least we don't have to worry about them," Dempsey told us.

"Maybe not," Kinsella responded, "but there's still the White American Bastion, the Bruder Schweigen, the Covenant the Sword and the Arm of the Lord, the White People's National Political Call, the National Alliance of Caucasians, the White American Rebellion, the Righteous Arm of Jesus and a host of others.''

"How many members all told?" I asked.

"No one knows for sure," he told me. "Best estimates run from two to five thousand hard-core and maybe fourteen to fifty thousand sympathizers. We haven't got near enough manpower to look into them all. And most of them are strictly political wings anyway; they're not involved in violence. And hence the crap they push is constitutionally protected free speech.''

"So," I said, "can we work under the hypothesis that this whole thing is a plot by white supremacists out to make the Nicaraguans look bad?"

"No."

"Why not?"

He looked annoyed, as if he were a teacher and one of his favorite students had asked him a particularly obvious question.

"First of all, a strict tenet of their faith is that you don't send white people to fight wars in brown nations. They could care less about what kind of government the Nicaraguans have. Communism, capitalism, it's all the same to these jaspers. They refer to the Russians as the eastern branch of ZOG.

"And secondly," he went on, "I don't think any of them are smart enough to have planned something like this. I haven't run across a white supremacist yet who knew enough to come in out of the hail.''

"They were smart enough to get three-point-six million dollars out of an armored car," I pointed out.

"And I believe that the first of them is due to get out of prison in 2026," he told me. "You really shouldn't have to be convinced that these people are idiots. They think the Holocaust was invented by the Allies to cover up atrocities we committed against the Germans.''

"What happened to all the money?" I asked.

He was suddenly embarrassed. "Well, ahhh, we recovered around a half million and they spent quite a bit on weapons and real estate. We think the rest of it was spread around the country to other extremist organizations. We'll probably never know for sure."

"I think I can tell you where some of it ended up," I told him bitterly.

I turned to Gagliardi. "Our witness saw at least two of them. Any idea what became of the other one?"

"When the APB went out there were six guys from Traffic right on top of the van. Terry concentrated his men at the bridges and tunnels and they were right there. The rookies went running up with their guns drawn before anyone could stop 'em and the guy blew them away with automatic rifle fire. Then the vets took care of him.

"A civilian who'd been behind the van ever since it turned onto Thirty-sixth saw two guys get out of it and enter a subway station. The description was just of two white guys in jeans and work shirts. Medium height, medium weight, no distinguishing marks."

"We have a book he can go through," Wallace told him, "but he's not likely to spot anyone."

"No one in the subway station remembers seeing anything unusual," Gagliardi finished up.

Chief Ostresky had made it in for the meeting. Maybe there wasn't a whole lot else going on in the sleepy hamlet of Toyon.

"Chief?" I looked over at him.

"There was a tap on the ambulance company phone," he began. "The FBI lab guy told me it was home built according to plans from some crazy book. The parts were all bought from Radio Shack. We'll never trace them.

"We found the place they were hiding the ambulance," he continued. "It was a filling station that's been closed for a couple of years. Seems like it must have been the same guy who rented out the building by the ambulance company.

Six months rent paid in advance with a money order drawn on Citibank. The garage looked clean but the crime lab people are going through it just in case.''

"There must've been people there every night for a couple of months," I told him. "Someone must have seen something. Can you make an announcement on a local radio station that we need information from anyone who might have seen anyone entering or leaving the garage or that store they were using to watch the ambulance company?''

"Will do," he said.

I turned to Sheldon. "You couldn't have been more right this afternoon," I told him. "What do you think they'll do next?''

Sheldon's prediction that the terrorists would shoot one of the psychotics full of amphetamines and let him loose in the city had sent his stock soaring with the law enforcement community. He rose to his feet looking every inch the conquering genius.

"Well," he said modestly, "it's unfortunate that I didn't foresee the car bomb. But I'm afraid we've all been guilty of underestimating their ruthlessness. As for what they'll do next . . ." He paused dramatically. "Assuming that their goal is to influence opinion and force a change of direction in American foreign policy." He looked over at the State Department people. "Of course, that's not very likely to happen, is it?'' They stared back at him stoney faced.

"Anyway," he went on unperturbed, "if they want to influence opinion they'll have to get to the middle class somehow. The middle class's opinion is the only one that really matters to the politicians.

"And they won't get to Middle America by striking here. Most Americans don't even consider New York City to be a part of the United States and they won't see things happening here as affecting them.

"So this time I expect they'll go after one of the suburbs. Probably a middle-class one and one within fifty miles of the city. They'd still want to take advantage of the media concentration here.

"I think they'll strike on the primal level. I think they'll go after someone's children. And I think they'll use one of the psychopaths."

"When?" I asked.

"Soon," he told me.

"Can we expect another little surprise like the car bomb?" Dempsey asked.

Sheldon paused for a moment. But, knowing Sheldon, I knew it was a dramatic pause. He'd have thought the whole thing through in advance. "Consider what they've done here, ladies and gentlemen. They told the world they'd be striking in the theater district. They practically begged people to stay away. That poor young couple in the video." He shook his head. "They shouldn't have been there.

"Now I'm not saying that excuses what they did or that the average citizen won't be rooting for you to get the bastards. What I'm saying is that, in the backs of their minds, folks will be thinking, *Pretty stupid place to have been hanging out*.

"The public isn't going to forgive the terrorists for what they've done. But along with the hatred for the terrorists, there'll be resentment against the police for not stopping them. In effect, they'll have shifted some of the public's anathema off of themselves and onto you people.

"What they'll most likely do next is predicated on what they hope to achieve. Assuming that they'll want to panic the middle class, they'll probably act against an individual or family that fits the public's image of average. They'll want people to be thinking, *Hey, that could have been my family!* They'll be attempting to shake the public's confidence in the police and sway public opinion toward giving in to their demands."

"Surely they don't expect the government to give in?" I asked.

The assistant secretary of state answered me: "No, not

really," he said. "What they really want is for the government to overreact and enact draconian antiterrorism measures: suspend the Constitution and crap like that. That's something we'll never do, though. The cure would be worse than the disease and all we would accomplish is making it easier for them to recruit."

I looked over at Wallace. "Where will they strike?"

He scratched his head. "If they're really located in Connecticut they'll probably strike in either New York or New Jersey. Should we let the local police know? It'll be sure to leak and then we'll have panic like you've never seen."

"I don't think we have any choice," I told him. "We have to give the local cops the best shot we can. I'll make a public announcement that we expect a strike within the next couple of days aimed at the suburbs. And then we'll get it out privately to the local police just what it is we expect the terrorists to do. Can anyone think of a better plan?"

No one could.

The assistant secretary of state looked troubled. "What exactly are you going to tell the press about the demands and the white supremacists?" he asked me.

I looked him over for a while. *Harvard*, I thought to myself. "My guess is that the terrorists won't be taking any chances that we'll try and keep their demands secret," I told him. "I'd be willing to bet my pension that half the news media in the country received a copy of their note along with some sort of proof that it was genuine.

"The question comes back to what we tell the press about the dead man. I gather that the State Department would prefer that we said nothing." He nodded. "And, in fact, I don't plan on telling anyone about him. We give" —I looked around the table—"the terrorists nothing.

"But let me make something clear here. If I begin to think that any of you has a hidden agenda that doesn't include getting the terrorists first, you will rue the day you came to New York.'' He wasn't very impressed; definitely Harvard.

"You fellows want to start contacting the local police in the suburbs?'' I asked Dempsey and the other two captains. They nodded.

"You want to handle the press?'' Dempsey asked me.

I nodded back. "Is there anything else?'' I looked over at Buchanen, expecting him to threaten me with the governor's wrath. But he didn't have anything to say. Maybe he was beyond making threats and was going to go directly to carrying them out.

"Unless something else comes up,'' I told them, "I suggest we all meet back here at three tomorrow. And before everyone leaves make sure both Sergeant Kane and Captain Dempsey have your telephone numbers. We may have to contact you at any time so make sure we have a number where we can reach you.'' I pointed out Kane to the ones who didn't know him. Dempsey looked amused.

People started lining up to give Kane their business cards. He was cheerfully stuffing them into his pockets, probably planning on handing them back out to women in bars. I could almost hear him describing himself as Ashly Blacksmyth, State Department.

Gagliardi came up to me and presented me with his business card personally. He was still a lieutenant and likely to stay one.

"After you finish preening yourself in front of the cameras,'' he told me, "the commissioner wants to see us. He says he'll be at City Hall all night.''

"Fine,'' I told him. I had averaged three hours of sleep two nights in a row and there wasn't any reason, other than impending collapse, to change my habits now.

Dempsey came up and gave me a copy of the videotape. "Good idea getting everyone's phone number,'' he told me.

"Yeah,'' I said. "Thanks.''

I talked with Dempsey for a while before going down to the auditorium, biding my time until the eleven o'clock news was over.

If anything, there were even more microphones attached to the rostrum than there had been in the afternoon. Six cops had been killed in the space of an hour. It was by far the worst day in the history of the department. I wondered if anyone on the chief of detectives' task force had made an announcement yet. Probably not, I decided.

I told the press what had happened and then dropped my little bomb on the suburbs. Then I answered questions for a half hour. Most of the questions from the print media were either about Kinta or the dead terrorist. The television people all wanted to ask about their slain comrade. The suburban reporters had a more urgent interest in what we thought the terrorists would do next.

I told them what I knew about Kinta and that the dead man had fallen on an incendiary grenade and been burned beyond recognition. It was the story we'd agreed upon at the scene. I didn't think it would fool the terrorists for a second, although it did have that Aryan warrior hero's death ring to it. I told the suburban press that they should urge their readers to remain calm and watchful. They were still howling questions at me as I left. I had to straight-arm the clown from ABC.

It was quarter to one by the time I got to City Hall. I took it as a good omen that they let me into the mayor's office. That meant that they hadn't decided to sacrifice me to public opinion yet. I guessed the memories of the CPF were still too fresh. They'd probably be fading by Monday.

The mayor had a TV and VCR built into one of the cabinets in his office. I plugged the tape into the VCR and gave them Dempsey's spiel. They all looked a lot happier when I told them Sheldon's analysis. It didn't mean all my troubles were over, though.

Chief Goldman handed me a black-and-white glossy print of Dr. Wilbur. He was relaxed and smiling—they'd given him a scalpel to play with.

"They sent this, along with a copy of their demands, to all the major dailies," he told me. "The courier service got them at nine-thirty and started delivering them a half hour later. Payment was by postal money order and no one at the courier service saw the person who dropped them off."

I told them about the Knights of Aryan Chivalry.

"You've got to be putting me on," the mayor blurted out. "We're being invaded by Nazis concerned about the health and well-being of the Sandinistas?"

"The FBI guys think it's a put-up job," I told him. "The problem is that no one can figure out why white supremacists would want to make the Sandinistas look bad."

Goldman looked up and addressed his comments to the ceiling. "No," he said, "but right off the top of my head I can think of one organization that would love to make the Sandinistas look bad."

The mayor shook his head. "Don't even think about it, Sy. They're crazy in Washington, but they're not that crazy." He turned to me. "Well, young man, what are you planning to do about these bastards?"

"They've left a trail, sir. It was really stupid of them to call the Worthington residence. We'll start tracking a sixty-mile radius upstream of the rest stop they called from. Worthington met one of their members at a shelter in Harlem and we think the shelter's director knew him. The FBI has penetrated the entire white supremacist network across the country and there's bound to be a trail. The pro-Sandinista organizations are fairly wide open. It's only a matter of time."

"Do you think they're really Sandinistas?"

"No, sir. They aren't doing the Sandinistas any favors with this crap."

"I don't think so either," he told me. "You look like you could use some sleep. Why don't you head home?"

"Thank you, sir," I told him.

I only vaguely remember the ride home.

CHAPTER 8

The alarm went off right on time at five o'clock. It took me a few seconds to figure out why I would want to be getting up at five. When it came to me I groaned and swung my feet down to the floor. Counting the twenty minutes I had in the car on the way home, it added up to almost three and a half hours of sleep.

I turned the cold water on full and stood under the freezing jet of ice water for as long as I could stand it; then I cranked the temperature control way over into the red zone. I didn't quite feel like a human being by the time I started feeling the heat. But I figured I was as close as I was going to get.

I found a taxi without much trouble; there were loads of them ferrying people home from the clubs. I was still the last one to get to the office.

"Father Dave still under wraps?" I asked. I figured an interview with the Saint of One Hundred and Forty-ninth Street was probably the first order of business.

"Yeah," Josh told me. "But you remember those two guys that got out of the telephone truck? They showed up

135

at his soup kitchen last night looking for him. They scared the shit out of some of his people.''

"He wasn't there, though?''

"Naah. He gave the guys we sent down to guard him a bad time so they busted him for running a bawdy house.''

I raised one eyebrow.

"He takes in both men and women and lets them stay in the same room,'' Kane informed me. ''And many of them aren't married to each other.''

"Of course,'' Josh added, ''he only has the one room.''

"Then he's lucky they didn't bust him for contributing to the delinquency of a minor,'' I told him. ''Let's go have a chat with him.''

I had Kane bring Worthington along. It turned out that Kane had had to bring Bryce home with him the previous night because he couldn't think of anything else to do with him.

"How was your night in the pleasure pit?'' I asked him.

"Swell,'' he told me. ''Do all cops keep leg irons in their apartments?''

I looked over at Kane.

"I didn't hear him complaining last night when I told him he could spend the night in the tank at the Twenty-eighth,'' he growled.

"That was before I met his two thousand six-legged roommates,'' Worthington told me.

Wayne shut his door and Kane burned rubber out into the street.

"Isn't that too bad?'' Kane told me from the front seat. ''He had to fight it out with some nasty old roaches.''

"You ever see macho man's bedroom slippers?'' Worthington asked me.

I shook my head. Kane was suddenly quiet.

"They're really great,'' Worthington told us. ''They're fleece-lined Hershey bars and they're just about the cutest little things I've ever seen.''

"Oh," I said. "And just where did you pick up these little treasures, Kane?"

He hunched over the wheel, ignoring me.

"I understand they used to call him Killer Kane in the marines," I informed Worthington. "On account of how tough he was. Did he show you his 'Kill 'em all and let God sort the bodies' T-shirt?"

"An old girlfriend gave them to me for Christmas," Kane growled. "They keep my feet warm."

"Toughest hombre in the Third Marines," I told no one in particular. "I always feel safer somehow when he's around."

Abrahms was being held in a holding cell in the 31st Precinct. They were treating him nicely, though more because he took in a lot of winos who didn't have anywhere else to go and saved them a lot of trouble than because of his reputation as a saint.

They told us down at the desk that an assistant from the mission had been to visit him earlier in the morning and had told him about the two guys who'd been looking for him. He'd quit threatening to sue for false arrest after that. I sent Josh down to his soup kitchen to get descriptions and told him to bring any witnesses downtown to see the police artist.

"Point out that the guys we're looking for want to see their boss dead," I told him. "That ought to get you some cooperation."

Abrahms was sitting dejectedly on the cot in his cell. He looked a lot older than forty-two and he did bear a striking resemblance to one of the saints I remembered from a fifth-grade catechism book. One of the martyrs, as I recalled. He glanced up when he heard us coming but looked back down quickly and didn't say a word when I sat down next to him.

"We've got a problem," I told him.

"I've got nothing to tell you," he said. He sounded like he'd just gotten the bad news about his kid's biopsy.

"They're looking for you," I said. "Eventually they'll find you. They seem to have a thing about loose ends."

He just looked down at the floor, ignoring me. I thought about threatening to let him go. Instead I dropped an eight-by-ten shot of one of the bomb victims between his feet. It could have been a picture of Frank Tadeutcher, but there wasn't a whole lot left and you couldn't be sure. It could have been his girlfriend.

He covered his eyes with his hands. "Were there nails?" he asked.

"Roofing nails," I told him. "Several thousand of them. They tell me it must have taken hours and hours to insert them all into the TNT. It would have to have been done by hand, one nail at a time."

He pushed his forehead down on top of his knees and wrapped his arms around his neck. "He's back then," he said. "I thought he was dead. I prayed he was dead. But he's not. He's back. People like him never die."

"Who?" I asked him gently.

"Stillwell," he told me. "Adam Stillwell."

I looked up at Wayne and motioned for him to go check on it. He looked like he didn't want to miss what Abrahms was going to say, but he went.

Abrahms straightened up and pushed himself back into the corner, away from me. He drew his knees up to his chest. "You won't understand. I know your kind. You're addicted to cashmere and Volvos. You have no goals higher than a twelve percent annual return and your ideals are manufactured for you by Ralph Lauren. If it can't be bought with your Gold Card you aren't interested and if there's nothing in it for you, you avoid it like the plague. You're the master of the zero-sum game, aren't you?"

I had a whole file folder full of pictures, and he'd already shown how easy it was to pull his chain. The next picture was taken from the video Dempsey had shown us, Mye and

Frank in front of the Globe. I kept my eyes on his and dropped the picture on the floor next to him.

He tried not to look, but he couldn't meet my eyes either. Finally he looked down and the juxtaposition of the smiling young couple and the hamburger that was left of them was too much for him. He closed his eyes tightly and tried to bury his face in his knees.

"Maybe I'm just a greedy yuppie," I told him. "But I haven't taken anyone out of the game lately. Your friend killed thirty people last night. And he's only just beginning. And don't give me any of that crap about there not being any innocents in this country. These two weren't even old enough to vote."

He was quiet for a moment, but then he began to speak. He pressed his forehead against his knees and talked into his lap.

"It started in the sixties," he began, "even before Vietnam. There was so much injustice. Overt racism in Congress and even on television. Squalor and wealth on the same blocks in the cities. Corrupt local governments that beat on the poor for the benefit of the wealthy." He looked up at me. "It wasn't that long ago, you know, that even lower-middle-class whites could afford to have a black maid come in twice a week.

"And then Vietnam came along and it was so obviously a corrupt war. The defense contractors gave it to us so they could sell more and better weapons to the Pentagon. More than a million people died so that Dow and its ilk could boost their dividends.

"And for the first time"—he clenched his fists tightly—"for the very first time, we mobilized the middle class in mass action. Before Vietnam we called for action and a hundred people would show up. And it was the same hundred people every time. But during the war it was thousands, hundreds of thousands. And suddenly Washington had to listen to us. We pushed for social justice and an end for white-skin privilege and things actually changed."

"And then the war ended," I said.

"Even before the war ended," he said bitterly. "That shit Nixon knew how to play the public for all it was worth. Peace with honor was his way of getting us out of Vietnam without actually letting on that we had lost. Kissinger had it worked out so that the South Vietnamese could hold out till 1976 and then the loss of Vietnam would have been blamed on the Democrats."

"Too bad about Watergate," Kane told him.

"Yeah," Abrahms said. "The rape wasn't quite complete when the South Vietnamese government had to move to Los Angeles."

"What did Stillwell have to do with Vietnam?" I asked.

"When Johnson stopped the bombing and the talks started in Paris the movement died. There were still protests, but it was over. Kent State should have burned down half the campuses in the U.S. But there was nothing. The middle class figured the war was over. They weren't even sending draftees to Vietnam anymore. The movement was dead."

"And I guess your aspirations for social justice went down the tubes along with it," I told him.

I regretted saying it immediately. I was afraid he was going to shut up.

"It's people like you that got the movement started," he told me.

I was tempted to tell him about the ZOG and ask how many police officials you had to blow up to become a Socialist Warrior. I managed to quash the urge, though; he was still talking.

"We had already split from the SDS and founded the Weathermen. We were more radical. We believed in direct action. We were going to set an example and bring the government to its knees."

"By blowing up buildings and killing innocent people?" I asked.

"We weren't setting out to hurt people. Not at first anyway. But people wouldn't listen. We blew up banks and chemical laboratories and the people didn't understand. The press told them we were terrorists and the people believed it. They didn't see that the things we were destroying belonged to their masters. They were happy being slaves.''

"And that radicalized you even further?"

"There was a split. One faction felt that we had to start hitting harder to make the government show its true oppressionist colors. The other faction said that that would only further isolate us from the people.''

"And Stillwell was the leader of the hit-harder faction?"

"No," he said. "Stillwell was the bomber.

"He never took the lead, but then he was never on the losing side of an argument either. He was always arguing someone else's position. Amanda Katz was the leader.''

The name sounded familiar but I really had to dig back. She had been part of the group that robbed an armored car in 1981 and murdered two police officers and an armored car guard. She was doing life for it, as I recalled.

It all began to have that familiar ring to it, though. Weathermen teamed up with black radicals robbing an armored car in a paramilitary operation planning to use the money to support their organization. It sounded an awful lot like what the Order had done in Ukiah three years later.

"How hard did they want to hit?" I asked.

He looked down. "They wanted to kill people. I was completely out of the movement by then, and I only heard about it afterward. We would have stopped them if we had known what they were planning. Stillwell went up to New England and bought fifty pounds of dynamite.'' He paused. "And fifty pounds of roofing nails.

"Sherill Walker's parents were out of town. They set up the bomb factory in the basement of their town house.'' He looked up at me. "You remember now, don't you?"

I did, but I let him finish.

"It was Stillwell's project. He showed them what to do and must've helped. They took the dynamite apart and formed the TNT into balls and then stuck hundreds of nails into the balls. All you had to do then was connect a battery through the terminals of an alarm clock into a blasting cap stuck in the TNT.''

''But something went wrong.''

''Yeah,'' he said, ''something went wrong. Diana Oughton and Terry Robbins were down in the basement when one of the bombs went off. There wasn't anything left of Terry but a few bones. They found one of Diana's fingers. The town house burned and collapsed. They found Ted Gold's body buried in the rubble.''

''I don't remember anything about another man in the town house,'' I told him. ''There were two women. They came running out naked. They'd had the clothes blown off them.''

He gave me a sardonic smile. ''And just how fast do you think you'd have been able to run if you'd just had your clothes blown off you, Mr. Captain of the NYPD?''

I hadn't thought about it. I looked over at Kane.

''Not very fast,'' he told me. ''You'd probably be dead.''

I looked back at Abrahms.

''The movement rejected the tired morality of our parents,'' he told me. ''To prove you were really dedicated you had to engage in acts of rejection: homosexuality, sex with different races, free love and other things. We found it was a good way to cut down on the FBI informers too. Ironic, isn't it? They wouldn't suck cock for old J. Edgar.''

''So Stillwell was upstairs with the two women then?''

He shrugged. ''That's what I figured, but how should I know? You could ask Amanda. I believe she'll be a guest of the state till well into the twenty-first century.''

''What happened to Stillwell after that?''

''I never heard anything about him after that. The hardline faction was in disgrace. Katz and Walker were deep underground. Ted, Terry and Diana were dead. The police planted the story that they'd been planning on leaving the bombs at Butler Library at Columbia. Amazing how little sympathy students had for the movement after that.

"I went to East Africa to work with a medical missionary group and was gone for six years. When I got back Jerry Rubin was a stockbroker. End of story."

"Who was the guy who came to visit you at the shelter? The one that Worthington went away with?"

"Adrian Deleux."

"Did he mention Stillwell to you?"

"No," he answered. "But he had that look in his eye. Deleux was Stillwell's pet; he used to follow him around everywhere. Stillwell didn't have any of the hang-ups Hoover's men had and Deleux's only hang-up was with women. I was afraid Stillwell was back when I first saw him. Now I know."

I thought about it for a while. I had arrived at Columbia in 1969 with an extremely high draft number and no particular interest in the Vietnam war. I'd have probably voted for Nixon if I'd been old enough.

The great riots and the takeovers had all happened the year before and the campus had been relatively quiet. We all knew the war would be over before Nixon had to run for reelection.

The town house blew up on a Saturday late in my freshman year and I remember being in shock reading the school newspaper the next Monday. The blast probably would have killed hundreds of students and the goddamned Weathermen weren't denying anything. Some of my fraternity brothers had gone out that night looking for SDS'ers, planning on beating them to death.

"The chem labs had already blown up that year," I told him. "A graduate student had both his legs taken off. You don't know anything about that, do you?"

He looked up at me. I could see the agony in his eyes and I knew what had sent him to East Africa and kept him in Harlem ever since. He didn't have the proper revolutionary zeal necessary to equate broken grad students with broken eggs. He started to say something, but I cut him off.

"Never mind," I told him. "They won't treat you any worse in Sing Sing than you're treating yourself where you are." I picked up the pictures and turned to Fred. "Get descriptions," I told him.

We left Abrahms sitting there holding his head. Most people can kid themselves that they're fighting for a just cause and if people get killed it's OK because the cause comes first. They tell themselves that people are dying every day in refugee camps or slums or insane asylums. Sometimes they can keep kidding themselves even after people start dying. Abrahms apparently hadn't been that self-deluding. If he'd have just turned himself in he'd be out by now. Instead he'd sentenced himself to life. Life without any possibility of parole.

We met Wayne coming back up the stairs. "Well?" I asked him.

"I talked to Hank Wallace," he told us. "He said Still-well's name didn't appear in any of his computer files. He says Abrahms must be pulling your chain."

I called Hank at Federal Plaza. "You got a file on a guy named Adrian Deleux?" I asked.

I had to wait a few minutes while he played with his computer. It turned out he did have a file on Deleux, several hundred pages worth.

"Pictures?" I asked.

"Full-face and profile," he told me. "But they're more than twenty years old. They're his mug shots from the 'four days of rage' protest in Chicago back in sixty-eight."

"I'll have Kane bring Worthington down to your office. Deleux's apparently his contact with the terrorists. You have an artist who can alter the photo to whatever Worthington says he looks like now?"

"No problem. You going to put it on the wire?"

"Every newspaper in the country," I told him.

CHAPTER 9

Hank Wallace was waiting for us in Mayes's office at FBI headquarters. He had his feet up on Mayes's desk and seemed to be enjoying the view of the harbor. Apparently his office in Washington didn't have any windows.

He'd been left in charge because Mayes had gone out to Connecticut to coordinate the search effort there. I hoped Mayes would be able to resist the urge to call a press conference and announce that the terrorists were hiding somewhere in southwest Connecticut.

One of Hank's assistants took Worthington away to look through their book of white supremacist mug shots; he'd been going through the Communist sympathizers the day before. I almost felt sorry for him. First it turned out that he'd been duped by a gang of homicidal maniacs and then it turned out that they didn't even share his political beliefs—quite embarrassing.

I flopped down on the couch and thought about stretching

out on it. But I decided Hank wouldn't appreciate my falling asleep in the middle of our conversation.

"What did the lab report on Branner show?" I asked.

"He was definitely chock-full of PCP. Apparently they held him down and packed his nose full of it."

"Messy."

"And stupid too. We got a large enough sample that we can do analysis on it and tell where it came from."

"How are you going to do that?" I asked him. "I thought PCP was pretty much PCP."

"Hey," he told me, "it's not like they're making the stuff down at Dupont. They cook it up in garbage cans. Every batch is as unique as a fingerprint. We're checking the trace impurities in the batch that came out of Branner's nose against samples that the DEA's confiscated over the past year. If it doesn't match one of those, we'll start in on samples from the local police departments."

"How long is that going to take?"

"Not very long. PCP abuse runs in cycles. It's almost as easy to make as Kool-Aid, you know; just add water. The problem with it is, by the time you're getting ready to market your second or third batch the consumers have wised up. By that time they all know someone who tried the first batch who doesn't speak so good anymore. So the dealers have to wait three or four years for the next group of suckers to make it to junior high school."

"So there aren't that many samples?"

"Maybe two dozen at the DEA. Three or four times that at the local PDs."

"Any word on the Front for the Total Independence of Nicaragua?"

"No, but that's not very surprising. These days most terrorist organizations have two or three official names and then think up a new one for every operation. It makes it seem like they're a bigger threat than they really are and it gives them a shield against reprisals."

"What are the Sandinistas saying?"

"They aren't being very cagey about it. They deny emphatically that they had anything to do with it, but they went on to say that the United States shouldn't be so surprised to find terrorists at home when we support terrorists abroad."

"That wasn't very smart of them, was it?"

"No, but it just goes to prove my point. They really didn't have anything to do with it. Just watch. Sometime this afternoon someone in their foreign ministry will call a press conference and denounce all forms of terrorism both in the U.S. and in Nicaragua. If they'd known about this in advance they wouldn't have let some loose cannon in Managua shoot his mouth off."

"What's the State Department doing?"

"Well now," he told me, "they *are* being cagey. They haven't denounced the Sandinistas yet, but they are making noises about the duty of every government to combat terrorism. I understand they're going to Capitol Hill today to brief Congress."

"Oh great," I said. "That's exactly what we need, a congressional fact-finding committee breathing down our necks."

"Any word on the van with the bomb in it?" he asked me.

"Yeah, Gagliardi was as good as his word. Same MO: it had commercial registration like the other two. This time it was International Bicycles and Mopeds, P.O. Box 1621 in Armonk."

"How cute. IBM in Armonk."

"We thought so. But that makes three in a row. Even money that there won't be a fourth. These people are too clever by a half. They've set a pattern and I'm betting they wanted us to see it."

"They're smart all right," he told me, "but it wasn't very smart driving a New York Bell truck through Connecticut. Someone must've seen it."

"Yeah, maybe. Dempsey has more than a hundred men

calling the registered owners of the cars in that video he made in Pelham. Then he's going back to Darien tonight and film Ninety-five at about the time they were passing through last night. And he's going to have another crew at Bridgeport and a couple more on the north-south routes that tie into Ninety-five east of Darien.''

"He's going to need an awful lot of people to man the phones,'' he pointed out.

"Yeah, well it's an emergency, you know,'' I told him.

"Tell me about it. We did an analysis on the clothes Branner and Hopkins were wearing—the dead man was positively identified as Gary Lee Hopkins, by the way. By the amount of pollen we found we can pretty much eliminate any city as their hiding place. They're out in the country somewhere.''

"That should really cheer people up in the suburbs,'' I told him. "Any fingerprints on the van?''

"Not one. It was wiped clean.''

"Any word on the white supremacist organizations?''

"Too early to tell. We have a lot of people in their organizations but we can't just call them. It would be kind of a breech in security. They'll have to call us. But I'm sure we would have heard from them by now if they'd heard anything related to our current problems.

"We're running a search now on known acquaintances of Hopkins. We'll probably come up with two or three names that haven't been seen in the past year and then we'll have a pretty good idea of who we're looking for.''

"And the radical Left?''

"Same story. We have a lot of people in their organizations. If I really wanted to I could go out tomorrow and arrest six known fugitives. We leave them out there because chances are we couldn't get prison sentences if we did arrest them . . . and being wanted tends to make them model citizens.''

"Seems like I read something about you guys arresting

a bunch of them out in Ohio a couple of years ago. They had gone deep underground and hadn't been seen since the seventies.''

"Since the seventies? Horse manure. I could show you a daily surveillance log. We'd still be leaving 'em alone today if'n they'd just been content to play fugitives. We don't go git 'em unless we have to.''

"What happened?''

"Eventually they got to thinking that they ought to be doing something to justify their images as revolutionaries. They decided to hijack an armored car, and after the disaster in Nyack we couldn't let them do it; too risky.''

"What happened? If you're so deep into their organization why didn't you stop that one?''

He looked around and then turned back to me and lowered his voice. "This is strictly between you and me. We arrested those idiots out in Ohio on fifteen-year-old warrants and they'll all be out of prison in five years at the latest. We knew the same thing would happen with Katz and her friends so we decided to catch them in the act and get them for armed robbery. The agent in charge figured we could put them away for twenty years.''

"What happened?''

"Their leader got too clever. He'd been preparing to hit a different armored car all along. The one they were supposed to hit was full of our guys and it would have been over in a second with no fuss. Instead, the change in plans made his people nervous and one of them came out shooting.

"After they'd killed an armored car guard they really panicked. They didn't have a chance in hell of getting away; the area was saturated with police. Within five minutes we were closing in on them and they knew it. One of them told us later that they thought they'd interrupted a police convention. They were stopped at a roadblock less than a mile from the scene of the robbery. That's where they killed a couple of cops and we captured about half of them. Rather than having another shootout we let the rest of them get away and picked them up the next day. It was a disaster of the first order."

"I can see why you wouldn't want to see that sort of thing in the papers. What happened to the agent in charge?"

"Well, they couldn't just fire him. What happened might have leaked to the press. He's probably sitting in a windowless cubicle in DC right this second, entering fingerprints into the Bureau's new computer system and counting the days till he's eligible to retire."

"That's the third armored car, you know," I told him. "First there was the one in Nyack, then the one in Ukiah and now one in Ohio. The Weather Underground, black radicals, white supremacists and maybe homegrown Sandinistas. How do you feel about conspiracy theories?"

"Not very good. I spent four hours one day trying to convince an idiot senator that Elvis really did die of constipation and that he wasn't assassinated by the same KGB agent who got JFK."

"How do you die of constipation?"

"Well, I saw the autopsy report. Apparently he'd been taking opiates for quite some time. And opiates slow intestinal motility down to just about zero. So it looked to the coroner like he hadn't been able to take a dump for a couple of days and he was sitting there on the throne straining away mightily and he blew a head gasket."

"That doesn't sound like terminal constipation to me."

"Call it what you want. Who is this Adam Stillwell person your guy was asking me about?"

I gave him the rundown on what Abrahms had told me.

"He's jerking you around. If there had ever been anyone of that name who had ever attended an SDS meeting in Podunk we'd have a file on him about three inches thick. Chances are we'd be able to tell you where he is today, what he's doing for a living and what his dog's name is. There is zero chance that anyone in the inner circle of the Weather Underground would not have a file."

"Maybe you missed it."

"You ever heard of computers in New York?"

I had. I knew they had Delete keys.

"Whatever," I told him. "It wouldn't be the first time I was lied to."

I borrowed an office and sat down to make some phone calls. My father answered on the third ring.

"Hi, Dad," I said.

"Johnny?"

"No, Dad, it's Michael."

"Michael?" he said. "Michael. You know it does seem like I have a son by that name. Of course it's been years since I talked to him. How do I know it's really you?"

"It's been about six days, Dad, and I've been busy. You sinking deeper into senility or something?"

"Hmmpft. I understand Dr. Spock finally admitted he was dead wrong about not beating on your kids. If only I'd known it at the time."

"Yeah, right, Dr. Spock. You raised us according to Dr. Hitler."

"Well, at least Dr. Hitler hasn't admitted he was all wet yet."

"Look, I didn't call up to discuss child rearing."

"No shit."

"What do you remember about the Walker town house explosion?"

"March 1970, three killed, two fugitives. Explosion blew a hole into their next-door neighbor's living room. Wasn't my case; Chief Seedman handled it personally. Hold on a second." He was off the line for less than twenty seconds. "You might try calling Frank Pito. He lives in Coral Gables now. You got a pencil?" I did. He gave me the number.

"You happen to remember anyone in the FBI who was in on the investigation?" I asked.

"Mylo Ketchem, but he must've retired years ago."

"Thanks, Dad. I gotta go."

"John, Marlene, the kids and I are going to the Yankee

doubleheader on Sunday after mass. You want to come along? Nettles is managing now, you know."

"So I've been told. You know I'd like to, Dad, but I don't think I'm even going to get a chance to get to mass. I've sort of got this problem with twelve screaming maniacs and a mad bomber that I don't think I'm going to have cleared up by Sunday."

"There's only eleven of them now," he pointed out. "It's giving the headline writers fits."

"I gotta go, Dad. Give the girls a big kiss for me."

"They like it better when they get them firsthand."

"When this is all over I'll do my best to deliver."

"I'll be going out to the cemetery on Saturday . . . ."

"I know, Dad. I'll go next week."

We said good-bye. Some fathers and sons go fishing together. My father and I go to visit our wives.

I was mildly surprised that I didn't need an access code to call Florida. The new government phone network was something else. Pito answered even faster than my father had. Maybe retirement's not all that it's cracked up to be— I could hear a television game show on in the background.

"Frank Pito?" I asked.

"Speaking."

I identified myself and we chatted about my father and the good old days for a few minutes before getting down to business.

"Yeah," he told me. "I remember it like it was yesterday. We had a bucket loader scooping out the basement. I nearly lost my lunch when they pulled out what was left of one of the bombers. He was burned pretty good and his arms and legs were missing. And what was left had been under water for a couple of days."

"I've seen worse," I assured him.

"Me too," he told me, "and it was only about three hours later. We pulled a wad of TNT about the size of a basketball out of the basement. It had about a million nails stuck in it. I nearly crapped in my pants when I seen it. And that was the end of the bucket loader, too. We cleaned out the rest of the basement with our mitts."

"I have a report that there were other people in the building when the bomb went off. You know anything about that?"

"Yeah sure, there were two girls who went running out in the street barcassed."

"No, there was someone named Adam."

"Oh yeah," he said. "Now that you mention it. The first guy on the scene tried to go in the front door but it was too hot. So he went around back. Seems like he heard two people talking inside the house. And yeah, seems like the women was calling out for someone named Adam.

"But there was a barred gate across the back door with a big padlock on it and it seems like he even took a shot at the lock but it was a no go."

"Why didn't any of that make the papers?" I asked.

"Well, it wasn't a secret, if that's what you mean. We figured we'd find the bodies down in the basement when we finally got it cleared out and we didn't want to scare the shit out of every mother in the country who had a kid named Adam.

"Then it was a couple of weeks before we got the basement cleared out and the only bodies we found pretty obviously hadn't been doing any talking after the first blast. But by that time nobody was much interested. I guess we were planning on asking the two women when we caught up with them. But then we never did catch them, so it got to be a dead issue. What's going on?"

"We think there's a connection between the bomb that went off last night in the city and the Walker town house bomb. It was the same type of bomb and we have a witness who claims that someone named Adam was involved. You have any idea who the guy who tried to break into the town house was?"

He thought for a minute befor admitting he had no idea.

"But he would have had to file a ballistics report. You should be able to track him down pretty easy."

I thanked Pito and then asked him not to talk about our conversation to anyone and especially not to talk to anyone about Adam and to try not to talk to anyone in New York for a week. He got a little huffy that I didn't think he could keep his mouth shut.

I poked my head out the door and called Wayne over. I told him about the policeman who'd heard voices from inside the burning town house and told him to go down to Central Records and look up the ballistic report. Then in a momentary spasm of guilty feeling I told him to find the cop and see what he had to say.

"And where's Kane?" I asked him.

"He was talking to one of the secretaries last I saw him."

"Great," I said.

I found Kane at the watercooler putting the moves on an impressionable young secretary who found his supposed ability to get by the doormen at the better clubs to be nearly irresistible.

"Don't get your hopes up," I told her. "You'll only be disappointed when you find out about his old war wound."

Kane clutched his right side and his face took on a look of comic anxiousness. "War wound?" he asked.

"Lower and to the left," I told him. I looked over to the girl, who seemed more confused than alarmed. "Mrs. Kane had to leave him, of course."

"Mrs. Kane?" she asked.

"Mrs. Kane?" he asked. "Oh yeah, Mom."

I started pulling him away. He came along but called out over his shoulder, "Mom couldn't stand the sight of suffering. She's better now."

"You just can't stand to see a guy having fun, can you?" he asked.

"Haven't you heard that a little variety in your sex life can be fatal these days?"

"Heh," he said, "I ain't scared. Doc says I got antibodies."

"Ho ho ho," I said. "Hey, Kane, say you were off duty in your personal automobile and witnessed a hit-and-run accident in which a pedestrian appeared to be seriously injured. What action would you take pursuant to Section Thirty-seven-point-two-point-five slash A of the NYPD administrative guidelines?"

"How the fuck should I know? I don't even have a personal automobile. What kind of a question is that?"

"You should know," I told him. "It was question thirty-four on the last sergeant's exam."

"Oh shit, they're not starting that again, are they?"

I nodded and then sadly shook my head.

Promotion to sergeant is based on your score on a civil service exam. If they need 150 new sergeants the top 150 scorers on the test get promoted. Ability, evaluations and commendations count for nothing. Naturally, if you came in 151st and had been decorated thirty times for heroism this would bother you.

After the last exam, the one on which Kane had shocked us all by coming in 140th, one of the borderline failers had sued the department. He found a judge who thought he knew more about police work than the college professor the department had paid $80,000 to make up the exam. The judge threw out a few questions here, accepted different answers there and awarded partial credit in a few other cases. Then he ordered the department to rescore all the examinations.

The department dutifully rearranged the list, and since they still only needed 150 sergeants, they handed out as many demotions as promotions—which led to at least one interesting case of role reversal in a precinct in Brooklyn. Kane got to keep his job, but he moved down to 147th on the list.

Naturally the new ex-sergeants were none too pleased, and since now they were borderline failers instead of bor-

derline passers, they decided to find a different judge and
sue the department themselves.

"Don't take it so hard," I told him. "I understand the
department didn't make the guys who got demoted pay back
the salary differential."

I brought him up to date on what I'd learned from my
father and Pito. Then I told him to call the corrections
department and find out where Amanda Katz was doing her
time.

I called Goldman to bring him up to date.

"So it's an old Weatherman," he said after I'd related
what Abrahms had told us. "Good work. But what about
the guy with the swastika tattoo? I don't see him being
welcome at an SDS convention."

"Stillwell's twisted," I told him. "We've known that
right from the beginning. Leaving notes in dead people's
blood isn't exactly normal. Maybe he thinks it's funny, or
maybe it's just another red herring."

"You think we were supposed to get the one with the
tatoo?" he asked.

"I hadn't thought about it," I told him. "I guess it's
possible."

"Can you be in my office at twelve-thirty?" he asked.
"There's going to be somebody here you really ought to
meet."

"I'll try," I told him.

"It's the secound consul to the Nicaraguan mission to
the UN," he said.

"I'll be there," I told him.

"See to it," he told me as he hung up.

Kane came in and flopped down into a chair. "Bernard
Hills," he said. "It's about an hour north of here."

"Thanks," I told him.

I called Traffic to arrange a helicopter. I told the boys in
Dispatching that I didn't give a damn how much it cost, it
had better be there when I arrived and that if it wasn't they

would be making friends with street people on a regular
basis in the future.

Hank came in just as I was hanging up. He handed me
a copy of the artist's reconstruction of Adrian Deleux based
on his old photograph and Worthington's description.

"And we got the lab report back on the PCP. Identical
to a sample confiscated in Norwalk, Connecticut, last
March. The Norwalk PD is about to start leaning on dealers
in a fashion the ACLU would not feel good about."

"It appears there was someone named Adam in the
Walker town house when it went up," I told him. "How
many other Adams were there in the Weathermen?"

He logged into the computer terminal on the desk and
called up a file and then played with the keyboard for a few
seconds. "None," he told me. "Nada, zilch." He deep-
sixed the file and turned to face me. "Who'd you hear it
from this time?"

I told him about the cop who'd tried to blast his way into
the town house and for the first time I saw an expression
of doubt cross his face. "That's pretty weird," he told me.

"It was eighteen years ago, Chief. What were you doing
back then?"

"I was chasing the Mafia in Kansas City."

"You know a fellow named Mylo Ketchem?"

"Nope. Should I?"

"He had your job in the late sixties."

"Oh," he said. He turned back to the terminal and called
up another file. He had to input about six authorization codes
and had to call someone to get a seventh, but finally found
what he was looking for.

"Ketchem, Mylo T., 1147 Tailings Creek Road, Grand
Junction, Colorado."

I dialed his number. Ordinarily I'm a firm believer in
hanging up after the tenth ring, feeling that either no one's
home or they don't want to talk to you. I know most people
won't even make an effort to go for the phone after the
tenth ring. But generally after the thirtieth ring or so they'll

get the idea that it may be important. It rang about forty times before someone answered.

"This better be fucking important," he told me. I knew I'd gotten Ketchem. He had a raspy voice that probably came complete with the kind of breath that chain-smokers who like coffee get after a few years. Ketchem wouldn't be the type who chewed Certs prior to a big meeting either.

"Life and death," I admitted.

"Yours or mine?" he asked.

"Thirty-six killed last night and we're expecting more this evening."

"Well, who are you?"

"Captain Michael Kelly of the New York City Police Department," I told him.

"How do I know it's really you?"

"We could play twenty questions all morning if you've got nothing better to do. My father, Tom Kelly, gave me your name, if that means anything."

"Stiff-necked old Irish fool Tom Kelly?"

"The same."

"What's his favorite brand of whiskey?"

"He doesn't drink."

"And a disgrace to his people because of it. What is it you want?"

"A bomb went off in the theater district last night. We think the Weather Underground may be connected with it somehow. We have a source that's identified someone named Adam Stillwell." There was dead silence on the other end of the phone. "The Bureau says that there was never anyone of that name connected with the Weathermen." There was still nothing but silence. "I was hoping you might remember something," I finished lamely.

"They say they've got nothing?"

"Not a thing."

"Then tell them to check their personnel files."

CHAPTER 10

The chopper was waiting for us at the Wall Street heliport, relieving me of the burden of having to arrange unpleasant transfers for various traffic officers. Transfers I probably wouldn't have been able to arrange anyway.

Hank Wallace had accompanied us to the heliport. He had decided to fly to Washington to examine the personnel files personally. He assured me he wouldn't let anyone shred anything. At least not until after I'd seen it.

Our pilot didn't have much to say. He waited for us to fasten our seat belts and then took off with a stomach-churning jolt. If he was trying to make the trip as unpleasant as possible he failed miserably. I was asleep within thirty seconds and didn't wake up until after we had landed.

Kane had to shake me a couple of times to get me moving. The pilot had already shut down the engines and the slowly spinning rotors made a *whop whop whop* sound as they passed overhead.

"Wait for us," I told the pilot. "This may take some time."

He ignored me. It seemed that my long career of not stepping on toes had come to a crashing end. I leaned forward and stared into the side of his face. "I've had seven hours of sleep in the last three days," I snarled at him. "And I'm not the same nice guy I was on Tuesday. Nothing would make me happier than charging you with insubordination, busting you to patrolman and shipping you out to the Bronx, where you can spend the next five years busting AIDS-infected junkies. I told you to wait for us here."

He turned to face me. "I'm sorry, sir. I didn't hear you the first time. I'll wait right here." He didn't tell us to mind the rotors as we left the chopper.

We crouched over and ran under the rotors and then walked up to the prison. The pilot had put us down in the middle of the long lawn leading up to the main building. It was actually kind of a pretty facility, given what it was.

"Kind of edgy, aren't you?" Kane asked me.

I glared at him but couldn't summon up any anger. I knew it would just make him feel morally superior. "Why yes," I told him, doing my best to sound sweet and reasonable. "Maybe I should cut down on caffeine."

The guards at the front gate had called upstairs and the warden had come down to greet us. I'd called her from the city and she'd said she'd be glad to help. She still examined our identifications closely and made us leave our guns at the door. We had to pass through a metal detector at the second gate. I'd never known about the stiletto Kane wore in a sheath strapped to his calf.

The guards relieved him of his knife and then they escorted us into a small interview room and told us to wait. The room wasn't much bigger than a closet. The table and mismatched chairs essentially filled it and the pastel-painted walls were bare of adornment. It was a horrible place to hold a meeting, but at least we wouldn't have to use telephones while staring through a glass wall.

"God, I can't take you anywhere," I told Kane.

"Sorry, I thought she just meant guns."

"Great, I am so embarrassed. Did you see the look she gave us when you came up with that pig sticker?"

"Look," he told me, "it could have been worse. If it had been Fred they'd have had to bring in a dentist."

"Why is it that I don't find that very surprising?"

Before he could answer, the door opened again and a guard escorted Katz into the room. The guard told us she would be right outside the door and that we should call her when we were through.

Katz sat down opposite us. She didn't much look like any revolutionary I'd seen on TV. I guess Hollywood had prepared me for olive-skinned, raven-haired beauties in jungle fatigues—not drab fortyish housewives wearing overalls.

Her father was Leonard Katz, one of the most famous labor union lawyers in American history. He had taken on Roy Cohn and Joe McCarthy back in the fifties when Joe was at his peak and the rest of the country was scared spitless. A tough act to follow, but I guess every child has to at least try to outdo her parents.

She sat across the table, eyeing us coolly. She didn't seem anxious to speak first. If nothing else, prison teaches you patience.

"We need your help, Ms. Katz."

"What makes you think I'd be willing to help the pigs against a revolutionary movement?" she asked.

"It's possible that I could help you with the parole board."

"I'm not eligible for parole for another seventeen years," she told me. "But even if I was eligible today I wouldn't help you. People are dying for the cause in Central America. Do you think I would betray them just to get out of this building into the so-called freedom of the United States?"

"I was talking to David Abrahms this morning. We were reminiscing about the good old days of the Vietnam war, back when people gave a damn. You wouldn't mind seeing another Vietnam, would you? Another chance to mobilize the great unwashed would suit you fine, wouldn't it?''

She didn't deny it.

"But it wouldn't be the same this time," I told her. "The war would be over in about two weeks and all you'd have accomplished is getting a hundred thousand people killed.''

"You wouldn't find the Sandinistas to be as easy an egg to crack as the Grenadian police force,'' she informed me.

I looked over at Kane.

"I did three tours in Vietnam, ma'am," he said. "This isn't Asia. They wouldn't even last two weeks. They got no place to run and the Commies got no way to resupply them.''

"And you know it won't take much of an excuse for us to do it,'' I added.

She just stared back at us. Appealing to her self-interest hadn't worked. Coming from me, I doubted she'd believe an appeal based on good intentions. And I knew she wouldn't start sobbing like Abrahms if I started showing her pictures of dead bodies; after all, people were dying all the time in Central America.

"It's Stillwell," I told her. "He's back.''

Her composure cracked. She shook her head from side to side and her lips mouthed, *But he's dead*.

"But he's not dead," I told her. "He's back and he wants to kill people. He doesn't give a shit about the cause or justice in Central America. He just wants to see people die. He's like a little kid with a stick poking at an anthill. He gets off on the turmoil.''

The little kid with the stick analogy brought it home to me and suddenly it all became painfully clear. "He's a psychopath, Ms. Katz. He's a sick, manipulative bastard. He can preach Marxist platitudes and white supremacist hatred with equal fervor. He's using both sides and playing them against the middle. He's trying to start a war. Surely you can see that. A hundred thousand corpses in Nicaragua would probably make his decade.''

She composed herself and stared at me. "Adam Stillwell

was a revolutionary hero. He died heroically on March 7, 1970, attempting to rescue his fallen comrades.''

"His fallen comrades?" I told her, my voice taking on an incredulous tone. "Ms. Katz, a nail-studded glob of dynamite the size of a basketball went off in an enclosed area. He would've needed a mop to rescue your fallen comrades. He sent you out into the street as a diversion and then got out of the town house some other way."

"Either he died in the house or the FBI murdered him," she told me. "If he'd gotten out he would have contacted us."

"Why would he contact you?" I asked her. "Your faction was in disgrace and you were wanted fugitives."

"Then the FBI murdered him."

"Why would the FBI murder one of its employees?"

She stared at me in disbelief.

"They set you up on the armored car job, surely you must know that. There were two hundred cops on top of you in five minutes. What did you think? That you'd run into a Saint Patrick's Day parade? And when the FBI rounded up the rest of the organization the next day, where do you think they got the addresses? They knew exactly who you were and what you were planning right from the word go.

"And they were setting you up in 1970 too. How else could Stillwell have gotten the dynamite? And why was it that no one ever got hurt when you blew things up? They were just waiting for you to build the antipersonnel bombs and then they were going to have some stooge at the library search your packs when you showed up. They'd probably have said they were looking for lost library books and boy would they act surprised when they found the bombs."

She was shaking her head from side to side.

"Don't tell me Stillwell was going to deliver the bombs personally. I can almost hear him telling you how much easier it would be for two women to sneak the bombs in than for a man. He probably even went so far as to buy you a couple of book bags. They were probably distinctive too, 'cause the FBI sure wouldn't have wanted to miss you coming in the door.

"And what a trial it would have made, because for sure they'd have gotten you all. They'd have made up mock-ups of the bombs to show the jury and the folks at home watching on television. They'd have probably set off one of the real ones inside a building the size of the reading room at Butler. Maybe they'd have hung some sides of beef in there with it so they could tell the press how many nails they dug out and show them pictures of the hamburger that was left.

"And that would have been the end of the movement, wouldn't it? The antiwar movement would have gone on, but without even a shred of moral justification because it would have all gone up in smoke along with your fifty pounds of roofing nails. I have to hand it to Hoover, it was a dandy plan.

"And the only one of you who wouldn't have gone to prison for two hundred years would have been Stillwell, because the rest of you revolutionary warriors would have gone to the gallows with his name unspoken. And he would have laughed and laughed down in Florida or out in California or wherever the Bureau had found him a new identity."

"Stop it," she screamed at me. "Stop it, you bastard. Nobody would have been hurt. The bombs were set to go off at six A.M."

"I don't know for sure," I told her. "But I'd bet you'd have a pretty hard time proving that."

And then she cried. Her whole life had been wasted and I'd made her see it. She'd thought she was in control of her destiny, the master of her fate. But all she'd really ever been was a puppet in a game she didn't even know she was playing. I was just the latest in a long string of puppet masters making her dance to my tune.

She sobbed like a child who knows there is no tomorrow. And for her, there really wasn't. She would be past sixty when her first parole date came up. Her sobs cut a hole through my stomach and I was ashamed of what I'd done.

Finally her sobbing died out. But I knew it would be a mistake to say anything. She would realize I was manipulating her and she hated me enough already. She would tell me about Stillwell or she wouldn't. It was out of my hands. Kane sat motionless by my side. Maybe it was easier for him. A lot of his friends had died in his arms.

"It's all true then, isn't it?" she asked me. "Except it wasn't going to be two girls. It was going to be me and Ted. We had borrowed the preppiest clothes we could find and Adam had bought two matching book bags—mine was rust and his was forest green. We were going to go as boyfriend and girlfriend, you see. We would have been holding hands and no one would have given us a second look.

"I was going to ask the librarian behind the circulation desk to hold mine while I went for dinner and Ted was going to leave his in a carrel on the main floor. People did it all the time. Scatter some books around and make it look like he was coming back Sunday morning.

"Adam wanted to wake people up. He said a blast at dawn would have great symbolic effect. But Diana . . ." She wiped the back of her hand across her eyes and sniffed back tears. "But Diana was a worrywart. She was afraid there might be a janitor or something in the building. But Adam was insistent, it had to be six A.M. So Sherill and I took Adam upstairs to distract him while Diana and Terry went downstairs to change the timers to midnight. They said they knew what they were doing."

"What time did the library close?" Kane asked her.

"Six o'clock," she told him. "It was a Saturday; they closed early on Saturday."

"Where was Stillwell from?" I asked.

"During the takeover of Low he just appeared. At first we thought he might be a spy, but we had contacts at Princeton who vouched for him. And he was a godsend.

He worked hard. He was dedicated to the revolution. He followed orders. He was a chemistry major.''

"Whose idea was it for him to make bombs?''

"Mine," she said immediately. Then she was silent for a moment. "Maybe he told me he could do it and I thought it was a good idea. He said he wouldn't have anything to do with hurting people, though. But that was fine. We were just going to destroy the property of the FG.''

"FG?" I asked.

"Fascist government.''

"Whose idea was it to make the bombs with the nails in them?''

She paused before answering, or rather before not answering. "On one of the earlier bombs someone had tacked on a little note about it being a present for Nixon. Adam found the tack and was quite graphic when he explained what the tack could do to anyone unlucky enough to get in its way. He was really steamed. No one would admit having stuck it in the bomb.''

We all knew who had left the note. But I doubted we'd ever know who first suggested making antipersonnel bombs. It didn't matter. Stillwell would have planted the idea in their head. I was beginning to get a real feel for how he worked.

"Do you have any personal information about Stillwell: where he grew up, who his parents were, any place he might be hiding?''

She shook her head. "He told us his parents cut him off because of their fascist political views and he had to drop out of Princeton. After that all he would say was that, as far as he was concerned, his parents were dead.''

"Do you have any contacts who might know anything about his current whereabouts?''

She shook her head. "I can ask.''

"Please don't," I told her. "It's rather important that he not know we're looking for him.''

"Of course," she said.

We got up to go and I could see her struggling with the last remnants of her pride. I knew her pride would lose, but I'd hurt her badly enough already.

"Thank you, Ms. Katz," I told her. "And even if you'd rather I didn't, I'll contact your trial judge and let him know how cooperative you've been. And I'll let him know about the FBI penetration of your group if I can find some way to do it unofficially."

There was no gratitude in her eyes, no hatred or disgust either—only despair.

I stopped in the warden's office and told her that Ms. Katz had been very cooperative and borrowed her phone to call Dr. Pendar at Columbia. Pendar was happy to hear that Worthington was cooperating and that it was possible that Columbia would be spared the embarrassment of a public trial.

He promised to call his opposite number at Princeton to see if an Adam Stillwell had attended back in the late sixties and to get the name of any roommates. He knew enough not to ask why we were interested in Stillwell. But I couldn't help but note the faint tinge of glee in his voice that Princeton's august name might be in for some dragging through the mud.

We retrieved our guns and Kane's knife and left.

"Did you catch the significance of the times?" Kane asked me.

"No."

"The bomb was originally set to go off at six A.M.; the library was scheduled to close at six P.M. At six, the lobby would have been packed with people lining up to check out books and there would have been another long line having their book bags checked for library books at the exit."

"But Diana was a worrywart and set the timer back to midnight," I finished. "And the bomb went off twelve hours early, at noon."

"Maybe she knew what she was doing after all," Kane mused.

The helicopter was waiting for us and the pilot treated me with exaggerated courtesy on the way back to the city. He even waited for us to get away from the prop wash before taking off after dropping us off at the East Sixtieth Street heliport. I hadn't been able to sleep on the way in.

We took a taxi to One Police Plaza. I stuffed the receipt into my wallet next to the other ones. I began to dread the day of reckoning when I had to fill out my expense report.

The Nicaraguan consul was waiting for us in Chief Goldman's office. He was of medium height, but powerfully built. His hawk nose, a vestigial reminder of some Indian forebear, looked strangely out of place between his pale blue eyes.

"Dr. Eduardo de los Toyos Hunnicut Marmolejo Ramos Morgan," Goldman introduced him. "Captain Michael Kelly of the New York Police Department."

"Pleased to meet you, Dr. Morgan," I said.

"And I am pleased to meet you, Captain Kelly," he replied. "But my family name is de los Toyos. The rest of it is merely genealogy. And while I personally find it fascinating, I would prefer that you simply call me Ed. That is what they used to call me at USC."

"Sure," I said. "And please call me Mike. Do you have any information about the Front for the Total Independence of Nicaragua?"

"I truly wish I did. But as my government, and all of my fellow government employees, have nothing whatsoever to do with any of the crimes this organization has committed, I can tell you nothing."

"The first reactions out of Managua were less condemnatory," I pointed out.

"My government can hardly take the responsibility for a minor Foreign Ministry official having a big mouth. The people of Nicaragua join peace-loving peoples everywhere in condemning acts of terrorism wherever they are committed.''

I looked at my watch and got up. ''Well it was certainly nice to meet you, Ed,'' I told him. ''But I'm kind of busy. Maybe we can get together in a couple of days and have a few drinks.''

He held up his hand. ''Please, I'll stop making speeches. I was just practicing for a press conference I have to hold later today. Let me assure you, anyone in Nicaragua with either the authority or the power to aid in this operation would not have been so stupid as to allow it to occur.''

''If you can help us catch the terrorists full credit will be granted to your government,'' I assured him, ''regardless of what any federal officials might want kept secret. Your government has as much to lose in this as anyone.''

''That is true,'' he said, ''and no one would like to see these criminals brought to justice more than we. However, the fact of the matter is that we cannot help you because we have had no contact with them.''

''Then why did you want to meet with me?''

''I believe that you have information that will totally exonerate my country.''

I looked over at Chief Goldman, who shook his head a few millimeters side to side.

''Where on earth did you get that idea, Ed?'' I asked him.

''I have made inquiries among people sympathetic to the Sandinista cause and they have informed me that the man who was killed at the tunnel last night was not who he appeared to be.''

''You're stretching, Ed,'' I told him. ''You know something but not very much or you wouldn't be here. Why don't you tell me what you know and maybe I can help you out.''

He took some time deciding what to tell me. I hurried him along by reminding him that we already had marines in New York and we weren't very concerned about getting more.

"I attended a meeting of concerned United States citizens in Brewster a few months ago. After the meeting a young lady came up to me and told me that soon a great blow would be landed against both racism and imperialism.

"Naturally I assumed she was an agent provocateur sent by your government to embarrass Nicaragua by involving me in some harebrained plot. I'm afraid I was quite short with her and said something about FBI spies being better looking in the old days. This seemed to hurt her feelings and I almost decided she might be genuine. She told me that I would one day realize she was a true believer and left me there. I realize now that I should have found out what she was planning."

"Why now?" I asked.

"Because she called the mission yesterday afternoon and told me that now I knew who the real patriots were. Before I could ask her anything she shouted out 'Long Live Sandino' and hung up."

"That doesn't look good for your side," I pointed out.

"Perhaps, but I also know that the man who died at the tunnel last night did so of gunshot wounds. His body was not burned beyond recognition and you must know his identity by now. But you are keeping it secret. I wonder why and can only presume that you wish to keep some embarrassing detail from the public."

"What kind of secret?" I asked.

"As of a few hours ago the FBI has put out an alert for Adrian Deleux, an ex-Weatherman who could be presumed to be sympathetic towards justice in Central America. If the dead man were also a member of an organization that might in some way be connected with Nicaragua, I am sure you would be trumpeting it to every ear that would listen. And then there is the cryptic remark the girl made about fighting racism."

"You're very sharp, Dr. de los Toyos. As it happens, however, my only interest is catching the terrorists. I could care less what's going on in Washington . . . or Managua.

The reason we haven't released any information about the dead man is to keep the terrorists off balance. We won't give them any information that we don't have to and their plans will have to be made in the dark."

"I did not mean to impugn your integrity," he assured me. "I hope you are not offended."

"No offense, Ed."

"But surely you must see that the stakes are considerably higher than what happens here in New York."

"I've already told you that I couldn't care less what happens in Managua," I told him. "It's not my job to care. It's my job to catch these bastards."

"I could go to the press."

"All you know is that an organization of Sandinista sympathizers have murdered nearly forty people and are apparently going to try and blame it on racists."

He thought that over for a few minutes. "But you know differently, don't you?" he asked. "If it were that simple you wouldn't even be talking to me. What is it that you want?"

"Tell me about the meeting in Brewster."

"It was very small, local people concerned that your government is getting them into another Vietnam. I do not think any of them were terrorists."

"Except the one," I pointed out. "How many people attended?"

"Perhaps twenty."

"And how much publicity did it get?"

"I don't know," he answered. "Presumably not very much or it would have been better attended."

"Then someone there must have known the girl. Get me her name, Ed, and I'll tell you what I think. But you better hurry. I don't care what's happening in Managua, but I might be the only one. The FBI and the State Department are already getting ready to push me aside. If I'm gone they'll be able to write the final report any way they want to. And we all know how that'll be."

He rose and said he would be in contact. He thanked Goldman for arranging the meeting and left. After he was gone Goldman looked over at me appraisingly.

"You were late."

"I was up in Bernard Hills interviewing Amanda Katz about Adam Stillwell," I told him. "Things are really getting to be complicated. I talked with the FBI agent who ran their antiterrorism office in New York back in the sixties: Mylo Ketchem. It turns out Stillwell was working for the FBI."

Goldman shook his head in disbelief.

"It gets worse," I told him.

"Does this have something to do with that town house that blew up in the Village?" he asked.

"It has everything to do with that town house. Apparently Stillwell was building bombs for the Weathermen. He had set them to go off at six P.M., when their target would have been crowded, and told his colleagues that they were set to go off at six A.M., when the building would have been deserted. One of his assistants went to change the timer to midnight, just to be on the safe side, and it went off at noon—right in her face.

"Apparently he was planning on killing a whole lot of people and dividing the blame equally between the Weathermen and the FBI. Or maybe he was going to let the world blame it on the Weathermen and then blackmail the FBI. Whatever he was planning, killing hundreds of people was a part of it."

"God," he whispered, "that's insane."

"He's crazy, all right," I told him. "I think he's pulling the same stunt today that he tried to pull back then. We know he's using the remnants of his old organization, the Weather Underground, and we suspect that he's also using white supremacists. He's going to kill a lot of people and when it's all over both sides are going to look real bad and the government is going to look like a first-class chump."

"You will hunt this man down," he told me, "and you will stop him. Any way you have to."

"Yes, sir," I said. It was the closest thing I'd ever heard to a "shoot to kill" order.

CHAPTER 11

"I got hold of the guy who heard the voices in the town house," Wayne told me as I walked into the school. "His name's Charlie Gertz. He's still with the force and he told it the same way you did. Two voices, one male, one female; the female voice was calling out for someone named Adam, and the male voice told her 'Over here.'

"You want to talk with the guy?" he asked.

"No, I was just checking. Good work."

There was a stack of pink message forms on my desk. I flipped through them rapidly and decided the only call I had to return was Pendar's.

"There was indeed an Adam Stillwell at Princeton," he informed me. "He matriculated in 1967 and took a leave of absence in 1968, for personal reasons, and never returned. He is originally from Greenwich, Connecticut. His parents' names are Elaine and Howard, although they aren't listed in the phone book; I checked. His religious preference is Episcopalian. He hadn't declared a major prior to taking

175

his leave of absence, although he was enrolled in a liberal arts curriculum.

"His freshman year roommate's name was Phillip Erickson. The alumni directory gives an address in lower Manhattan, on Charles Street, but no phone number."

"And who did he live with the next year?" I asked.

"I was getting to that," he told me. "That was his personal reason for leaving school; his second roommate committed suicide."

"Details?"

"Just that Stillwell found the body on a Sunday night and requested a leave of absence two weeks later. The boy who killed himself's name was Roger Crampton. He was from Rhode Island. I'm afraid I didn't get any of the details on him."

"That's OK, Dr. Pendar. I can get them if I need them. Is there anything else?"

"No, that's about it."

"You've been of great help. Thank you."

"I'm happy to oblige."

I found Kane and Bret drinking coffee and arguing as usual. I asked Bret to take a quick trip up to Connecticut to see if anyone in Greenwich remembered Elaine and Howard Stillwell and their son Adam. I told Kane to get the Erickson telephone number on Charles Street and see if Mr. Erickson was at home.

I called a reporter at the *Times* who had done favors for me in the past and repaid the favors by lying to him shamelessly—off the record. I told him we were concentrating on organizations known to be sympathetic to the Sandinistas and that we expected to make a major arrest at any moment.

I figured it couldn't hurt. Stillwell would certainly see the article and have a good laugh at our ineptitude. I didn't want him to get spooked, seeing as how he didn't know that we were on to him. I didn't want him to go to ground. I also saw it as a way to light a fire under Eduardo.

Kane came in and I had to cut the conversation short—

I acted like I was doing something under the table.

"I called Erickson's house," he told me. "The guy must be loaded. His maid said he was at work and that she couldn't give me the number."

"So what'd you do?"

"I figured if the guy was rich my buddy Sally would know him."

"And did Sally know him?"

"Not a chance; guy must be gay or something. So I called Fred's friend at the phone company."

"Never mind," I cut him off. "What's the bottom line?"

"Erickson's the controller of First Manhattan Savings. Here's his number," he told me, handing me a scrap of paper he'd been clutching like it was the answers to the next lieutenant's exam.

"Thank you," I said. "Fine work, I'm sure."

"You don't know the half of it," he told me as I dialed the number.

I had a very pleasant conversation with Erickson's secretary while she dialed police information on another line. When she had decided I really was a cop, she finally put me through to the boss.

"Phil Erickson here," he said. "How can I be of assistance?"

"Mike Kelly," I told him, assuming that his secretary had informed him who I worked for. "I'm running the investigation into the murders and kidnappings out on the Island."

"I would have had to have been on the moon not to have known that, Mike," he told me. "Is there some way I can help with the investigation?"

"Yes there is," I told him. "What can you tell me about Adam Stillwell?"

"Great guy," he said immediately. "It was a real shame what happened to him."

"What exactly did happen to him?" I asked.

"His roommate killed himself—Roger something or

other. It really screwed up Adam's life. He took it real hard.''

"Crampton was the roommate's name," I told him. "Were you there when it happened?"

"No, I had joined a fraternity and was living at the house.''

"Stillwell didn't rush the fraternity with you, then?"

"Ahh," he said, "I tried to get Adam to rush too, but he said he didn't go for all the brotherhood crap.''

"What was he like?"

"Great guy. I saw him literally give the shirt off his back to this fellow who'd spilled a drink on himself at a fraternity party. Everyone really liked him. He was really social and a hard worker. The girls were all over him.''

"Did he have any really close friends?" I asked.

He thought about it for a while, but he couldn't think of anyone in particular. It seemed that everyone had been his friend, but no one more than anyone else.

"What was Crampton like?"

"He was one of those high-pressure guys. He'd had straight As all his life and he figured that was why his parents loved him. Apparently he had never talked to them very much. Anyway, he got to Princeton and suddenly he was a B student, a low B student. Most guys in his shoes could handle it; they figured if they were failing, at least they were failing at a pretty high level.

"But Roger couldn't see it that way. He fought it and fought it. He must have studied twenty hours a day and he never took a day off. But it never did do him much good. He just didn't have the tools.''

"How did he kill himself?"

"It was bad. He used Adam's Princeton tie to hang himself from a coat hook. His feet weren't even off the ground. He just tied the knot and then relaxed his knees. He could have stopped anytime, but he just hung there till he died. Must have been a lot of pain inside for him to have been able to do that.

"Adam found him. He'd been away that weekend at his parents' and when he came back on Sunday, there was Roger hanging there. He took it pretty hard. It was ten minutes before he could pull himself together enough to call for help. He was in shock, and he didn't get any better.

"I went to see him and told him it wasn't his fault but he wouldn't listen to me. Kept saying he should have been there. He was all broken up."

"How long had Crampton been dead before he found him?"

"Since early Sunday morning, they thought."

"Why did he want to room with someone like Crampton, anyway?" I asked. "He doesn't sound like he would have been a very attractive roommate."

"Yeah, at the time I wondered about that. But Adam convinced me Roger would be the perfect roommate. He would never be there while the library was open and he'd never ask Adam to go sleep in the lounge because he had a girl over."

"Adam got along well with women, you say?"

"The original lady-killer," he told me. "When he left we all figured he'd be back because he hadn't broken the school record yet. He was only a sophomore, but he was pretty close as it was."

"I don't suppose you have a picture of him, do you?"

"I must, but I can't think of any offhand."

"Did you ever meet his parents?"

"No, but he used to talk about them all the time. Elsie and Howard or something like that. He had their picture up on the wall, handsome old couple."

"Did you ever visit them?"

"No, never had a chance. But it seemed like Adam went up to Greenwich every other weekend. He really was the perfect roommate, a great guy and never there when you didn't need him, if you get what I mean."

"Yeah, great guy," I told him. "Would it surprise you to learn that he's a psychopathic killer and the reason he took Crampton as a roommate was to see if he couldn't push him over the edge?''

Erickson choked and coughed and it was a few moments before he could speak. "That wasn't very funny."

"No," I agreed, "it wasn't.

"Mr. Erickson, I'm going to send a patrol car to pick you up and take you back to your home. I want you to look through your photo albums and see if you can find a picture of Stillwell."

"I can't possibly leave the office," he told me. "I have an important meeting at three o'clock."

"Thanks for reminding me," I said. "But look, Mr. Erickson, this is literally a matter of life and death. I'm afraid I'll have to insist."

"It's totally out of the question," he shot back at me.

"If you won't help me willingly," I told him, "I'll send a pair of uniformed officers into your office and have you taken out in handcuffs."

"On what charge?" he started to say, and then changed it to "Oh, never mind. Have them meet me at my town house and I'll see what I can dig up for you."

"Thank you, Mr. Erickson. That will be of great help."

"But let me tell you something, Captain Kelly. I'm going to look Adam up and I will relish testifying at your slander trial."

"If you find him first, let us know," I told him. "Or at least leave a note with your next of kin where we can pick up the body."

I heard sputtering noises on the other end of the line and hung up.

"You still interested in how the other half lives?" I asked Kane.

"Maybe I can pick up some decorating tips," he told me on the way out the door.

"Meet him at his town house," I yelled after him.

I fought traffic over to Federal Plaza by myself. It took me ten minutes of block circling to find even an illegal parking space. I was almost late for the meeting. That would have been bad, or at least it would have made a bad situation worse.

Dempsey caught me outside the conference room.

"How's the telephone campaign going?" I asked.

"Laugh all you want," he told me, "but a guy three cars back from the telephone van had been following him all the way from the Ninety-one interchange in New Haven. He actually saw it pulling onto the turnpike."

"God, that's a break."

"Ain't it? We're going back to Ninety-one tonight. We're going to have crews at every freeway entrance from New Haven to Springfield."

"That's going to be a lot of people to be calling."

"We're not going that route this time. We're having blowups of the telephone van made, life size. We're going to station them along the highway with signs asking people who might have seen it to stop and tell us about it."

"How are you going to do that?"

"Like in the old Burma Shave ads. We'll put one word on a sign and space them out over a quarter mile."

"Think people will stop?" I asked.

"They may not stop at the first one, but by the time they see the twentieth they may get the idea that it's important."

"I guess the Connecticut state troopers are cooperating then."

"I say 'Squat' and they say 'How deep?'" he told me.

"Have you alerted the local news media yet?"

"Why would we want to do that?"

"There's not much you can do about it if one of the terrorists sees one of your little billboards on the way home from picking up a pack of cigarettes," I told him. "But if they see it on TV or hear about it on the radio you'll feel mighty foolish."

"Good point. I'll have the Connecticut boys call around to the local stations and ask them not to broadcast what we're doing. How are things going on your end?"

"Pretty good," I told him. "The guy we're looking for's name is Adam Stillwell. He was active in the Weather Underground back in the late sixties and could be presumed to be sympathetic to the Sandinistas. The problem is, we think he was probably an FBI informant and was keeping them informed about the bombs he was building for the Weathermen. And just to add a little spice to his character, I think he had his own private agenda as well."

Dempsey shook his head in disbelief. "Sweet Christ, ain't that going to shake things up in Washington? They already want to dump you, you know. And when they find out about this they're going to be even more anxious."

"Yeah," I told him, "when they find out it's one of theirs, they're going to be mighty anxious to make sure there aren't any outsiders present when they shoot him."

"Think they'd go that far?"

"Did Dillinger have three feet?"

"That's the rumor," he told me.

"Mayes is back from Connecticut," he continued. "He's got quite a task force set up: most of the Connecticut National Guard, five hundred FBI agents, three dozen army helicopters and assorted armored personnel carriers, mobile kitchens, portable command posts and, most importantly, crews from all three networks."

"And when you tell him where the terrorists got onto Ninety-one he's going to saturate the area and start searching house to house?"

"Roadblocks on every passable road within ten miles of the exit and then start closing in towards the center."

"I sure hope it's not just an exit where they stopped to get gas," I told him.

"We'll check that, but would you stop if you had Branner in the backseat making noises like a water buffalo on speed?"

"Good point," I told him. "Let's go see what our water buffalo have to say."

The meeting lasted three hours. I let everyone else go

first. Mayes had a huge map of Connecticut pinned up on a wall with little blocks representing all of the units he had mustered. I felt like a Wehrmacht general listening to Hitler describing Operation Barbarosa. He went into loving detail on interdiction and methods of house-to-house searching. The helicopters were for rapid deployment of the FBI SWAT teams when the terrorists made their inevitable break for freedom.

He droned on and on for more than an hour. After about twenty minutes I managed to tune him out completely, though I kept an attentive look plastered across my face. I started to daydream. But something was all wrong. I couldn't shake an uneasy feeling I'd had all afternoon.

I wended my way back through the afternoon and into the morning. The trancelike state Mayes had put me in made things considerably easier. I traced the feeling to something Hank had told me that morning: fingerprints, there hadn't been a single fingerprint on the van, inside or out. That made sense though; Kinta had seen the van and other people had too. They must have been planning on taking it through the Midtown Tunnel into Queens and abandoning it there.

But the other two men from the van had gone uptown to Father Dave's shelter. How had they been planning to get back to wherever they'd come from? They must've had a car stashed somewhere. And then it hit me what was bothering me. They had carefully wiped all the fingerprints off the van, but had still driven a New York Bell truck through Connecticut. They might as well have placed a huge neon sign on top of it that said "Remember this van."

It would have been so much cleaner to use a plain, windowless panel truck with Connecticut plates to deliver Branner to the city; there's only about a million of them on the road at any given time. And then transfer him to the telephone truck—essentially invisible in the city—somewhere in Queens. So they must have wanted the van to be remembered.

And why hadn't they just abandoned the van after releasing Branner? Because they didn't want it found right away, probably. A few more days of fruitless searching and we'd have been that much more ready to grasp at straws, to mobilize the Connecticut National Guard for a house-to-house search of New Haven.

I already knew they wouldn't be there. When they had gone underground, they had gone way underground. If they hadn't, FBI informants would have known about the Toyon operation way in advance. Hank had told me that morning they were going to start looking for friends of Hopkins who had dropped out of sight. Men who'd stopped attending meetings and hadn't been seen by their friends for quite some time. And then we would know who we were looking for.

The same thing applied to the Sandinista sympathizers. They'd have stopped attending meetings, they'd have cut themselves off from their old friends. The girl at the meeting in Brewster wouldn't have driven across half the state to get to it. She hadn't been able to resist the temptation to attend the meeting because it was right in the neighborhood.

The last question was, how had they been planning to get us to look for them in Connecticut? It wasn't likely that they had been counting on Dempsey having a video camera mounted on a highway overpass. I leaned over to Jake, who was sitting in Hank's place during the meeting. "Were there any maps of Connecticut in the van?" I whispered.

He shook his head.

The Connecticut state police captain, who'd taken Mayes's place during my reverie, and was talking about isolated farmhouses, started shooting me dirty looks. "Anything that might tie it to Connecticut, then?"

"Receipt from the Darien Ho Jo," he whispered back. "Three cheeseburgers and strawberry milk shakes."

I leaned back in my chair and smiled at the trooper. How convenient; they spend six months in an empty garage and don't even leave a coffee cup behind, and now they leave us a receipt from a Howard Johnson's in Connecticut. Once we started looking on 95 we were bound to find someone who remembered the telephone truck. I wondered what else they had done to make sure people remembered them: driven the whole way with their brights on maybe.

I slapped the interested look back across my face and started daydreaming again. The trooper gave way to Mayes again, and then to an army type and then to a National Guard type.

Kane came in during the National Guardsman's talk and handed me a picture. Six friends sitting on a couch drinking beer. One of the men had two girls sitting on his knees. He had his arms around the girls and a stein of beer in each hand. He looked to be near six feet tall and had thick black hair cut just like Prince Valiant's. He was grinning and he had deep dimples on either side of a mouth full of large white teeth. He really did look like a swell guy. I pointed at him and Kane nodded.

I handed the picture back to him and told him to get copies. He smirked and handed me a stack, which I flopped down on the table in front of me where everyone could see them and wonder what they were.

I went back into my daydreams with a vengeance—the result of too little sleep over too many days—and hadn't even realized the assistant secretary of state for Central America was speaking until I noticed him pointing at me and speaking my name. I glanced at Jake out of the corner of my eye and he mouthed, *Sandinista at Goldman's*.

I turned back to the assistant secretary and returned his sneer, though mine wasn't nearly as good as his, and replied, "If I thought it would help, I would go to Cuba and talk to Castro."

"Just so you'll know who you're dealing with in the future, Captain Kelly, Dr. de los Toyos is suspected of being the head of the Sandinista secret police detail in North America. I don't see how any misinformation he may have supplied you with could help this investigation."

"If you had been listening at the meeting last night," I told him somewhat hypocritically, "you would know the Sandinistas are probably more interested in capturing the terrorists than some branches of the federal government."

"I think you had better take that back," he snarled at me.

Dempsey saved me from saying something I would have felt good about for a long time—despite having been transferred to Staten Island on account of it. He stood up and glowered at both of us.

"Gentlemen," he began, "I have to agree with Captain Kelly that all avenues must be pursued; but I cannot believe that any branch of the government, on any level, is not one thousand percent behind this investigation."

"My apologies," I told the assistant secretary.

"Perhaps you'd like to tell us what you've found," Dempsey said to me.

I handed the stack of photographs to one of the Feds and motioned for him to pass them along. "The man on the left end of the couch, with the two women sitting on his legs, is Adam Stillwell. He's the leader of the terrorists we're chasing." It was quite a bombshell—especially so after the hours of mind-numbing organizational details we'd just been treated to. The passing of the photographs took on a new urgency and they came in for a great deal of close scrutiny as soon as each person got theirs.

"Stillwell was the chief bomb maker for the Weather Underground back in the late sixties," I told them. "His last known efforts on their behalf were two basketball-sized, nail-studded time bombs similar to the one that went off outside of the Empire Globe last night. A close associate of Stillwell's was Worthington's contact with the organization. I believe that Stillwell is the only possible leader that could have melded white supremacists and Communists into a cohesive terrorist organization."

"What direct evidence do you have tying him into the organization?" Mayes asked me.

I was stuck. The only "evidence" I had was Abrahms's gut feeling and Katz's confession. And neither of those was worth spit. But I had more than evidence. I had three brutally murdered prison guards and that sick helpless feeling of being manipulated. There was an animal out there, hunting. And its name was Adam Stillwell. I didn't need any eye-witnesses.

"None," I told him. "All I have is the guesses of two of his former colleagues and a pattern. He fits too neatly into the pattern."

"Pretty weak, Kelly," Mayes sneered. "But we'll know for sure when we catch this Deleux person. What did the Sandinista have to say?"

I told them about the girl at the meeting and how she had called de los Toyos the day after the hit at Toyon. I tried to explain my theory about how the terrorists had to be close to Brewster. And I tried to explain to them why it didn't make any sense for them to drive a New York Bell truck through Connecticut. But nobody wanted to hear it. They had their lead and their big operation. The operation every-one understood and felt comfortable with. They felt my theory was flawed because it was based on tainted infor-mation from a Sandinista. I was too tired to argue with them.

Dempsey got up and announced that he would be available all night. If the operation he had set up on 91 was successful and they found the exit the van had pulled in on, the strike for the next day would be on. He gave them a number they could call to find out and told them that anyone interested could hitch a ride on a helicopter to the command post in Connecticut if they could make it to JFK by five o'clock the next morning.

I adjourned the meeting.

Jake, Kane and I took the elevator down to the floor Hank's team was using.

"You tell Mayes about Stillwell's connection to the Bu-reau yet?" I asked him.

"Not my job," he told me. "If Hank wants to tell him he will." He looked me over carefully and didn't say anything about the dark circles under my eyes. "If it's true—and don't forget, maybe it isn't—he'll have to let the director know. Anything could happen then."

"Yeah," I told him, "anything."

I went back into the office I'd been using that morning and called my own office. The switchboard operator at the 9th precinct answered. She gave me a message from Bret. He was visiting with the Greenwich police department and wanted me to call him. I dialed the number.

"Spooky," was the first thing he told me when they got him on the line. "Very very spooky. If I wasn't up here already thinking this guy was a motherfucker, I'd be feeling real bad for the sorry son of a bitch."

"Had some troubles, has he?"

"They have a file on his family here. He had two little brothers. One was playing with his father's gun; it went off. Three weeks later the other got into the medicine cabinet. Apparently it nearly killed their mother. Family friends reported she walked around in a daze for weeks afterward. They should have taken her car keys away from her. She ran the family station wagon under a freight train about a month after the second kid died.

"Mr. Stillwell went off the deep end after he lost his wife—used the same gun his son had been playing with."

"When did the father kill himself?"

"1965."

"So where did young Adam go to live after that?" I asked.

"His maternal grandmother, Mrs. Dorothy Braemar. She had a home in Providence, Connecticut; that's about thirty miles north of here. He went to live with her."

"And when did she pass away?"

"She had a stroke in 1967. They say she lingered a few days, but never regained consciousness."

"And what do people say about him up there?"

"Folks who remember him are uniformly positive. He was a hard worker, friendly, mature, social, everyone's favorite potential son-in-law.

"But we've been going through the unsolved crimes files up here. You ready?"

"Hit me."

"In 1961—Stillwell would have been twelve—a ten-year-old boy disappeared. They found his body floating in the harbor a week later. There was no evidence that he'd been molested. He died of asphyxiation.

"In 1963, a week before Stillwell's little brother shot himself, a drunk was doused with gasoline and set on fire. Six months later, another drunk, and two weeks after that Stillwell's other little brother swallows sixty-five sleeping pills. The coroner's report states that his stomach was distended by the number of pills and candy it contained.

"In 1964, a young woman is found strangled in the Episcopal church the Stillwell family attended. There was no evidence of rape.

"In 1965, Stillwell's father is found dead of a single gunshot wound to the head. The autopsy reveals a blood alcohol content of point-two-four. The coroner reports being surprised that he managed to get the gun up to his head. But Adam Stillwell states that he heard his father stumbling around in his den followed by a gunshot. He didn't leave a note.

"Stillwell's roommate killed himself in 1969," I told him.

I heard Bret relaying the news to someone in the room with him. Someone said something and then he was back on the line.

"They aren't too thrilled up here. The next unsolved murder in Greenwich was in 1972, and it was apparently over drugs. We called up to Providence, but they didn't have any unexplained deaths between 1966 and 1968."

"No, of course not," I told him.

"Why 'of course'?"

"Because he was sixteen," I told him. "He would have had a driver's license by then."

"Oh," he said. "Sure."

"His freshman year roommate told me he spent every other weekend visiting his parents." I didn't wonder out loud where he'd actually been going. We could always call the New Jersey and Pennsylvania state police and ask them about unsolved murders during the late sixties. It would give us a pretty good idea what he'd been up to.

I told Bret he could come home. My head began to feel extremely heavy so I rested it on the desk for a second. I was jerked awake a few moments later by the sound of the phone ringing. It was Jake.

"Gotta minute you could spare?" he asked me.

"Sure," I told him.

"Then you might want to come down to the garage. I'll have someone come get you."

"I think I can find the garage," I told him.

"Sure you can, but you don't have a key to the elevators. You just wait by the doors and I'll send someone up."

He was as good as his word. I hadn't been at the elevator bank for more than ten seconds when the doors of one of the shafts opened and Kane called out, "Twelfth floor. FBI counterterrorism, yuppie police captains, sushi bar."

"How do you rate a key?" I asked him.

"Jake lent me his," he told me.

"Jake's just dying to get into a new line of work, isn't he?"

"Not that I know of, why?"

Jake was waiting for me over by the ventilated telephone truck. He was standing behind it holding the kind of lamp you aim at your houseplants to kid them into thinking they're living in the Amazon Basin. I walked over to see what he had. He waved at Kane, who had stayed by the elevator, and Kane hit the lights. Jake turned his light on and pointed it at the van.

"See it?" he asked.

In the black light there was a rectangle of darker paint around the telephone company logo on the door. He swung the light around so that it illuminated the logo on the side of the van and there was a larger rectangle of dark paint around it.

"What are they?" I asked.

"You can buy them anywhere," he told me. "They're magnetic signs; printer's shops sell them: 'Your ad or logo here.' It costs about fifteen dollars plus twenty-five cents a word. They protect the wax underneath them, it isn't exposed to as much sunlight as the rest of the body.

"What do you suppose the signs said?" he asked me.

"International Bicycles and Mopeds," I hazarded.

"Pretty good guess," he agreed. "And why would you want to cover up your perfectly good telephone company decals?"

"Because they'd tend to stick out if you were driving your telephone van around in the wrong state."

"And why, then, would you take the signs off while driving around in the wrong state?" he finished.

"So people would remember you," I told him.

"Yep, you were right. Going to tag along in Connecticut tomorrow?"

"No," I told him, "I think I'll sleep in."

CHAPTER 12

Dempsey was in Kinsella's office waiting for us. He had his feet up on the desk and seemed to be at peace with the world. He was having trouble wiping the grin off his face and the small black cigar stuck between his lips was about to ruin his blouse.

"Cheshire, Connecticut," he chortled. "Two witnesses saw it get onto the freeway in Hamden. Twenty-two additional witnesses reported seeing it south of Cheshire and only one, unreliable, witness claims to have seen it to the north. And," he added, "we have an extremely reliable witness who followed it down Route Ten from the center of Cheshire."

We all sat down and stared at him. "Cheshire seem like a suitable location?" I asked.

"Two major interstates cross through it and it's almost exactly halfway between the city and Boston. The local cable company carries stations from both cities. It has a high enough growth rate that new folks in town won't be noticed. And it's far enough out that there's still privacy. It's perfect.''

"Sounds like they really put some thought into it then," I told him.

Nobody else had anything to say. Dempsey looked from face to face, puzzled over our lack of enthusiasm. Finally, Jake told him what the van looked like under black light.

"Shit," he said. "Now whadda we do?"

"Let Mayes do all the talking," I suggested. "And maybe we can do a little quiet poking in the Brewster area."

"Sure," he told me, "we can each take a few square miles and be done by Christmas—next year. You may have to do a little better than that."

I sighed and picked up the telephone. Ketchem answered after only the twentieth ring this time. I put him on the speaker so everyone could listen.

He didn't bother to ask who was calling. "Looks like you should have figured out by now that I don't have anything to say to you."

"Mr. Ketchem," I told him, "if you were in the shit as deep as I am now, you might be a little slow worrying about other people's feelings yourself."

He gave an evil old laugh. "I been there, boy. And that's why I'm where I am today. In the great state of Colorado you can shoot trespassers, Lord's Prayer or no."

"I need to know what makes Adam Stillwell tick," I told him.

"Boy, there's a lot of things you need in this world, but believe you me, knowing what makes Adam Stillwell tick isn't one of them. In this particular case, ignorance is bliss."

"He played you for an idiot, didn't he?"

"Never felt half as stupid, before or since," he admitted.

"Well, he's doing the same thing to me now," I told him. "And he's pushed the stakes higher. I'm not exactly sure what he has in mind, the worse-case scenario is World War Three."

He sighed. "I broke the oldest rule in the book, boy. I

let him recruit me. We had plenty of people watching the SDS, more than was warranted, considering they were the sorriest excuse for an organization you ever hoped to see. I remember laughing till I cried when I read the transcript of their Chicago convention. That was back in sixty-seven.

"That was the meeting where the various SDS factions started wailing on each other and the really lunatic fringe broke off to form the Weather Underground.

"Now, if I'd been half as smart as I used to think I was, I'd have taken my time infiltrating people I could trust into their little cabal. Generally all we had to do was go down to the NYPD and tell them we needed to catch a negro with at least a kilo of horse. Bingo, instant FBI informer. And the Weathermen were so screwed up that a black hide meant instant acceptance."

"Why didn't you?" I asked.

"Because I was catching all sorts of flak from the director's office," he barked at me. "The goddamned Weathermen had evidently taken the Mafia's spot in old J. Edgar's nightmares and he wanted results. That's when Stillwell found me. He came to me in New York, all earnest clean-cut American, we've got to do something about these darned Communists. He told me he'd been attending SDS meetings at Princeton and had terrible tales to tell.

"He told me the same things I was getting from the other five spies we'd planted on that particular chapter of the Students for a Dimwitted Society. But the one thing he had going for him that none of my other informers did was that Bernie Stockman had taken a liking to him. Bernie ran the local chapter of the Weathermen. So rather than thank him and send him on his way and suggest that he should stick to studying in the future, I gave him a code name and a contact number."

"And I bet you were real happy you did," I told him.

"Oh, you betcha—best move I ever made." His voice dripped acid. "That boy was a godsend careerwise. He made me look so good my shit stopped smelling. We foiled bomb plots here and break-ins there. We had your secret testimony in front of grand juries and your sealed indictments.

"The kid was a genius. And you know what his cover was? He joined ROTC. He was cadet of the year at Princeton. I don't know which of us thought that was funnier, me or Stockman. By the end of Stillwell's freshman year we had enough evidence to roll up their entire organization in New Jersey. He had done such a good job that the boss wanted to see him personally and thank him for his patriotic efforts.

"Ol' Adam flew down to Washington and had a private interview with J. Edgar Hoover hisself. You would not believe what my performance evaluation looked like that year."

"And then it all started to unravel?"

"I told you Stillwell was a genius. Hoover suggested that my boy had done such a fine job in New Jersey that maybe we should transfer him up to New York where he could do some real good. And was I ever glad we did.

"The Weathermen—this is all according to Stillwell, you understand—had a plan to shut down Columbia. They were going to plant antipersonnel bombs around the campus and set them off at odd hours. They figured if they could force an evacuation for a couple of weeks, Columbia might have to cancel an entire semester. At least that's what Adam told us.

"We were all concerned about that. We didn't see it doing the country any good to let some half-assed Communist terrorist organization have that sort of power. If they could do it at Columbia, then a telephone call would be good enough to shut down Harvard. And then maybe the rest of the universities all across the country."

"Pretty farfetched."

"Yep, pretty crazy. But as you'll recall, the domino theory had a lot more currency back in those days. Anyhow, the director was concerned and he wanted to know what we were going to do about it."

"And I guess Adam had a plan."

"A plan, did you say?" he asked me. "It was no mere plan, boy. It was a dandy plan, a jim-dandy crackerjack of a plan!" His voice dropped down, managing to become both conspiratorial and heavily sarcastic. "We were going to supply him with a hundred pounds of dynamite. He would build some bombs—we would show him how—and then we would catch the ringleaders of the Weathermen delivering them to a crowded place and arrest them all and send them to Leavenworth for two thousand years."

"And you went along with that?"

There was a long pause on the other end. "Son," he told me, "I can look back on my seventy years of mortal existence, in which I have made more than my share of dumb mistakes, and I can proudly say that I have never been that stupid."

"But you were overruled?"

"The director hisself authorized it. Though I would be willing to bet my entire pension and all my worldly goods against a day-old donut that you would never be able to prove it."

Jake nodded his head.

"I imagine you looked pretty good in retrospect when the bombs went off a little early."

He gave an even longer sigh and I could picture him shaking his head out in Colorado. "Son," he said sadly, "J. Edgar Hoover may have been a petty, evil, cowardly, tyrannical sodomite. But even he would never have been stupid enough to give anyone a hundred pounds of dynamite and real blasting caps. You might say we were all just a tad surprised when that town house vaporized."

"And I guess it didn't do you much good, having been against giving him the dynamite?"

"You let a snake into the house, boy, and you take responsibility for who it bites. I didn't get any black marks on my record, seeing as how officially nothing had happened. But I spent the last four years of my career reading purchase requisitions at all the finer defense contractors. That's the equivalent of chasing prostitutes in your department, only you don't get laid as often and your eyes go bad.''

"I talked to Amanda Katz," I said.

"Lucky you."

"She told me he only had fifty pounds of dynamite."

"Makes sense. Your boys recovered twenty-five pounds and we figure the blast was only good for another twenty-five at best."

"What do you suppose happened to the rest of it?"

"Well, I personally would not want to work with twenty-year-old dynamite. But if you'd stored it in a cool dry place and had exceptionally steady nerves, it wouldn't be any problem."

"Any other cheery thoughts?" I asked.

"Jest if you run into Adam, tell him I managed to live happily ever after anyway. That ought to tick him off something terrible."

"Tempting fate, aren't you?"

"It's like I told you, son. We can shoot trespassers in these parts."

"Thanks for your help, Mr. Ketchem."

"No problem, son. You look out for yerself. And tell that father of yours I said hello."

I pushed the Disconnect button and looked around the room. It was hard to tell who looked unhappier, Jake or Dempsey. Kane was studiously checking his fingernails for dirt. "Cadet of the year," I told them. I shook my head. "Let's go look at the map."

We took the elevator back up three floors and trooped into the conference room. Hank was already there. He had his hands jammed in his pockets and was staring moodily at the map of Connecticut and the various little markers symbolizing helicopter squadrons and National Guard units.

"Well?" I asked.

"You know what the penalty for unauthorized destruction

of our files is?'' he asked me. "It's five years in federal prison,'' he answered his own question. "So I ask you, how could someone go through more than two dozen closed and sealed files and cut numbered pages out of controlled reports? There were indexes missing. How do you lose an index? How do frames from microfilm reels disappear?''

There was an embarrassed silence. Kane and I didn't see it as our jobs to tell him and I knew Jake wasn't real anxious.

"There may have been material, possibly embarrassing to a former employee of the Bureau, in those files,'' Jake told him.

Hank brightened immediately. Suddenly the planet was back in its orbit, water was running down to the sea and FBI files were not disappearing, or at least not disappearing mysteriously. Nobody had to tell him who the former employee was.

"Say,'' I asked, "speaking of which, whatever happened to that former employee's secret files? The ones the *National Enquirer*'s been looking for all these years.''

Jake and Hank looked at each other. "Well,'' Hank told me, "it's entirely possible that an exhaustive search of the late employee's home and office did not turn up any secret files.''

"Even so,'' Jake added, "there is some circumstantial evidence that said files may have existed at one point.''

I looked back at Hank, expecting more information. "Consider the most unlikely presidential candidate of the previous two decades—and I'll give you a hint: he got elected.''

"And the news media was certainly surprised at how easily he got his agenda rammed through Congress,'' Jake finished.

"Oh,'' I told them, "sorry I asked.''

We took seats around the conference table and I brought Hank up to date on what we'd found out about Stillwell and what the plans were for the next day. He walked up to the

map and found Cheshire—it's just north of New Haven.
He placed National Guard unit symbols over all of the roads
within ten miles of the town center and then plopped the
helicopter icons down in the middle.

"I think the good citizens of Cheshire are going to be
more than a little PO'd after they have the livin' bejezus
scared out of them for no reason," he told us.

"Not to mention the good citizens of Wallingford, South-
ington, and Hamden," I added. "But what were they doing
in Cheshire anyway?"

"They had to stop someplace," Jake pointed out.
"They'd want to take off those magnetic signs covering the
phone company logos."

"Those hypothetical magnetic signs," Dempsey told
him. "I'm still not convinced. We're breathing down their
assholes strictly on account of them making one dumb move:
calling Worthington from that rest stop. If they hadn't done
that we'd still be back at square one."

"There was a receipt from the Darien Howard Johnson's
in the van," I told him.

"What?"

"It didn't seem important," Jake said. "We already knew
they had stopped there."

"It didn't make any sense," I told him. "They had
cleaned the van off completely, not a single fingerprint. It
just seemed pretty foolish to me to go through all that trouble
and then leave something with an address on it under the
front seat. What did they need a receipt for anyway—their
expense accounts?"

I retraced the van's route back to New Haven and then
north to Hamden and then farther north into Cheshire. The
other interstate near Cheshire is I–84. I followed 84 west
through Waterbury and Danbury, across the border into New
York, and stopped in Brewster, just over the border. I picked
up the black magic marker Mayes had left behind and drew
a twenty-five-mile-radius circle around Brewster on the
map.

The circle took in a lot of things: Bernard Hills, where Amanda Katz was rotting; Armonk, where the van had been registered, and Providence, Connecticut, where Stillwell's grandmother had lived. I stepped back from the map and sat heavily on the end of the table.

"What's the matter?" Kane asked me.

"Providence," I reminded him. "It's where he went to live after his parents died."

"Get Josh and Fred," I told him. "Have them start calling around. Try and find out whether he inherited his grandmother's place."

"He was his parents' only heir, too," Jake reminded me.

"Have him check that too, then."

"He knows we have Abrahms and the kid," Hank told me. "He knows Abrahms knows about his connection with Deleux and that we have a fourteen-state alert out for Deleux."

"He won't know that Abrahms connected him with Deleux or that Abrahms has talked. Tomorrow morning he'll turn on the television and see long traffic jams at the roadblocks around Cheshire. He'll think he's safe for a few more days at least. He'll have another hole to crawl to, probably a couple more. But he won't want to take that circus on the road until he has to."

"So when are we going to Providence?" Kane asked.

"Tomorrow," I told him. "Tomorrow is plenty soon enough. Mayes is going to buy us some time."

CHAPTER 13

I t was still dark outside when the phone began ringing. I sat up in my much-too-large bed and fumbled for the receiver.

"What?" I snarled into the phone.

"It's Dempsey," he told me.

"Didn't I tell you I was sleeping in?"

"We've found Roble."

I had to think about it for a second.

"The insurance agent?" I asked.

"The same."

"Where?"

"Greenwich."

He didn't elaborate, just Greenwich. I felt suddenly cold and pulled the comforter around me.

"How many?" I asked.

"Four," he told me. "One survivor. Evidently Roble's in good shape.

"The helicopter will be landing outside your apartment

in the same place it did Wednesday," he finished. "You have twenty minutes."

"I'll be there," I told him.

Kane answered on the second ring. He didn't sound surprised or angry and I knew he wouldn't need anything to keep himself warm as I gave him the news. He told me twenty minutes was no problem.

I decided to shave and skip the shower. I figured I was going to feel terrible regardless, but might as well look good. At least I wasn't hung over.

The helicopter came in out of the west and landed near the pitcher's mound. Dempsey was already on board. I had to scream to make myself heard telling him we had to wait for Kane.

Dempsey made a cutting gesture to the pilot, who killed the engines.

"How do I rate a first-class greeting committee?" I yelled over the whine of the dying rotors.

"I'm not letting you out of my sight anymore," he answered.

"Why?" I asked, my voice dropping down to near normal.

"Alex Webber."

"Who?"

"Alex Webber. He drives a bus on the Connecticut Turnpike. Every day it's the same route, Stamford to New Haven and then back. He wasn't likely to forget the telephone van. The driver cut him off just this side of New Haven as he was pulling onto the turnpike. Then he gave old Alex the finger as he pulled away."

"Wasn't very professional of him, was it?"

"Neither was getting shot two dozen times," he pointed out.

"Yeah, but that wasn't intentional."

"Think so?" he asked me. "I'm not so sure anymore."

"Chief Goldman was thinking the same thing yesterday," I told him. "Maybe you're right."

Kane showed up a few minutes later. A white Mercedes pulled up and Kane piled out of it and ran for the chopper. I caught a glimpse of the driver. She seemed to have inordinately long blonde hair.

"Who's your girlfriend?" I asked.

"Just someone I know from the neighborhood," he told me.

"Yeah," Dempsey added, "she turns tricks there."

I would have asked Kane how he happened to know her, but the pilot had already fired up the engines and anything I might have said would have been lost in the roar.

The pilot took a direct route, low over Long Island Sound. The whole trip lasted barely thirty minutes. He flew across Greenwich, getting directions via radio from the local police. They were waiting for us in the parking lot of a grocery store. Two cruisers had parked facing each other about fifty feet apart with all their lights flashing. The pilot put us down between them.

The local police turned out to be Connecticut state troopers. They saluted Dempsey and ignored the rest of us. Kane and I got into the back of the first cruiser and Dempsey sat up front with the trooper.

"What exactly happened?" I asked Dempsey.

"I haven't heard the whole story," he told me. "All I know is they got Roble and there's four dead." He turned to the driver. "Fill us in," he said.

"The local police got a call at quarter to four," the driver told us. "Caller didn't identify himself, but reported seeing a prowler entering a home at Twenty-six Vista Terrace. Said he was sure it wasn't someone who lived there.

"Two units responded and started looking around. They went around back and spotted someone in the kitchen cooking breakfast. They knocked on the door and the guy cooking flipped on the porch light and invited them in for some eggs. One of the officers recognized him. They say if they hadn't realized it was Roble, they would have written the

whole thing off as a crank call and gone back on patrol. He
was that cool.

"They made the arrest and then started looking around
in the house. It was a family of five. The parents were
butchered in their bed. The two youngest children—" His
voice broke. "Christ, one of them was only a baby. . . ."
It took him a second to regain his composure, to reassume
the professional air of coolness that all cops affect. "They
were also killed. The oldest child, a ten-year-old boy, was
left alive. They found him downstairs hiding under a bed.
He hasn't been able to give a coherent statement."

"Any ID on the prowler report?" Dempsey asked.

"No, sir. We've started canvassing the neighborhood,
but as of twenty minutes ago, there was nothing."

The sun was well clear of the horizon as we passed
through the police roadblocks. Greenwich is a wealthy town
and the Vista Terrace neighborhood must have been above
the mean as far as money goes. The homes were all large
and were separated by large expanses of lawn: the kinds
that need professional attention. The street itself was a dead
end and the local police had blocked off the entrance and
were keeping the reporters and other assorted vampires out.

Twenty-six Vista Terrace turned out to be a two-story
expanded white colonial with a one-story extension that cut
back into the backyard. All the neighbors had gathered on
the adjacent lawns to comfort each other and watch. I knew
they were all asking themselves why it hadn't been them.
They watched us as we pulled in and drove around back.

"So much for Sheldon's theory about them striking at
the typical middle-class family," I told Dempsey.

"He was close enough." Dempsey replied. "I wouldn't
sweat the details."

We got out and I walked over to the three-car detached
garage and peeked in. There were only two cars, a Porsche
and a sensible Volvo station wagon. The other bay was
taken up by a home workshop.

Dempsey started walking up to the back door. "You coming?" he asked.

"Yeah," I told him. "I'm coming."

We entered the house through the back door into the kitchen. Roble was sitting at the kitchen table with his hands cuffed behind him. He was going to have a beautiful shiner by midafternoon. Along with the Connecticut state police captain attached to the task force, whom I had expected to be there, was his boss: the commandant of the Connecticut state police. He was leaning against a closet door staring at Roble. His look was matched in intensity by the faces of the other five men in the room. In a different age, Roble would have already been dead.

The commandant looked over at us and turned his head to indicate the stairs. Dempsey and I looked at each other and then trudged toward them; dreading it, but knowing we had to go look.

"I'll just stay down here, if you don't mind," Kane told us.

We were only gone for a few minutes. Strangely, it was harder coming back down than going up. Maybe it was because the world had changed for me in ninety seconds; gravity had increased or something. We came back down wishing we lived in a different age.

I sat down at the kitchen table across from Roble and tried to figure how someone could have done what he'd done and still look like a normal human being. He wasn't emotionless; he looked angry and upset. But not angry and upset over having chopped four human beings into hamburger. He looked more like someone who'd just gotten into a fender bender at the local grocery store. And I knew why. It was his black eye. Knowing why didn't help me understand how.

I remembered what Sheldon had told us about the mask of sanity that psychopaths wear and how there was no way anyone could see through them to what lay beneath. I tried to picture Roble hacking the family to pieces, but I just couldn't do it. It would have been like trying to imagine Santa Claus with an ax.

A strange thought came to me while I sat there trying to get into Roble's head, all the while wanting to leap across the table and rip his heart out. It occurred to me that all of us in the room were wearing masks. Roble was pretending to be human and we were pretending to be civilized. We were all pretending we wanted to send him back to the asylum rather than take him out into the street and shoot him down like the mad dog that he was. I mentally adjusted my mask so he couldn't see the animal behind it.

I turned to the commandant and asked him to have the cuffs taken off Roble.

"Don't tell me how to keep a prisoner," he told me.

"Take the cuffs off him," I repeated. "Maybe he'll try to escape."

He didn't move.

"We need his help," I pointed out. "You are not getting anywhere, so why don't we at least try it my way?"

He gave me a sour look and then motioned to one of his troopers to remove the cuffs. Roble stretched and then rubbed his wrists and gave a baleful look at one of the local cops. I pointed at the guy Roble was staring at and told him to get lost.

Roble turned to me after the guy was gone and smiled. "I'm glad to see that there's at least one police officer in this country who understands the importance of common courtesy."

I could understand how he'd sold all that insurance. His voice was rich and warm and full of all of those Cronkitian warbles that bespeak warmth, understanding and honesty.

"From day one at the police academy," I told him, "they stress the importance of being courteous when dealing with the public."

"Then perhaps you'll be courteous enough to arrest that brute who just left for assault and battery."

"He assaulted you?"

He pointed at his eye. "I certainly didn't get this by walking into a door."

I gave him a Gaelic shrug—from one man of the world to another. "There's not much I can do for you, I'm afraid. It's really not very likely that any of his partners will be willing to testify against him. Realistically, what can I do?"

He thought it over. "I guess nothing," he told me.

"Do you know where you were being held?" I asked.

He curled his fingers into his palm and started inspecting his fingernails.

"Mr. Roble," I reminded him, "it's your duty as an honest citizen to help us locate your kidnappers and punish them."

"Your storm troopers didn't exactly treat me like an honest citizen when they burst in here and beat me," he told me.

"That was all just a misunderstanding."

"I haven't eaten well for days," he told me. "If it was all just a misunderstanding, then perhaps you would be so kind as to finish cooking my breakfast?"

"Of course," I said.

I ignored the looks all the local cops and troopers were giving me and walked over to the range. It was a modern one: a stove with a microwave built in and one of those stovetops that heats up without burners. I examined the controls for a moment and then pressed a few buttons. It was a few seconds before the grill started heating up and I knew I'd done everything right.

I flipped the half-cooked eggs into the sink and went to the refrigerator for fresh ones. There was a carton of Tropicana fresh-squeezed orange juice next to the milk. I got it out and poured him a glass and set it down in front of him. He thanked me and took a sip. I couldn't help noticing that all of the troopers shifted their hands onto their pistol butts.

The grill had heated up nicely and I cut a pat of butter and put it on to melt. When it had turned brown I dropped a pair of eggs into the middle of it. He had left a box of English muffins out on the range. There was a half-eaten one sitting next to the box. I took another muffin out, split and buttered it and dropped it on the grill to toast. I would have added a few strips of bacon, but the thought of touching raw meat made me ill.

"You were about to tell us where they were holding you," I said.

He smiled at me. "Of course," he said, "it's my duty, after all. I can't tell you exactly where we were. But I can describe the room we were held in. That might help."

I nodded encouragingly.

"It was an extremely old house. We were kept in the basement. I know it was old. The basement had a dirt floor and the stairs were a dead giveaway. The risers were two tree trunks, about twelve inches in diameter. They still had the bark on them. They made the treads by cutting four-foot-long logs into quarters, lengthwise." He made motions with his hands indicating how it was done.

"A huge waste of timber. They stopped building that way after the sawmills got efficient, say early nineteenth century."

"How do you like your eggs?" I asked.

"Over easy, thank you."

"So you were all down there together?"

"Yes, all twelve of us. They kept us in straitjackets and they sedated all but three of us. And they even gave the three of us something to keep us quiet."

"Which three?"

"Myself, Dr. Wilbur, and one of the screamers—black curly hair, stocky . . ."

"Branner," I told him. I scooped up his eggs and put them on a plate next to the English muffin and handed them to him. "More orange juice?"

"Please."

I poured him more juice.

"It was really quite dreadful," he continued. "There

were no facilities except a few buckets that they changed once a day. And since we were in restraints . . . '' He paused. "Anyway, it was quite terrible and I was glad to get out."

"What sort of deal did they offer you?" I asked.

He looked around uneasily. "Maybe I shouldn't go into that without my attorney."

"I really doubt any purpose would be served by prosecuting you," I told him. "Waste of the taxpayer's money."

"Well, in return for doing a couple of jobs for them, they offered to give me a new identity and set me up in Argentina."

"And this was the first job?"

"Yes. They gave me an hour here, then they were going to pick me up and take me to another job tomorrow night." My expression must have betrayed something of what I was thinking because he leaned forward and became earnest. "Look, I didn't have any choice. It was either do it or spend the rest of my life in that stinking prison. I made it as painless as I could for them. I don't get any pleasure out of hurting people."

"No," I told him, "of course you don't. How did you happen to miss the one kid?"

"He told me to leave a survivor. He told me that's where I'd gone wrong in Buffalo. He said that a survivor would triple the news coverage."

"Who's 'he'?" I asked.

"Their leader. I didn't get his name."

"How long did it take you to get from the place you were being held to here?" I asked.

"Ninety minutes."

"Are you sure about that?"

"When they put the hood on me in the basement it was two o'clock—I got a look at a wristwatch. When I got here it was three-thirty by that clock over there," he said, indicating a wall clock. "And ninety minutes seemed about right. I used to spend a lot of time on the road, you know."

"Did you get any feeling that they were driving around in circles or taking a circuitous route?"

"Not that I could tell."

"Did you see what kind of vehicle you were in?"

"No, I was hooded the whole time. They dropped me off here with another man and then took off. The man took off my hood and watched me until I was in the house. He was supposed to come get me at four."

I took the photographs out of my jacket pocket and slid the first one over to him. It was the artist's reconstruction of Deleux. "Recognize him?" I asked.

"Yes," he said. "He took the hood off me outside. It's not a great picture."

"How about this one?" I asked, sliding him a picture of my father.

"No," he told me. "But I didn't see them all."

"No problem. Anyone in this picture?" I handed him the shot of Stillwell and his college friends.

"The fellow with the two girls on his knees," he told me. "He was the one who offered me the Argentina deal. Of course this picture is three or four years old."

A strange look came across his face. He grabbed his stomach with both hands and gave me a wild look and started to moan. He stood up unsteadily and three or four guns left their holsters.

"Don't," I barked.

Roble's eyes rolled up in his head and he fell over backwards, hitting his head sharply on a countertop. He hit the floor with a thud and didn't move. Kane knelt down beside him and felt for a pulse.

"Careful," Dempsey told him.

Kane stood up. "I will be," he told him. "I won't eat any of Mike's cooking."

CHAPTER 14

I wasn't even surprised. I reached over and picked up the photograph of Stillwell and turned it over. The date was written on the back of it: "March 28, 1967—Just back from Lauderdale."

"Three or four years old," I mumbled to myself. "The years must have been very kind to him."

"What the fuck happened?" the commandant bellowed at me.

I turned to him tiredly. "He'd seen Stillwell. Of course he wasn't going to be allowed to testify in front of a grand jury." I sighed and sat back down and looked down into the photograph at Stillwell's smiling face. "There's any number of ways of doing it. Coat a few grains of cyanide with Ivory soap and then put that inside a gelatin capsule. Depending on how thick the layer of soap is, it can take up to a day to dissolve. They probably told him it was a stimulant to counteract the tranquilizers they'd been feeding him."

213

"Looks like they cut it too close," Dempsey told me. "He talked before it hit him."

No one seemed to be in any hurry to try resuscitating Roble. I bent down and looked under the table at his rapidly cooling body. The lower half and sides of his face had turned light blue and his face was frozen in a horrible grimace. He was long past the point where resuscitation might have helped. I wondered vaguely if anyone would have rushed to save him if he'd been hit with a coronary.

The commandant turned to one of his subordinates. "How long does it take to get to Cheshire from here?" he barked.

"Ninety minutes," I told him.

He turned back to me. "You an expert on Connecticut highways, son?"

"No," I told him. "But maybe I'm an expert on Still-well—kind of scares me. I have a pretty good idea how he operates. He wants us in Cheshire, so it'll turn out to be a ninety-minute drive. And there'll probably be something else on Roble's body that the lab boys will be able to trace back in that direction—a Cheshire JCs booster button he swallowed or something.

"Stillwell probably has a couple of cases of beer and big box of microwave popcorn. He's going to sit in front of the TV all day today and watch us make idiots out of ourselves."

"You saying we're just going to be wasting our time in Cheshire?"

I nodded.

"Well how the hell did they know we were going to catch Roble and that he'd be so cooperative about helping us? It's stretching it mighty thin that everything he told us was according to some master plan. You must have Stillwell on the brain, son. Nobody's that smart."

"How'd he know we were going to grab Roble?" I asked him. "He knew because it was his people who called it in. Or are you still looking for some late-night jogger?

"They didn't have to take any chances," I told him, "so

why do you think they did? Think about it. If they really were in Cheshire, taking ninety minutes to get here was incredibly stupid. You have to believe an organization as disciplined as Stillwell's would have driven around for a few hours before heading in this direction. And the more I think about it, Roble getting a look at somebody's watch before they blindfolded him seems to be just a little too convenient.''

The commandant bit his lower lip and looked over at the trooper next to him.

"At that time of night ninety minutes is about right between here and Cheshire, sir. Given that you would assume they'd be obeying the speed limit.''

The commandant looked back at me. "I still don't buy it.''

"Nobody bought Stillwell yesterday,'' I told him. "What aren't you going to buy tomorrow: sunrise? They tipped us off that Roble was here and they knew he hadn't resisted arrest when he got nailed in Buffalo. They wanted him alive long enough to answer questions but not long enough to finger any of them in a lineup.''

I could see he was just a little disturbed. Made me almost wonder what he'd told the governor the night before. Four dead in the state's wealthiest suburb followed quickly by a fiasco in Cheshire wasn't going to sit too well with the politicians.

"It's too goddamned late to stop the operation in Cheshire,'' he told me. "Even if I was sure you were right, which I'm not, it wouldn't make any difference. The roadblocks went up before dawn. Like it or not, we're committed.''

There was an uncomfortable silence. I couldn't think of anything to tell him. But I figured I better say something because we were sure going to need all the help we could get when the house-to-house search in Cheshire turned up empty. I'd want to redeploy the troops in Providence, but the politicians were going to scream bloody murder. They weren't going to be so ready to listen to us a second time.

And it wouldn't be easy convincing them to let us roust two different constituencies in the same day. Maybe the commandant could convince them it had to be done. I thought about it for a second and decided that he probably couldn't.

"I hope I'm wrong," I told him. I crossed my arms on the table and rested my head on them. I wasn't too optimistic about our chances. It was getting to be time for Stillwell to be moving on, and I was sure he had thought long and hard on where he would be going. We wouldn't find him.

Mayes trotted in accompanied by his usual phalanx of steely-eyed G-men. He looked around, and in almost no time detected the body sprawled out at his feet.

"I was told he was taken alive," he said flatly.

"He was," Dempsey told him. "But they must have given him some kind of time-release poison. He checked out about five minutes ago."

"Damn. Did he say anything?"

The commandant answered. "He identified Stillwell, he told us it was a ninety-minute drive to get here and that he had been held in the basement of a house that was at least a hundred years old."

Mayes mulled that over for a few minutes before he pronounced it excellent news. "But can we believe him?" he whined.

They all looked at me. "He was trying to be an honest citizen and help us out," I told him. "And he had a chance to identify any number of innocent civilians as terrorists and didn't. I think we can believe him. I would guess he disliked them even more than he did us."

"And the ninety-minute drive is consistent with the distance to Cheshire," Mayes told me. He seemed to be unusually happy. "I think we really have them in the trap; it's only a matter of slamming the door."

I almost pointed out that he was mixing his metaphors. But at the last second I decided to be political.

"What's going to happen if you search all of the nineteenth-century farmhouses in Cheshire and come up empty?'' I asked.

He ignored my question but did fill me in on some news I hadn't heard yet. ''You'll be pleased to know, Captain Kelly, that the federal government is finally taking this matter as seriously as it merits. At two this morning the president authorized a special federal task force to take charge of the investigation.''

''With you in charge?''

''Naturally.''

''And I guess it supersedes the old multistate task force?''

''As you know,'' he told me, ''the FBI is the lead agency in any matter involving either foreign agents or terrorism in the United States. The multistate task force was an aberration of accepted procedures brought about by political interference. The new task force simply corrects the aberration.''

''Then of course,'' I told him, ''you have my full support.''

''Thank you,'' he replied. He turned to Dempsey and the commandant. ''I'm going back to Cheshire. Can I give anyone a lift?''

There was a momentary, painful silence—followed immediately by a series of hems and haws. Dempsey begged off because he had too much work to do back in New York. The commandant decided he was needed in Greenwich to ease the minds of the worried citizens. Mayes looked slightly perplexed that they didn't want to be there at the kill. But he didn't question his good fortune too closely. He left to go bask in the glow of the adoring and grateful public by himself.

''Well, son,'' the commandant asked me, ''if not in Cheshire, then where?''

''Providence.''

''Why Providence?''

''Because if they aren't in Providence,'' I told him tiredly, ''then we haven't even got a clue and we might as well all go home and wait for someone to drop a dime on them. That's the traditional FBI investigative technique, I believe."

"Son," he said, "if you know something the rest of us don't, you had better let us in on it. There's still ten lunatics out there and I think the level of general panic is going to go up a notch when folks start finding out what happened here last night."

"Someone from his organization attended a meeting in Brewster," I told him. "The meeting was lightly attended and couldn't have had much publicity. If they aren't in Providence, they've got to be close to Brewster."

"You told us that last night and it still doesn't carry any weight," the Connecticut state police captain pointed out. "She could have been visiting a friend. She could have been passing through on the way somewhere else. She might even be another of your red herrings."

"I don't think so," I told him. "Their organization doesn't work that way. They were completely underground before the main operation. I don't think they would have broken cover in advance and had us looking for them. We might have found something.

"And besides," I told him, "she told de los Toyos something that hinted at the white supremacist connection. Stillwell wouldn't have wanted to do that."

"What else is there?"

Dempsey spoke up for the first time. "The PCP the FBI pulled out of Branner's nose. It was from Norwalk. Norwalk's probably the closest city to Providence where they'd be able to find someone selling it."

"And Stillwell spent a couple of years in Providence when he was growing up," I added. "He knows the area and may even own property there that he inherited from his grandmother. My people are running it down now."

"Son, your people are from the wrong state to be checking something like that. What was the grandmother's name?"

I checked my notebook. "Dorothy Braemar," I told him.

He asked me to spell it and then turned to one of his men and told him to check it out.

"We have to find them soon," I told him. "The next logical thing for them to do is break camp here and head for LA and we'd be back at ground zero."

"What do you suggest we do?" he asked.

"We can't check everything," I told him. "But we can check as much as we can. I'm guessing Providence—it fits Stillwell's personality. He thinks he's a whole lot smarter than the rest of us. Hiding in his old hometown probably gets him off.

"And even if I'm not right about Providence, I still think I'm right about the Brewster meeting. They're no more than twenty-five miles from Brewster."

"Great," Dempsey said, "you've narrowed their location down to a mere thousand square miles of densely populated high-value real estate first settled during the seventeenth century. There's probably more than ten thousand hundred-year-old homes within twenty-five miles of Brewster."

"So you're going to be busy with your half of it," I told him. "It'll do your men some good to get off the phone and out in the field to do some investigating."

"And we'll know we've found them when one of the search parties doesn't report back," he told me.

"So tell them to be careful," I told him. "What about your side of the border?" I asked the commandant.

"If we haven't found anything in Cheshire by noon, I'll pull fifty men and send them to Providence. In the meantime maybe I'll get the local PDs on the horn and see if they've noticed anything suspicious in the past six months."

"You aren't worried about what the head of the federal task force might say when you start pulling men?" Dempsey asked him.

"You worry about New York and I'll worry about that little pissant," the commandant said. He looked over at me. "Any way you can narrow the location down some, son?"

"De los Toyos was going to check with the people who sponsored the meeting in Brewster. He was going to try and find out what they knew about the girl and how she might have heard about the meeting."

He nodded in the direction of the telephone. "Go ahead, son—the owners won't mind."

I checked the number de los Toyos had given me and dialed it. I did feel vaguely like a grave robber. But as he'd said, I didn't think the owners would mind. De los Toyos answered on the third ring.

"Good morning, Ed," I told him. "It's Mike Kelly of the New York City Police Department. Sorry to get you up so early."

"It is no problem," he replied. "In fact, I am already up and even now I am speaking to you courtesy of GTE Mobilnet."

"On your way somewhere?"

"As you probably know, there has been some unpleasantness in Greenwich, Connecticut. I am on my way there to extend my country's condolences and condemn acts of terrorism against innocent civilians. We feel it will be much more effective a statement if delivered at the site of the crime."

"Where are you now?"

"I crossed the Throgs Neck Bridge fifteen minutes ago and should be arriving in Greenwich in another ten minutes. And where are you?"

"I'm already here," I told him. "You haven't been listening to the news, have you?"

"I have heard that the FBI has trapped the terrorists in a ring of steel in Cheshire, Connecticut, if that is what you are referring to."

"Some of us have our doubts whether they're really hiding in Cheshire. What did you find out about the girl?"

"The meeting was sponsored by the Unitarian Church in Brewster. They meet once a month to discuss human rights issues. The only publicity the meeting had was a note in the church bulletin and also a public service announcement by the radio station affiliated with a local community college.

"The people who invited me to speak at the meeting were doubtful that the station could be picked up more than ten miles from the school, even on a clear night."

"Did they know the girl?"

"No," he told me. "They had never seen her before that night and no one at the meeting knew her."

"How can they be certain no one knew her?"

"Because they remembered her quite well. They heard me accuse her of being an FBI spy and discussed it among themselves. I think they were secretly pleased that the FBI thought they were sufficiently important to warrant sending a spy."

"There is one more thing," he added. "She came to the next monthly meeting as well. But when she found that the topic was repression of the Baha'i in Iran, she did not stay. They have not seen her since."

"That's very interesting," I told him. "After you've made your statement to the press—you won't have any trouble finding them—give your name to the police at the barriers and I'll see that they let you in."

"Thank you, but it is an image I would not wish to see on the evening news—Nicaraguan consul drives up to death house. I will await you beyond any roadblocks. As you will recall," he added, "we have a deal and I have now fulfilled my part of it."

I told him I would be out to see him.

Then I brought everyone else up to date on what he'd told me.

"So she attended a second meeting," Dempsey mused. "That dovetails very nicely with your theory that they're close to Brewster."

The commandant got on his radio and told someone on the other end to patch him through to someone named Nolan with the task force in Cheshire. He had to wait a few minutes but eventually got through. He quizzed Nolan on who the police chief in Providence was and what he was like. He listened for a moment and then told Nolan to call the chief and tell him I was coming to visit and to ask him to co-operate.

"The chief up there's an old coot named McNamara," he told me. "There's only four or five guys in the entire department, but Joe Nolan says he's a good cop—if a little old-fashioned. Nolan's commander of the Stamford barracks and knows him. Says McNamara'll cooperate if you treat him right."

"Right being like he's a cross between Wild Bill Hickok and Melvin Purvis?" I inquired.

"Didn't know you knew the man," he told me.

"I've known plenty just like him."

"I'll get you a car and driver."

"Thanks," I told him.

We found de los Toyos expounding on the virtues of the Sandinista revolution to anyone who would listen. There not being anyone else to listen to, he had gathered quite a crowd. Of course as soon as I showed up the news scum lost interest in the excesses of the Somoza regime.

Apparently my sudden appearance confirmed that the Front for the Total Independence of Nicaragua—better known as the Deranged Dozen—had struck locally.

I immediately had two dozen microphones stuck under my nose and all of the video cameras had their red lights blazing. The questions, as far as I could tell, were: how many dead, which one did it, how gruesome was it, why haven't you caught them yet, are they in Cheshire, how much blood was there, and were there any survivors. I've always felt that "No comment" is an idiotic response to any question, so I ignored them instead. That seemed to infuriate them.

"Is it true you've been fired, Captain Kelly?"

I would have ignored that one too, but she had managed

to get directly in my path and I didn't want to shove a five-foot-tall, hundred-pound woman into a fence. Not with the videotape running anyway.

"What makes you ask?" I asked her.

"Special Agent Mayes, of the FBI, announced this morning that a new task force was being formed in order to better prosecute the investigation and that the new task force superseded the task force you were commanding." She stuck the microphone back in my face.

"Then I guess I'm out of a job," I told her. "Now if you'll excuse me."

I pushed my way past her and got to de los Toyos.

"Morning, Ed."

"Morning, Mike."

"Is this the scene you'd rather see playing on the evening news—you and me conferring together and then racing off into the distance?"

"I am sure it will go over better than Sandinista examining his people's dirty work. Have you had breakfast?"

"I'm not very hungry," I told him. "There are some things I have to tell you."

"And no doubt they are things I need to know."

I conferred with our driver, Sergeant Takach of the Connecticut state police, as to a place we could meet out of microphone range. He suggested the Howard Johnson's off the turnpike just west of Darien. It seemed appropriate and Eduardo didn't seem to mind.

Takach got on his radio and had a pair of cruisers block the road behind us to keep any nosy reporters off our trail. We would have lost them anyway; Eduardo turned out to be a madman behind the wheel—something diplomatic tags tended to make you. Takach had to turn on his lights and we played Daytona 500 through the morning commute. Eduardo still beat us to the restaurant by five minutes. He was drinking coffee and flirting with the waitress when we got there.

"Well, Michael," he started, "as I recall our arrangement, I would discover what I could about the girl and you would inform me who is behind this madness.''

I filled him in on Adam Stillwell's checkered career. He stopped me every once in a while to ask questions—mostly about the rest of Stillwell's organization and its possible ties with Nicaragua.

After I finished he smiled at me. ''I am very relieved to find that my country has been totally exonerated in this affair.''

''What makes you think your country's been exonerated?'' I asked.

''Have you not just finished telling me that this is all the responsibility of a lone madman?'' he asked.

''No,'' I told him. ''It sounds more to me like a lunatic Sandinista on the loose in the States. Or at least it wouldn't be very hard for me to make it sound that way if I wanted to.''

He sighed. ''What is it you want from me now?''

''The FBI informs me that you're the head of the Sandinista secret police detail in the United States,'' I told him. ''It would seem to me that there's probably a whole world of things you could do for me if you really wanted to.''

Being accused of being a secret policeman really set him off. He fixed me with one of those looks that only people with heavy doses of Spanish blood can pull off without looking silly. The kind that are supposed to lead to cutlasses at dawn.

''First of all,'' he bristled, ''the State Security Department of the Interior Ministry of the Nicaraguan government is no more—and probably much less—of a secret police than is your FBI. And second of all, I have absolutely no connection with state security.''

He banged his fist on the table. ''Why is it,'' he asked, ''that every time there is a revolution somewhere, you Yankees immediately assume that some spiritual descendant of Joseph Stalin is running it?

''Let me explain something to you,'' he continued. ''Getting rid of those pigs the Somozas was the best thing that ever happened to Nicaragua. And do you know why? It is because for the first time in fifty years, the American—and I do mean the North American—dream is alive in Nicaragua. For the first time you do not need to be the cousin of some pig in the National Guard to go into business and be successful. You do not need to worry that some swine in a uniform will rape your wife because he thinks she is good looking. You do not need to worry that your land will be expropriated because the generalissimo wants to put a banana plantation on top of it.''

''That's all very nice, Eduardo. And I'm sure the peasants go to sleep every night blessing their government for the bounty it's producing for them. But that doesn't exactly solve my problem, and as you know, my problem is your problem.''

''What is it that you want?'' he asked.

''Stillwell is using Sandinista sympathizers. I think you can find out who they are.'' I looked at him for a few moments; he didn't blink. ''I need to know who they are.''

The more he looked at me the less I believed what he'd said about not working for Nicaraguan state security. Finally he told me he would see what he would see. I had no idea what that meant.

CHAPTER 15

The Providence police department was headquartered in one of those standard red-brick municipal buildings with the fake cupolas. It could have been a Domino's outlet. Sergeant Takach wheeled his patrol car into the parking lot and we got out to meet Providence's answer to crime. We were disappointed.

Chief McNamara had been called away on important business and couldn't be disturbed by anything as non–earth-shattering as a visit from the former head of the (presently defunct) multistate task force for the investigation of the Toyon murders. He had left his lieutenant behind to take care of routine matters like us.

"I think Chief McNamara would really appreciate you letting him know we're here," I told him. "I think he'll probably be pretty annoyed if the first he hears about it is from CBS."

"Now why don't you just let me decide what the chief wants?" his lieutenant told me. "I think I know the chief just a little better than you do. And I'm tellin' you he don't want to be disturbed.''

I've been accused of making snap character judgments and then sticking with them in spite of subsequent evidence to the contrary. Maxwell made a good case in point. I had sized him up in about thirty seconds and it was going to take a telegram from the Nobel Prize committee to get me to change my mind.

"Have you heard from the commandant of the state police yet?" I asked him.

"Not from the commandant hisself. One of his boys called me, though. Askin' me about ol' Dorothy Braemar and her grandson.''

"And what did you tell him?''

His eyes narrowed and he pulled his head back a little. "Now, maybe what I told him is, like, private.''

I forced my anger down. I reminded myself that I would be going back to New York soon and nothing I did in Providence was going to make Maxwell any less of a congenital idiot than he already was. I told myself I could deal with him for fifteen minutes without blowing my stack.

"He mentioned we would be coming here, didn't he?" I asked. "He was supposed to ask you to cooperate with us.''

"Well if'n he did, don't mean I have to.''

"I'm sure we'd all be very grateful if you did, though.'' I tried to sound sweet and reasonable. It required effort.

He thought it over for a few seconds. "Well, shit, guess it can't hurt none. It was before my time, of course. 'Cept I knew her. She taught at the elementary school. Not me though; she was too high-an'-mighty to teach kids like me. She only wanted to teach her kind of kids—candyassed four-eyed little snots with rich parents.

"She kicked back in the sixties. I guess I was still in middle school, well, maybe it was my first year in high school. Had a big old house just outside of town, probably a pot full of money too; people like that always do. Really pisses me off, people with money thinking they're somethin' special like.''

"What happened to the house?" I asked him.

"She must've left it to the SPCA; they have it now. Seems like people could find better use for a nice old house than takin' in strays and castrating poodles. But rich people are usually nicer to animals than they are to their own kind anyhow.''

"Did she own any other property in the area?"

"Ah, beats me. I called old man Dryden—always a good idea to do favors for the Staties 'cause you never can tell when you might need somethin' in return. But you think that old shyster'd give me the time of day? Oh no siree, that's con-fee-den-shal. I tell you, try to run an investigation in these parts, like pullin' teeth.''

It took only five more minutes of teeth pulling to ascertain that "old man" Dryden had been the Braemar family lawyer, that he still practiced part-time and that his office was in his home. Maxwell insisted on coming along to keep an eye on things.

Dryden lived, and worked, in a fine old colonial on Main Street a few blocks down from the Congregational church on the town green. I asked everyone to wait in the car, but Maxwell insisted on coming with me. He seemed to be worried I would tell Dryden that he'd called him a shyster.

Dryden came to the door promptly. Despite it being Saturday, he was dressed in full lawyer regalia: three-piece suit, wing tips and Phi Beta Kappa key. Maxwell had told me he was eighty-something, and he looked even older than that. But he had bright blue eyes that recognized me instantly and he seemed to radiate energy. His expression changed from interest to disdain when he saw Maxwell.

"Yes?" he asked.

I showed him my identification and told him why I'd come to see him.

"I'm sorry," he told me. "But I'm afraid attorney-client

confidentiality will prevent me from helping you. I'm sure you understand.''

He didn't make any move to slam the door in my face. I looked at Maxwell out of the corner of my eye and didn't have any trouble understanding.

"Then perhaps you could help me out on another matter," I told him. "A personal matter."

"I doubt there's much I can do for you," he said. "But perhaps there's something. Why don't you step into my office?"

He moved back out of my way. I followed him through the door and turned to block Maxwell, who had started to follow me. "It's a personal matter," I told him. "I won't be a minute."

I paused expectantly and then gave him a hint. "I'm sure Sergeant Takach will be happy to give you a lift back to the station."

"That's okay," he told me. "I'll wait."

I shut the door in his face.

"I think we can talk in the parlor," Dryden said. "Unless you think I might need any of my references."

"No, sir," I told him. "The parlor's fine."

The furniture was all professionally restored Early American, or damn good reproductions. Dryden lowered himself carefully onto the settee while I made myself comfortable in a chair that had bird legs for feet. As I sat down I could see the patrol car through the bay windows. Maxwell was leaning against it smoking a cigarette.

"How did you become so lucky as to acquire a native scout?" Dryden asked me.

"Chief McNamara is off doing something too important to be bothered by anything so trivial as the Toyon Terror," I told him, referring to the new name the headline writers were using now that "Deranged Dozen" wasn't appropriate anymore.

"Somehow," he told me, "I find that difficult to believe. However, Lieutenant Maxwell is being groomed to take over the chief's position, so perhaps it is best that he learn to deal with emergencies.''

"He's being groomed to take over?" I asked incredulously. "Has the chief lost his mind?"

"I don't believe that it is the chief's idea," he told me. "But the Maxwells are a rather large clan in these parts. They've lived in the town since before the American Revolution and they seem to run in packs. Young Maxwell is their star—apparently his parents were only second cousins. There's some talk that Chief McNamara is dissatisfied with young Maxwell's performance. But the chief is getting near retirement and the Maxwells make up a large voter block.''

"Well, as serious as your problems are," I told him, "I have bigger ones. I need to know about Dorothy Braemar and her grandson Adam Stillwell.''

"I'd like to help you, Captain, truly I would. But what I told you outside still holds. The canons are clear about the confidentiality an attorney owes his clients.'' He held up his hand to stop me from whining about how important it was. "Of course I've broken the canons in the past. And I've always had good reasons . . . but good reasons are such a slippery slope. I know you must have a good reason for coming all this way. But you'll have to give it to me before I can talk to you about Dorothy.''

I outlined what I knew about Stillwell. From the deaths in his family, to his FBI informer days, to his bomb-making days with the Weathermen. I told him about the FBI's dynamite and the vaporized town house—and the roofing nails we'd found on Fifty-second Street. He took it all in without a word, but he paled and a look of almost tragic sadness came across his face.

"I guess you're about to tell me how wrong I am," I told him. "How it would be impossible for Adam to have hurt a fly, let alone be an indiscriminate psychopathic killer. But believe me, Counselor, it's all true.''

He shook his head. "Oh no," he whispered, "I believe you. You build an impressive case, conjecture and hearsay though it is. But I believe you. I've lived a long time and I don't believe in coincidence." He buried his head in his hands. "I should have known then. There was too much death following that boy around—too much tragedy for one lifetime. But he was such a game lad. He bore up so well and he never complained. He told us he had to be strong for his father's sake—it nearly broke my heart. He fooled us all. But I shouldn't have let him fool me. It was my job to protect Dorothy. I failed her so."

He looked up at me. "I suppose you want to know about the money?"

I nodded. "And especially about any property Mrs. Braemar might have owned in this area."

"You don't think he's hiding in Providence, do you?"

"Yes."

He gave me a funny look. Almost as if he hoped it were true.

"Adam's parents were well-to-do, not wealthy, but certainly not hurting. Adam received their estate in its entirety. Although shortly after his mother died, his father changed his will, leaving the bulk of the estate to the Catholic Church. But of course his subsequent suicide showed that he was non compos mentis—he was, after all, an Episcopalian. There were technical errors in the new will as well and it would have left his son almost destitute. On behalf of Dorothy, Mrs. Braemar, I moved to have the new will declared void. The church didn't fight it.

"Do you think Adam's father knew?" he asked. "And meant to write him out of the will?"

"No," I told him. "I don't think so. Stillwell doesn't operate that way. He manipulates people and drives them into their own private hells. I think he probably drove his college roommate to suicide by convincing him that he was stupid and didn't deserve to go on living. I think he murdered his little brothers and then made it look like it was his parents' fault. Or at least made it easy for them to blame themselves. He wouldn't have wanted to give his father an out, some way to believe that he wasn't responsible. His father probably left the money to the Catholic Church because it believes in an angrier God than the Episcopalians.''

I tried to concentrate on what I was saying. But the more I talked about Stillwell manipulating people and driving them deeper and deeper into private hells the louder Amanda Katz's sobs echoed in my head. I kept reminding myself that I had done it for a good cause.

"Dorothy became his guardian, of course," he continued. "Adam's mother had been an only child, so Adam was Dorothy's only living relative. She was rather overprotective of him. I used to warn her about mollycoddling the boy. When she died she left everything but her home to him. The home went to the ASPCA. I became Adam's guardian. Including what his parents left him, his net worth was around one and a half million dollars. There was no real estate; the bulk of his trust fund was in corporate securities.''

"And when he turned twenty-one he came and got the money?''

"No. After fourteen years a cousin from his father's side moved to have him declared legally dead. I fought it, but the courts agreed with the cousin and awarded the entire estate to him and his brothers and sisters and some other cousins. By that time it had grown to more than six million dollars.''

"And you never heard from Adam that entire time?" I asked.

"No, not to this day. The court assumed that I was just trying to hold on to the money because of the leverage that kind of wealth can give you. But it was really because I couldn't stand to have Adam declared dead.

"I never married, you see. And he was like a son to me.''

"I'm sorry I had to break it to you," I told him. His face had taken on the appearance of a death mask. He was carrying more of a load than any man was meant to bear. But he was doing his best, because Yankees don't cry. It would have been a lot easier for him if he were Irish.

"I don't know anything about where he might be now," he finished.

"He's hiding in an old farmhouse," I told him. "I think in this area. They'd want to be as far away from the neighbors as possible. And I think he's been planning this for a long time. He might have bought the property years ago."

Dryden wasn't listening to me. He seemed to be lost in a fog. I had to repeat my question. But he just shook his head. He told me that Dorothy had had an old farmhouse out by the lake, but that it had been sold years before, long before Adam had come to live with her.

"She was very much alive," he told me as I got up to go, "and then one morning she was in a coma. The doctors called it a stroke, but I doubt they looked very closely. He murdered her too, didn't he?"

I shook my head. "I don't think so. It's not his style to let people go that painlessly. She probably really did have a stroke—she was lucky."

I left him there, his blue eyes not so bright as they had been. Just another victim of Adam Stillwell and his chief publicity agent, Michael Kelly.

"Well, whaddid he say?" Maxwell asked me.

"He suggested I could have all my problems solved in Reno," I told him. "And he mentioned that Stillwell's grandmother once owned an old farmhouse out by the lake."

"Yeah, I guess she could've," he told me.

"What lake?" I asked him.

"There's only one lake," he told me. "Lake Candlewood. But it's probably twenty miles around it. Take all day to check it out."

"You folks keep records up here?" I asked. "Maybe we could spend a few minutes in the Town Clerk's office?"

I opened the car door for him.

"Learn anything?" Kane asked.

"Not really," I told him. "You can probably chock up Stillwell's grandmother in the victim column."

"I thought she died of natural causes."

"Maybe," I said. "But I don't believe in coincidences. Another thing: he isn't motivated by money. He passed on a six-million-dollar estate, let them declare him legally dead and redistribute the money to his cousins."

"Maybe six million don't mean much to him," Maxwell hazarded.

"I hope not," I told him. Stillwell with mega-millions was a nightmare I didn't want to even think about. "He probably wanted everybody to think he was dead. I would guess he probably thought the FBI was keeping an eye on the money and he wanted them to think he had been blown into unidentifiable bits in the basement of the town house."

At the town hall Maxwell made a big deal out of having keys that fit all the right doors. My guess was that he doubled as a night watchman. In the clerk's office there was a row of ledgers lined up neatly on top of a filing cabinet. The ledgers contained all the property transfer records for the town dating back to the eighteenth century.

There was a single ledger covering the eight years between 1958 and 1965. It didn't take very long to find what we were looking for: August 5, 1961; 1517 Lake Farm Road; Dorothy Braemar to Richard Estes.

In the seventies real estate transactions had picked up and there was a single ledger for each year beyond 1974. We all took three and started going through them to see if the property had changed hands again.

Kane found it. December 3, 1985; 1517 Lake Farm Road; estate of Richard Estes to CIFE Corporation. I looked questioningly at Maxwell.

"Never heard of them," he told me. "Whadda you think? Think it might be him?"

"No," I said. "But we might as well go out and take a look. Maybe we'll learn something." I finished thumbing through the ledger for the current year. I'd been looking for familiar-sounding names but I hadn't found any. "Let's go," I told them.

We drove out to the lake and started driving around it. Lake Candlewood is enormous and seemed to be a favorite spot for millionaires to build their summer cottages, the kind of cottages you can't see from the road because of the high stone walls and the quarter-mile-long driveways. The only saving grace was that there weren't a lot of roads in the area we would have to set up roadblocks on, given that we got permission from the politicians to do it.

WABC had a crew live at Mayes's headquarters in Cheshire and we got their reports on the half hour—or rather we got the same report every thirty minutes: nothing. I almost turned the radio off. The only thing that kept me listening was to see how long it took for Mayes's tone of absolute confidence to start changing. I was betting on four o'clock.

The drive was, however, quite pleasant. I idly thought about coming back in a month or so, after the foliage had begun to change. It could only get prettier.

Takach slowed down and then did a U turn. "Last mailbox was Fifteen Thirty-nine," he told me. "We must have passed it."

He slowed as we came to an old dirt driveway on the right side of the road with a rusty chain strung across its entrance. There was a No Trespassing sign, but it was so rusty it was hard to read.

We got out and looked past the chain up the driveway. There were faint tire tracks leading up to a bend in the distance. Evidently there wasn't a lot of traffic going that way. The chain was rusty, but it wasn't rusted to the posts it was attached to. It came free without sticking.

"Kind of overconfident, ain't they?" Maxwell asked.

"If it's them," I told him, "there's nothing they could put out here that would keep us out. Their best bet would be to look as innocuous as possible. This looks pretty damned innocuous." I stepped over the chain.

"You want to call in reinforcements?" Kane asked.

"No point," I told him. "I've been crying wolf all day and they haven't been listening."

We made our way up the driveway. As we got closer to where we figured the house was, we moved over closer to the woods. The road bent sharply and the house came into view. We all crouched down.

It was old. It was old and it was shabby and there were blackout curtains in the upstairs windows. Someone had grafted a front porch onto the house back in the last century. It looked like an ugly pimple. No Puritan would have built it and no one with any taste would have kept it. Worthington had stood blinking on a front porch before being ushered in to see Stillwell.

"And we'll know we've found them when one of the search parties doesn't report back." That's what Dempsey had told me when I'd suggested looking at all of the old farmhouses near Brewster. I felt the hairs rising on the back of my neck.

I turned to Takach. "Time to call reinforcements," I told him. "See if you can get some regular army combat troops and a few helicopter gunships. We'll wait here and keep them under surveillance. If you see us hurrying past you, figure we've been spotted."

He took off at a trot. I was almost going to call after him and suggest that the closest available men might be Dempsey's in New York and he shouldn't be shy about calling them. But I decided yelling after him wasn't too good of an idea. I was watching him, though. I saw him step on the mine.

He must've felt it, because he tried to stop himself. But his momentum carried him past it. The explosion blew him five or six feet in the air, his arms and legs twisting independently of each other like a drunk gymnast's. He seemed to fall in slow motion. And like a leaf, he was dead before he hit the ground.

CHAPTER 16

Maxwell and I stood there with our mouths open while Kane moved into action. His .44 was in his hand before I had had time to swallow hard. He was scanning the driveway for depressions and when he didn't see any he ordered us to turn around and squat in place.

He squatted down next to us and, with his left arm across his eyes, aimed his weapon down the driveway and emptied it, kicking up divots at eight-foot intervals.

"Follow me," he yelled. As he took his first giant step (coming down on bare dirt) he was reaching into his pocket for a speed loader. He made another jump, onto the first of the divots, and came to a screeching halt, dropping his pistol onto his shoes. Over his shoulder I could see the man in jungle fatigues holding a machine pistol.

Kane, sensibly, put his hands over his head and I couldn't think of anything else to do so I followed suit. Maxwell reached for his pistol, but pulled his hand away when a shot rang out from the woods, digging up the dirt in front of him. Then he raised his hands too.

A girl wearing sixties-vintage marine fatigues came out of the woods to our right. She was carrying a machine pistol too, and she was close enough for me to see that it was a MAC 10. I recalled the way the prison guards had been taken care of and wished that I'd made a move for the woods back when I had a chance.

"There are red rocks scattered at random in the driveway," she informed us. "Walk in a straight line between the red rocks. Do not deviate from a straight line. Move."

We were very careful to do as she said. She didn't have to tell us what the penalty for straying was. When we reached the porch they had us lean on the wall and spread our legs. They must've had the same training we did, because they made sure our feet were at least three feet from the wall. They didn't miss Kane's knife.

They ushered us into the farmhouse parlor and invited us to sit in straight-backed wooden kitchen chairs. To ensure that we stayed seated they wrapped ten turns of duct tape around our arms and legs. They seemed to like duct tape. They had used it to fix the earphones to Branner's head, I recalled.

We only waited a few minutes. Stillwell came in and sat on a table facing us. He was dressed like a model from the L. L. Bean catalog and the years had been remarkably kind to him. I looked for plastic surgery scars. But if he had had any, the surgeon had been very very good. He had the photograph his people had found in my shirt pocket in his hand.

"I was quite gratified this morning to learn that you had been removed from command, Captain Kelly," he told me. "Especially considering the dispatch with which you dealt with my former associate Mr. Santiago."

"I should have known you were behind the CPF," I told him. "All those punks we captured were in strictly for the bucks. They just followed Santiago because they thought he knew what he was doing."

He laughed. "And he did know what he was doing. He

was listening to me." He held up his photograph. "I admired your efficiency in dealing with him, but I must say that I was guilty of underestimating you."

"I try to be a credit to the old Alma Mater," I told him. "Unlike some people."

"Where did you get this picture and how did you find this house?" he asked.

"We tailed your assassins back from the soup kitchen in Harlem," I lied. "We lost them just south of here, but we knew you were up here someplace. We pretended to fall for your Cheshire gag because we knew you were so conceited you'd stick around here thinking you were safe. There's ten thousand National Guardsmen closing in on you now. We just happened to be the lucky party that found you."

He grinned at me. But it wasn't the kind of grin you see down at the Elks lodge after you've told a particularly funny one. He hopped off the table and came over to me.

"Lucky?" he asked. Then he hit me, twice. And whatever he hit me with, it damned near put my lights out. The room got all fuzzy for a second and then came back into focus. My mouth began to fill with blood from where I'd cut my lips against my teeth.

"Lucky for someone, dear boy, but not for you. Those men did not return here, so there is no way you could have traced them back here. Now how did you find me?"

By this time my mouth was full to capacity with my blood. I squirted it out in a stream that ended up at his crotch. He looked down at the bright red stain streaming down his leg and threw back his head and laughed.

He looked over at Kane and Maxwell and pointed at Maxwell and said "Bring him" to the men standing behind us. The two men picked up Maxwell's chair and followed Stillwell out of the room. We heard a door opening and then the sound of feet clumping down the stairs.

"I sure hope you have a plan," Kane told me.

I tested the duct tape—it might as well have been steel.

"Wild animals often relax their sphincters there at the end," I grunted as I strained at the tape. "Has something to do with trying to make themselves smell inedible to the thing that's about to eat them."

"Good plan," he told me. "Except I don't think it worked for Maxwell. Got any other ideas?"

"Couple of hours and it'll be noon. The commandant said he'd come looking for us at noon."

"I don't think I want to wait that long," Kane told me. "In fact, I'd just as soon be moseying along in the next couple of minutes."

Pulling hadn't worked, so I tried moving my arms left to right. They might as well have been set in concrete.

"Don't let my rank intimidate you," I told him, wanting to say something that might take my mind off what they were doing to Maxwell. "If you have any suggestions I'd love to hear them."

We heard the door opening in the next room. "Don't spit any more blood on him," Kane suggested. "I don't think he liked that."

Stillwell came back into the room accompanied by Dr. Wilbur. Wilbur was wearing a straitjacket, and I couldn't help but notice the blood spattered on his shoes.

"Lieutenant Maxwell assures me that we have several hours of relative tranquillity ahead of us," Stillwell informed me. "And quite frankly, I believe him. Now about this picture?"

"How'd you waste your grandmother?" I asked. "I've been wondering about that all morning."

"Really," he said, sounding offended. "She was extremely old."

"Yeah," I told him. "You probably had to hurry because you were afraid she would check out without any help from you."

He drummed his fingers on the desk—an actor pretending he was impatient. "Captain Kelly, I would hate to see our conversation degenerating into a mudslinging contest.

Surely we're both above that sort of thing."

"My first thought was oxygen starvation," I told him. "Just put a pillow over her face and hold it there for a few minutes. Then take it off and let her recover a little bit and then slap it back on. But that just doesn't seem to be your style. I couldn't see you getting your hands dirty that way."

"Dr. Wilbur," he said, "has been reading in the papers about a new surgical technique called radial keratotomy. Perhaps you've heard of it? It involves precise radial cuts in the cornea. He tells me he has been dying to try his hand at it."

Dr. Wilbur came over and stared down into my eyes. "Oh, yes," he said. "This man is in dire need of the procedure."

"And I guess the next thing you're going to tell me is that you let your malpractice insurance lapse while you were in the nut hatch," I told him—apparently without offending him in the least.

"Go ahead and carve me up," I told Stillwell. He stared at me, perplexed, wondering why I wasn't reacting the way I was supposed to. I knew it would never occur to him to hold a knife to Kane's throat to get me to talk. That would've required some form of human empathy.

"Fair is fair," I told him. "How'd you do in Granny?"

"I told her the truth," he snapped at me. "If you must know, I told her in loving detail how my little brothers came to meet their unfortunate ends and how I tried to convince my parents that it hadn't been their fault and how I made their lives a living hell until my mother, poor dear, forgot to look where she was going one day—which I blamed on my father for not caring enough about her to see that she was in too much pain to have been driving by herself." He took a deep breath. "The picture."

"Well, that was pretty risky," I told him. "Suppose she hadn't checked out?" I could see he was beginning to get annoyed. "Although I suppose you had a contingency plan. Oh yes, the picture. Once we knew who you were it was fairly simple to get a hold of one of your old college chums, who gave us the picture.

"So where have you been for the last twenty years anyway?"

"Allaa hu Akbar, Captain Kelly. How did you find out about me?"

"Remember the video cameras at Toyon?" I asked him. "The feed split at the DCX box and went to two different machines. One was a monitor for the guard station that played continuous loop with voluntary feedback and zoom. The other went to a PC with a CD ROM player for storage and editing so they could get still shots."

It was all bullshit, but I figured there wasn't any need to do him favors. All you have to do is reel off initials like you know what you're talking about and most people tune out and nod their heads and try not to look like morons. He looked like he was eating it up.

"The picture quality isn't that great, you were pretty blurry, but not so blurry that one of your ex-associates at the FBI didn't recognize you. But we got the whole thing, you pausing dramatically and then giving the signal. F. Lee Bailey won't be able to get you off after they play it back for the jury."

"They have a video of the whole operation?"

"No," I told him. "It's a CD scan of the video. Something like every two seconds it samples the feed and stores the signal on a CD—compact disk," I explained helpfully. "So the motion looks pretty jerky, but they can store forty hours of live action on a disk about the size of an LP. Then if there isn't anything interesting on the disk, they just wipe it and start over."

He chewed on that for a second and I decided I had better get him onto another subject before he realized it was all crap. "How'd you get out of the town house?"

"There was a rather large hole in the living room wall," he told me. "I just crossed into the house next door a few minutes after the ladies and went out the front door. I even picked up a souvenir on the way through. Why aren't there really ten thousand National Guardsmen surrounding us?''

"They believed when you told them Cheshire," I told him. "How are you keeping the Nazis and the Commies from slitting each other's throats?"

"It's simply a matter of telling each of them what they most want to hear. My friends on the Left think they're going to make the government look very bad and discredit the whole white supremacist movement as a bonus. They feel this will relieve some of the pressure on the Sandinista government.

"My friends on the Right are thinking this will push the United States into a protracted war in Central America. They think the war will lead to domestic unrest in which they will be able to secede from the Union and found a nation based on Adolf's good ideas. And both sides hope to get their hands on the twenty million dollars the government is going to pay to get the last six of the lunatics back." He looked over at Wilbur. "No offense."

"None taken," he responded.

"Who is this Mayes person who seems to have put you out of a job?" Stillwell asked me.

"I wouldn't worry too much about him," I told him. "He thinks effective administration is a substitute for talent. He's a firm believer in getting the paperwork straight and the rest will take care of itself. You know the type."

"Hmm. You're telling me that unless I call him and tell him where I am, I don't have to worry much about him finding me."

"Something like that. But then again, I found you."

"Which just goes to show that sometimes it pays to be stupid."

"The FBI was certain you were an American, why was that?" I asked.

"Have you ever wondered why you aren't any busier?" he asked me.

"I'm busy enough."

"Yes, but you aren't very busy with the Germans or the Italians or the Japanese or the Palestinians or the Libyans. Your main problems, as I understand them, are Puerto Ricans, black and white extremists, Armenians and Jews. Now what does this group have in common that they don't have in common with the first group?"

"You tell me."

"Of course," he said happily. "Everyone in the first group gets their financing from the KGB; everyone in the second group buys their own. Does this not strike you as a little odd?"

"Plenty of Americans have been killed overseas," I pointed out.

"Yes, and a great many Russian boys came home from Afghanistan in little boxes as a result of our country's enlightened foreign aid policy. But, as far as I know, there have been no bomb blasts in Kiev lately. No Uzbekistani has lately assassinated his Russian overlord. The Marine Corps has not rushed to free the Baltic states."

It had been the State Department that had been so sure that the terrorists weren't from overseas, I reflected.

"So you think our governments are in bed together?" I asked.

"I think they wish to keep the world safe for empires, yes."

"Then why have they supplied the Sandinistas with weapons?" I asked. "How's that fit in with your deal?"

"I wasn't there when Stalin and Roosevelt divided the world up between them, just like the Pope did back in the sixteenth century. We will never know what they decided was of vital strategic importance to each other. I know you will never see Russian arms in Mexico, just as you will never see American arms in the Ukraine. It is quite likely that it just never occurred to Roosevelt that Central America would ever become something other than the feudal estate it had always been. Maybe it never occurred to Stalin that someday some idiot on the Central Committee would decide to rescue Afghanistan.

"Another thing I know. After the Soviet economy goes bankrupt next year, the Russians will need all the goodwill they can get from the United States and my friends in Nicaragua will be in the shit deep," he told me as he stood up.

"Thank you very much for your time. I have enjoyed our short time together, but now I must be leaving. Come along, Doctor."

Wilbur looked at him aghast. "But this man needs help."

"I'll get glasses," I told him. I looked over my shoulder at Stillwell. "One thing before you go."

"Yes?"

"Do you ever feel guilty . . . any remorse?"

"No, of course not. Why do you ask?"

"Lately I've been worried about myself."

He looked me over. "Am I to believe that you sometimes feel these things?"

"All the time," I told him.

He came over and patted me on the cheek. "Not to trouble yourself any further then. You are not like me. You lack a certain quality that you would not understand. Call it Olympian detachment."

He smiled at me. "Soon," he said, "soon you will be able to see that it has all been a dream, a nightmare of obscene proportions. Soon, so soon, all your troubles will be over." This time as he patted my cheek it was almost a caress.

I watched him as he led Wilbur out the door and then turned to Kane. Kane had turned an interesting purple color trying to pull his arms out of the duct tape. Most cardiologists wouldn't have approved and probably would have prescribed two weeks of bed rest if they'd seen him.

After another few seconds of straining, without discernibly affecting the tape, he let his breath out in a burst and sagged in the chair. "I have a very bad feeling about this," he told me. "I think that blood-spitting idea was not the best one you've had all day."

We heard the basement door opening and for the second time in an hour I felt the hairs rising on the back of my neck. It's a natural reaction. As the skin forms into goose pimples the hair follicles are forced away from the body. I craned my neck around and saw her framed in the doorway.

I made the sort of noise that men aren't supposed to make. It was Florence Moore. They must've been planning to let her loose in a city somewhere, because they'd given her a waist-length blond wig and she was wearing a tight black minidress. She had taken some time with her makeup. If I hadn't been petrified I would have taken a few minutes to admire the results. She had Wilbur's scalpel in her left hand.

I tried to think. It wasn't easy. I pictured the screen with Moore's face projected across it and Sheldon standing in front of it fatuously lecturing about how dangerous she was. "She hates men," he'd told us. And then I remembered the part about her penis collection and I started wondering what had become of it when they locked her away. I felt really stupid because I couldn't get it out of my head. Had they tried to match them up with the bodies? I wondered.

Finally I latched onto the thought that she had been abused as a child. I thought about that and wondered if I could use it. I had to latch onto something because she had started walking in my direction. She stopped in front of my chair.

"The fat one screamed for me," she informed me. "*He* told me that you would scream for me too." She paused and then asked, "Won't you scream for me?"

"No," I told her huskily. "You scream for me."

She played the scalpel along my temple, just to the right of my eye. And then she cut me with it. She ran it down the side of my face, slicing a shallow cut down the entire length of my face. The scalpel was sharp and I barely felt it. Actually, I probably wouldn't have felt it if it had been a rusty Lady Schick.

"Aren't you afraid?" she asked.

"I've known since I was five that life is pain," I told her. "I've lived with that pain every day of my life. And I've been waiting for you. I've been waiting for someone to come and release me." It was even worse than the crap I'd been feeding Stillwell. But it apparently meant something to her. At least she hadn't tried to cut my nose off yet.

She brought the scalpel up to her shoulder and cut a line down the sleeve of her dress from her shoulder to her elbow. A bright red trail followed the scalpel. She repeated the process on her other sleeve and then brought the blade down along her left side and then her right.

The dress literally fell off her. She stood there, naked, covered with blood: her own mixing with Maxwell's, sheathing her in crimson. "I love you," she told me.

And then she began to cut my clothes off. It was a ritual. The blade cutting skin as well as cloth, leaving a long trail of blood behind it.

She grabbed me and whispered in my ear. She told me it was all right and that she would never hurt me. She stroked me until I was erect and then mounted me. She kissed me full on the lips and then bit my lip, hard. She pulled back a moment and I knew what I had to do.

I did what I had to to survive. As she drove down on me, her motions getting wilder and wilder, I began to frantically twist my arm inside the duct tape—it was the only motion it was capable of. She was oblivious and after a while I could rotate my wrist a hundred and eighty degrees. I could see the blood leaking out from under the tape, and I tried not to think about what I was doing to my arm.

As she climaxed, I screamed and pulled my arm free—leaving a big patch of skin still attached to the tape—and caught her wrist as it came down with the scalpel to castrate me. With every bit of panic-driven strength in my body I drove her arm down onto the arm of the chair. Her forearm snapped, driving the scalpel into my leg, her broken wrist making a right angle with the rest of her arm.

I barely felt the blade going in. I grabbed her real hair and butted her as hard as I could until I was nearly unconscious. Exhausted, I dropped back into the chair and her body slumped over mine.

"Who says there are no bad orgasms?" I asked, as I pushed her off me onto the floor. I sat there breathing heavily, wondering how I had ever gotten myself into a situation like this and what I would do if she was pregnant.

"You know," Kane said admiringly, "you are one kinky dude."

I looked over at him. "When I get the strength," I told him, "I'm going to pull this pig stikah out of my leg, and then I'm going to cut myself loose and go over to where you're sitting."

I didn't get to finish the thought. Kane's eyes got bigger and he tried to shout out a warning, but he was too late. Stillwell pinned my free arm to the chair and pivoted around on it until he was staring into my eyes.

"You really didn't think I was going to leave until I was certain you were dead, did you?" There was a hypodermic in his other hand and I was too weak to move. He pushed the needle into my arm and rammed the plunger home.

He stood up, ignoring me, and nudged Moore with his foot. "You realize you've destroyed my faith in duct tape, don't you?" he asked. "I'm afraid I'm going to have to go back to rope with all the attendant problems that means." He sighed. "What's a fellow to do?"

The room was beginning to spin around me and the lights from window and ceiling had begun to multiply.

"So Dave Abrahms tells us you like to take it up the ass," I heard Kane telling him.

"I'm not a taker," Stillwell told him. "I'm a giver. Would you like a sample?"

"Go ahead, dick nose," Kane said. "I'll clench my cheeks so hard it'll . . ."

I had to ask him what it would do later. The lights went out for me with a crash.

CHAPTER 17

It took me a long time to regain consciousness. I was only vaguely self-aware and my universe seemed to revolve around the twin realities of a blinding headache and a horrible case of nausea. Finally, after the nausea got to be so bad that I had to do something about it, I rolled over onto my side and vomited. I felt like I would throw up forever. Each new spasm produced an agonizing pain in my head that felt like a dull knife being pushed into the temple. I managed to get control of my stomach but didn't have the strength to push myself back onto my back.

I heard footsteps through the drumming sound that came and went in rhythm with the surging colors I was seeing through my closed eyelids. A woman's voice told me to "drink this" and I felt something pushed up against my lips. I couldn't swallow; the thought of putting anything into my stomach was too horrible. She held a towel up to my mouth as I spit the water back into it.

She rolled me back onto my back. I noticed that my hands weren't following my body. But with my stomach empty, my body saw no reason for me to still be awake and I passed out.

When I awoke the next time the nausea was gone. No such luck with the headache. I groaned and tried to sit up and found out why my hands had been behaving so mysteriously during my last adventure in consciousness; they were handcuffed to the side of the bed.

I pulled my legs up to my chest and got them around my arms and managed to sit up. I was still naked, but someone had cleaned me up and there were neat bandages on my arm where I'd pulled it out of the duct tape, and also on my upper thigh, where Moore had stabbed me. As I moved I opened up the long scalpel cuts along my arms and legs and bled a little. It was the least of my problems.

My bed was in a long dormitory room with two rows of steel bunk beds along the walls. Dr. Wilbur was on the bed to my left. His hands were cuffed to the side of his bed the same as mine and I noticed they had chained his legs to it as well. He twisted around in my direction and asked how I felt.

"Terrible," I told him.

"Any numbness in the extremities?" he asked.

I started to shake my head but thought better of it immediately. "No," I told him. "Just a headache."

"Chloral hydrate probably," he told me. "He slipped you the old Mickey Finn."

I looked down at the bandage on my arm and felt suddenly queasy as the thought of who might have attended to me sprang unbidden. I looked up questioningly at Wilbur.

"I offered," he told me, "but they insisted on doing it themselves."

The shades were drawn on all the windows, making it difficult to make out who was lying in the other beds. Four beds down was Kairos. I could tell because his feet extended at least a foot beyond the end of his mattress. I counted seven people all together but couldn't make out any of the faces.

"Allow me to introduce you," Wilbur said. "You already know your friend there." He nodded over my shoulder. I looked behind me and saw Kane asleep. I was glad to see him. "On my immediate left," Wilbur continued, "is Dr. Felix Durand, computer scientist and raving maniac. Please excuse Felix for being so reticent. I'm afraid his bloodstream is rather full of tranquilizers.

"To the left of Dr. Durand is Charles Lasuen," he continued, nodding his head in Lasuen's direction, "psychotic and connoisseur of fine gems. Immediately to his left is Konstantine Aristotle Kairos, who is not to be trifled with by the way, not even in his current state of drug-induced torpor.

"Just beyond him, and one hundred percent drug free, is Marcus Twain, rogue, bon vivant and stealer of hearts. And beyond him are Jason Roth and Angus Whitman, with whom I have not had the pleasure of conversing."

"Where are they keeping the women?" I asked.

"Lucy Stern is no longer with us," he told me. "The result of an unfortunate choice of tranquilizer. Pity they didn't choose to consult with me prior to injecting her with five hundred milligrams of oxazepam. As for Florence, the last time I saw her she was on the way to chat with you."

"She was still breathing last time I saw her," I assured him. "Where's Crothers?"

"They took him away this morning. They said something about a day-care center."

"Where are we?"

"We appear to be in some sort of summer camp," he told me. "Apparently in the Poconos."

I chewed on that for a moment. There was no way Dempsey was going to find us. We were going to live as long as Stillwell had some use for us and not a second longer. He was probably planning on enclosing parts of our bodies with his ransom demands when he got around to asking for his twenty million.

"I have to take a leak," I told Wilbur. "How do you call room service?"

"There was an unfortunate incident with one of our keepers last night," he told me. "Since then we've been left to shift for ourselves. If I were you I would use the floor. Take my word for it, lying in one's own bodily wastes is not a pleasant experience."

As he mentioned it I took a deep breath and it became apparent that at least a few of us were already experiencing it. I decided to wait. I wasn't much bothered by being naked in front of Wilbur, but I couldn't make myself urinate in front of him. At least not until I was desperate.

"Roble told us they were heavily sedating all but a few of you."

"Too true, even I have been subjected to the indignity of it. However, they seem to have backed off in the past day. Of course, Lasuen and Durand have to be continuously sedated. Otherwise they'll try to harm themselves. And they're keeping Kairos in a straitjacket and pumped full of oxazepam, an even larger dosage than they gave poor Lucy, I think. Of course, that's because they're afraid of what he might do should he get loose."

"How many of them are there?" I asked. I didn't have anything else to do. I decided I might as well try to investigate.

"Hard to say," he told me. "I think there may be as many as ten all together. They seem to be evenly divided between the Bible thumpers and the hippies."

A door opened and the girl who'd been carrying the machine pistol (probably the one who'd come to see Eduardo in Brewster) came in carrying a bucket. Two men carrying clubs followed her around as she watered the prisoners. That seemed to be an apt expression for what she was doing: watering. She had to hold the cup up to their mouths to let them drink.

Twain said something to her that made her laugh. She didn't offer to take his cuffs off though. When she got to

Wilbur the two guards stood over him with their clubs poised as she held the cup up to his lips. She seemed poised to pull the cup away at any second.

She gave me my water and watched me carefully as I drank it. I thought about asking her about Brewster, but decided it could wait. I didn't want to expend my only leverage over her, not with her two friends standing right behind her. She glanced at Kane and then left. She hadn't offered to bring me any clothes.

"The incident with one of your keepers didn't involve you by any chance, did it?" I asked Wilbur.

"I think I'll take a nap now," he told me. "Wake me if anything interesting happens."

It took about fifteen minutes for something interesting to happen: a visit from Stillwell.

He brought his own chair and sat down at the foot of my bed. He shook his head sadly and brought up a Polaroid camera and took a quick shot of me sitting there looking as miserable as a human being can look. I wasn't reacting fast enough to turn my head. He didn't say a word until the photograph had developed.

"You'll be heartbroken to learn that your investigation is falling completely apart in your absence."

"I'm sure Mayes has everything under control," I told him.

"Alas, no. The operation in Cheshire, as you've probably guessed, was a total debacle. Some millions of dollars of taxpayers' money spent for no apparent reason. While on the other end of the state, the former head of the investigation—who had been displaced due to the bureaucratic machinations of this Mayes person—was hot on the trail of the terrorists. Unfortunately, his fine police work went for naught due to his lack of support and he was captured and is apparently being tortured by the terrorists—they found the farmhouse and what was left of Maxwell yesterday afternoon. You'll be relieved to know that Ms. Moore is in satisfactory condition at a nearby hospital.

"Anyway, the mayor of New York is up in arms and the federal government has quite a bit of egg on its collective face. The entire nation is watching this melodrama unfold now. They're all on the edges of their seats waiting to see if the hero of the piece, that's you, can somehow escape from the clutches of the evil genius terrorist, that's me. Don't count on it.''

"And I guess the photograph is supposed to make me look less heroic and you look more like an evil genius."

He laughed. "You do look somewhat bedraggled," he told me. "But cheer up, you may get out of this alive after all. I may throw you and Sleeping Beauty''—he nodded at Kane—"in with the rest of this merry crew and ask for twenty-five million."

"What did you do with Crothers?"

"Gave him a machine gun and dropped him off at an elementary school in New Jersey. He was still holding the police off at noon. Lord knows what kind of mess he's made in there."

"And this evening, if we can get him moving, we'll be dropping Mr. Kairos off at the Cheshire Youth Center— just to rub it in, you know. The local high school's having a 'back to school' dance there this evening."

"Where exactly are we?" I asked.

"Camp Rachael in the Poconos," he told me. "We specialize in caring for young Jewish women with eating disorders. Perhaps you've seen the advertisements in the *New York Times Magazine*?"

"I haven't been looking for a good summer camp lately," I told him. "Where're the girls?"

"Unfortunately, there wasn't enough interest in the camp to merit opening it up this year."

"Really?"

"Well, no story is perfect. The girls just had to go elsewhere this year. Now if you'll excuse me, I have to go drop this in the post," he said as he waved my photograph at me.

I hadn't asked him for any clothes. I didn't want to ask him for anything. I tried to make myself comfortable and wondered if he would really mail the picture. My lips had been forming an O and my fingers had been shaped into a C and an O. Maybe someone would be smart enough to add NOS to the end and figure it out.

"I feel better now," Kane whispered from behind me. "It's nice to know someone's finally recognized my true worth."

"They'll probably deduct it from your pension," I told him. "And besides, it's probably five million for me and they'll throw you in as a sweetener."

"It's people like you who drive honest working men into the arms of the Commies," he told me.

"I thought you saw the light at the Worthingtons'?"

"I was momentarily seduced by materialism," he told me. "What's the plan?"

"We hope the Treasury Department can convince the Japanese to buy another twenty-five million dollars worth of T-bills," I told him.

"And people wonder if America is really in decline," he muttered. He rolled over onto his back and seemed to go back to sleep. Since I couldn't think of anything better to do, I joined him.

"Wake up," Wilbur hissed at us. "This may be interesting."

I opened my eyes and looked around. The sun was beginning to set and there was much less light filtering in through the shades. The two men who'd accompanied the woman on her rounds were back. They were bent over Kairos, trying to lever him out of the bed.

I could hear them grunting and cursing as they tried to shift three hundred pounds of dead weight.

"Motherfucker," one of them said. "This guy is a fucking monster."

They managed to get him sitting up with his back to the wall.

"You got the needle?" one of them asked.

"Yeah, I got it," the other one said. "You really think he needs it?"

"Fuck, you wanna take the straitjacket off him without shooting him up first?"

The man shook his head and took a needle case out of his shirt pocket. I looked over at Wilbur. He was watching very carefully. I sensed the anticipation.

There was a hole in the sleeve of Kairos's straitjacket where they must have been injecting him. I winced as the needle penetrated his arm. Kairos didn't even blink.

"Shit," the guy with the needle said. " I don't think the captain's gonna be able to get this one moving when the time comes."

"You worry about you and let the captain worry about that," his friend told him. "You got the cuffs?"

"Extra large," he replied.

The first one grabbed Kairos by the hair and pulled him forward to expose the straps on the back of the straitjacket. He undid them and then heaved Kairos back upright and pulled the jacket off him. Wilbur had stopped breathing.

The first one took hold of Kairos's right arm and brought it up for his partner to snap the handcuff onto it. He had to struggle to keep the giant arm up in the air. Except suddenly it wasn't a struggle. The arm shot out and grabbed him by the throat. His partner tried to back away and reach for his pistol simultaneously. He was way too late.

Kairos had them both by the throat and brought their heads together with a thump. Then he pushed them out to the full extent of his reach and brought their heads crashing together again. And then again.

"They hadn't been using oxazepam on Kairos at Toyon for years," Wilbur told me, his sentences punctuated by the wet, thumping sound Kairos was making with the two corpses. "He'd built up such an immunity to it that they had to switch him over to ethchlorvynol. Imagine, he's been lying in his own feces for four days now pretending to be in a coma. He's been waiting for them to take him out of the restraints.''

"Another case where they could have benefited from your advice?'' I asked.

"Indubitably.''

Kairos had shifted his grip to the sides of their heads and was doing his best to make their noses meet. Each time he pulled the heads apart there was a sucking noise as he broke the vacuum. I hoped he was getting all of his frustrations out.

Finally he dropped them and rummaged through their pockets and came up with a set of keys and a pair of pistols. I noticed one of them was Kane's. He unlocked Twain and then motioned for him to move down our way. The gun he was using for motioning was totally superfluous.

They bypassed the beds where the patients were too drugged to be aware of what was going on and stopped at the foot of my bed.

"You will help?'' Kairos asked.

"Yes,'' I told him.

"Can I trust you?''

"Until they're dead you can.''

"Unlock him,'' Kairos told Twain. He rushed to obey. Kairos turned to look at Kane.

"I'm up for it,'' Kane told him.

Kairos gestured at Kane. "Him too, then.''

Kairos turned to Wilbur. "And you?''

"I'm afraid not,'' Wilbur told him. "I'm a doctor, not an assassin. I'll be happy to follow along and treat the wounded, however.''

I thought I almost detected a smile from Kairos. In retrospect I guess not, though. Kairos passed on the offer.

I rubbed my wrists and looked up at him. "Weapon,'' I told him.

He looked at me questioningly.

"Until they're dead," I said. "I want him dead a lot worse than you do."

"No, you do not," he told me. He threw Kane his spare pistol. It was a .38. I doubted Kane would be able to kill him with it. Not unless he hit him in a weak spot. I didn't see any weak spots.

I made my way over to the bodies and thought about taking some clothes. Their clothes were spattered with blood and feces though, and I decided I didn't mind being naked.

But because I had gone over to the two corpses, I happened to be the closest to the door when it opened. Apparently the man standing in the doorway looking surprised was a hippie. At least he looked like he'd spent his formative years in San Francisco. He stood there in the doorway with his jaw hanging slack for fully a second before he started for his gun.

He shouldn't have just stood there. I felt the bullet pass by my ear on its way to his forehead. I turned around to see Kairos sitting on one of the beds taking his pants off and Kane smiling at his marksmanship.

"There goes the element of surprise," I yelled. "Follow me."

I raced out of the building, stopping to get the hippie's pistol, into a quadrangle surrounded by other dormitories. There was a two-story administration building at the head of the quad and I ran for it. I killed Eduardo's friend as she came out the front door and took her MAC 10.

Pausing on the stoop, I looked up and saw a window shattering as a man knocked it out with his rifle butt. He leaned out of the opening and took aim at something headed our way. I gave him a burst in the chest and felt a rush as I saw the body slump in the window. Kairos landed on the stoop next to me. He was naked from the waist down and even in the excitement I couldn't help but notice the smell. Kane was right behind him.

"Where's Twain?" I asked.

"I will kill him later," Kairos told me.

"He headed south," Kane added.

Kairos stood up and kicked the door off its hinges and barged into the building shooting. We followed.

"It wasn't locked," Kane called out.

The door opened up into a wood-paneled lobby. Wings branched out in either direction and a double set of stairs led upward from the back. Kairos was leaning against the stairs breathing heavily. He'd been shot at least twice, once in the stomach and once in the leg. I stepped over the body of the man who'd done the shooting and picked up his automatic weapon, an M16, and threw it to Kairos.

He picked it neatly out of the air and motioned down the corridor to our right. I turned into the corridor with the trigger of the machine pistol halfway home. There was no one there. At least no one stupid enough to have his head sticking out where I could see it.

We picked our way carefully down the corridor and stopped a few feet short of one of the offices. Kairos pointed at it meaningfully.

The number-one rule of urban warfare, as I recalled it, was not to hide behind gypsum board walls. The instructor had been quite sarcastic about the shielding ability of a half-inch-thick piece of semisolid talcum powder. Most people don't know this, so I put a twelve-shot burst through the wall next to the office door about three feet off the ground in a Z-shaped pattern. I only hit him six times.

Another very good rule is: don't fire off bursts that empty your weapon. I believe the instructor referred to this as "leaving your dick on the chopping block." Apparently the second man had never heard that rule either because he came charging out expecting to find Kairos with an empty weapon. As it happened Kairos blew him away. I could have done it.

I picked up his weapon and threw it to Kairos and got the other man's for myself.

"Are there no bullets for this one?" Kairos asked me, holding up his M16. He seemed oblivious to the hole in his belly. There was a steady stream of blood pouring out of it, running down his leg to meet with a smaller stream issuing from a hole in his thigh. I figured he probably had plenty of blood.

"You're better off with a full load in a new weapon," I told him.

He broke his M16 across his good leg, reminding me that I was dealing with three hundred pounds of bleeding paranoiac. Rather than give him any ideas, I led the way back to the stairs.

Kairos pointed at Kane. "Check this floor," he told him. And then he followed me up the stairs. We paused on the second-floor landing.

"We got one in the city," I told him. "You got two in the bunkhouse and two in here. Kane got one in the bunkhouse and I got three in here. If Wilbur was right, that only leaves Stillwell."

"He is mine."

I didn't argue with him. He could have him if he got to him first. I reminded myself that he would probably come for us after he was finished with Stillwell. Which got me to wondering if he would wait until after Stillwell was dead. The thought bothered me and I couldn't just write it off to paranoia.

"Right or left?" I asked.

"I will take the right," he told me.

"There was someone in the second room on the left," I told him. "I got him on the way in."

"I know," he said. "Is why I go right."

We stepped out into the hallway with our backs to each other and began to search the rooms. Kairos found him.

I heard the shots and a scream of rage and went running back down the hall. Kairos had been carrying a MAC 10. All I had heard were pistol shots.

I didn't pause outside the door with my back to the gypsum board. I went in low with the trigger on my machine pistol half depressed. It was a classroom of some sort and

I took cover behind a student's desk that was almost as bulletproof as a sheet of quarter-inch plywood. Luckily no one was shooting at me.

In the gloom it took me a few seconds to find them. Or find Kairos, rather. I could see his massive legs sticking out from behind the teacher's desk in the front of the room. It took me a moment longer to see Stillwell's legs sticking out from under them.

I approached warily, leaning over the desk, ready to blast away if anything moved. Nothing was moving. Stillwell was conscious, but immobilized beneath Kairos's body. Kairos was dead. I couldn't see any exit wounds in his back, but he was definitely dead.

I came around the desk and found Stillwell's pistol. It was empty.

"I can't breathe," he whispered.

"Tough shit," I told him.

I felt for a pulse in Kairos's wrist but there was none. I was surprised. I would have thought it would take a grenade launcher to finish him.

"Please," Stillwell whispered.

I decided not to give myself a hernia trying to move Kairos. I figured it wouldn't be safe to put my weapon down and there was no way I was going to move him one-handed. I stepped behind Stillwell and grabbed him by the collar and heaved. As I pulled, he screwed up his eyes tightly and whimpered. When Kairos's head hit the floor I dropped Stillwell. His head hit with a thump.

"Thank you," he whispered. "I hit him with all six shots, but he was like a dinosaur. It took thirty seconds for the message to get up to his brain that he was dead."

"Have some broken ribs, do you?"

He grunted.

I picked up Kairos's weapon and fired a burst into the rear wall of the classroom. It worked fine. I would never know why he hadn't used it. It occurred to me that he had probably stopped thinking rationally on first sight of Stillwell. But I realized immediately that that couldn't be it. He hadn't been rational in years. I wondered what my excuse was going to be.

I picked Stillwell up by the shirt collar and jammed the barrel of Kairos's weapon under his chin. The barrel was still hot and I could see that it was burning him.

I heard Kane in the doorway clearing his throat. "I'll just take a look around and see if I can't find Twain," he told me. "Whistle if you need anything." And then he was gone.

"Go ahead, Captain Normal," Stillwell told me. "I don't believe in hell and there's nothing left for me here."

He saved his life. Maybe he'd planned it that way. Maybe he was manipulating me to the end.

"You don't believe in hell?" I asked him. He didn't answer.

"You will, though," I told him.

Then I reversed the pistol and brought it down on the side of his head, knocking him into unconsciousness.

EPILOGUE

The ambulance from Toyon finally arrived. It was nearly nine and I'd told my father I'd be home by eleven. The bomb squad was making a final sweep for booby traps, although they hadn't found any yet. The orderlies from Toyon led Dr. Wilbur past us to the ambulance. He nodded to Kane and me on the way by and I couldn't stop myself from automatically nodding back.

I was wearing Stillwell's clothes. They fit me pretty well; we both shopped at Brooks Brothers.

Dempsey made his way back across the quad along the path the bomb squad had marked as clean and sat down next to me on the stoop of the administration building.

"You still going to remember your friends after you're elected?" he asked me.

"Sure," I told him. "How'd you like to be my special executive assistant in charge of press relations?"

"I'd rather be dropped naked into a tank full of piranha."

The phones had been working at Camp Rachael. While I'd been having my little chat with Stillwell, Kane had been

267

using them to call Dempsey. Apparently they'd been sitting around waiting for a phone call from the terrorists—the Federal Reserve Bank of New York had been standing by with an undisclosed amount of cash. Mayes hadn't been there; he was either on vacation or headed for Fairbanks. No one knew for sure.

The first helicopter had set down twenty minutes after Kane first said hello.

Dempsey had arrived thirty minutes after that. His people had left me alone until he got there.

"Any word on Twain?" I asked.

"No," he told me. "We think there may be a car missing and some of the dead terrorists were missing their wallets."

"You'll find him," I told him. "He's going to leave a trail. He can't help himself."

The orderlies from Toyon came back for their last patient and led him back to the ambulance. He went along docilely until he saw the word *Toyon* on the ambulance. And then, in spite of his broken ribs, he started struggling wildly. He smashed his head on the door as he fought with the orderlies. They literally threw him into the ambulance and shut the door so we couldn't see what happened after that.

"How long do you think they'll be able to keep him there?" Kane asked.

"I think the deal is," I told him, "that once you get to hell, they keep you there forever."